CW00735303

MY PERFECT REMIX

SWATI M.H.

SMH PUBLISHING

Copyright © 2021 by Swati M.H.

All rights reserved.

No part of this book may be reproduced in any form or by any electronic or mechanical means, including information storage and retrieval systems, without written permission from the author, except for the use of brief quotations in a book review.

This is a work of fiction. Names, characters, businesses, places, incidents, and events are either a product of the author's imagination or used fictitiously.

Cover: Cover Me Darling

Editing: Silvia's Reading Corner

Publicity: Give Me Books PR

❀ Created with Vellum

To my incredible Dad. Though he'll never read this book, he's my biggest fan. Thank you for giving me the most invaluable gift: your belief in me.

"Love is a friendship set to music."

— Joseph Campbell

PLAYLIST

"**Summer**" by Calvin Harris

"**Skateboard**" by Jacob Sartorius

"**Kryptonite**" by 3 Doors Down

"**Umbrella**" by Rihanna, JAY-Z

"**One Kiss**" by Calvin Harris, Dua Lipa

"**Magic**" by Kylie Minogue

"**Miracles**" by Colton Dixon

"**Something Just Like This**" by The Chainsmokers, Coldplay

"**We Found Love**" by Rihanna, Calvin Harris

"**Don't Speak**" by No Doubt

"**Lovefool**" by Twocolors, Pia Mia

"**Titanium**" by David Guetta, MORTEN, Sia

"**Peanut Butter Jelly**" by Galantis

"**Cry for you**" by September

"**Find U Again**" by Mark Ronson, Camila Cabello

"**Promises - David Guetta Remix**" by Calvin Harris, Sam Smith, David Guetta

PROLOGUE

"You better watch it, *Batgirl*. You're not in a BMX competition," I caution Anisa as she jumps her bike over the concrete speed bumps around our school parking lot. Her jet-black hair flies underneath her helmet as she hovers over the saddle.

"And if I were I'd be kicking everyone's ass!" Breathing heavily, she zig-zags her bike between the speed bumps. "Try it with me, scaredy cat!"

"I'll pass. I like my bones intact." I turn my bike around, getting up from the saddle as well, and take it for a spin through the parking lot, though I keep an eye on Anisa. She might act like she's tough, but she's prone to injury.

In the spring, Anisa's parents invited a few of her friends over to hang out in their backyard and we all jumped on their huge trampoline. Anisa got it in her head that she wanted to not only jump, but flip. She lost her balance and landed awkwardly on the edge, and while she barely winced, she came to school the next day with a cast on her wrist.

It's nearing the end of summer, and we've done this

almost every day--I ride to her house and ask her parents if Anisa can come out with her bike. Then, we take the long trail behind the school and ride around for an hour, talking about everything from last year's classes to comic books, movies, and video games. Mainly we argue about movies and video games.

I've never had a friend who's a girl before, but strangely, hanging out with her has become something I look forward to every day. Maybe it's because she doesn't act like a typical seventh-grade girl. She's nerdy and hilarious and thinks she knows more about comic books than me. The girl has no idea that most of the time, I'm not even listening to what she's saying. All I want is to watch her talk. I've developed a strange fascination with her mouth and the plumpest, prettiest lips I've ever seen. No matter how hard I try, my eyes fixate on them when she's eating or talking, like they're some sort of homing device.

"Hey, so why didn't Wayland come out today?" She takes me out of my musings about what her lips might feel like on mine. Being thirteen is starting to suck with all the damn involuntary reactions my body keeps having . . . it's like I'm possessed.

I shrug. "Probably because you gave him a hard time about Jeena the last time he came with us." Sometimes our friend Wayland joins us on his bike, but I'm pretty sure the only reason he comes is to grill Anisa about her older sister, Jeena. The boy has a good old-fashioned crush.

I wouldn't know anything about crushes though, because I've never had one.

She laughs, a chirpy sound that's sweeter than baby birds in the morning. "It's borderline obsessive, don't you think? Every time we come out, he asks where she is, what she likes, who she talks to. I'm telling you, it ain't healthy."

"Right. And your obsession with a guy who wears tights and wields a big hammer is . . .?"

"His name is Thor, and it's not just any old hammer. Anyway, I'm not the only one who thinks he's hot. Anyone with a functioning brain and eyes can see it."

"I don't."

"I rest my case."

She's a real comedian. I roll my eyes and ride closer to her, remembering her plans for this evening. "Are you still going to watch the new Avengers movie with your dad and sister tonight?"

She lifts her bike on its back wheel and rides for a few seconds, making my heart race. I get a vision of her flipping backward and breaking her spine, but I keep my mouth shut, knowing she already thinks I act like an overbearing dad. Setting her bike back down on both wheels, she shrugs, a grimace playing on her lips. "I don't know. I might just stay home with Mom and Scooter and let Dad and Jeena go alone."

Scooter is Anisa's twelve-year-old greyhound. She picked him up at the local shelter last year and begged her parents to give him a home instead of one of the younger dogs because she didn't want him to die without a family. The girl has some sort of Mother Teresa complex when it comes to old homeless animals.

My brows furrow. Anisa would never miss an Avengers movie. "Why? You've been looking forward to seeing that movie all year. You're going to miss your chance to see Thor on the big screen?"

She shrugs again, but I can tell there's something else. I've only known her since the middle of last year--when my family moved to Austin and I started at the same middle school--but Anisa wears her emotions on her face like a mood ring. There's never a question as to how she's feeling about something because her face usually gives her away.

I still remember meeting her on my first day of school. I didn't know anyone and hated the fact that I was going to have to make friends in a new town. I was putting in the combo for my locker when she shut hers next to mine and her face came into view. She turned completely toward me, her intelligent, light brown eyes trying to assess me. Her black hair hung in a ponytail, with loose pieces framing her face. Her even, tan skin only enhanced the natural color of her pink lips. I think it was the first time I'd felt winded without having run an all-out sprint. I recall wondering if I needed to spend my first period in the nurse's office because my heart was beating so fast. It was the first time I'd had such a reaction to a girl.

She was wearing a black hoodie--two sizes too big for her--and some sort of psychedelic tights with a hundred neon colors that made me wonder if that's what people saw while they were on drugs. Maybe I was on drugs and just didn't know it. It would explain the hammering in my heart at least.

Her gaze traveled from my chest to my eyes. "The Joker is probably the *only* character in the DC universe that's mildly respectable. Honestly, all the others need to be shelved."

I looked down at my shirt with the Joker holding out a card with his namesake, smiling like a lunatic. He looked like what I felt inside at the moment. "Right. Because, let me guess, you think Tony Stark can hold a candle to Bruce Wayne, who he was obviously a cheap copy of." I met her light brown eyes with a wry smile.

"Please. Iron Man doesn't hide in the shadows, is way more intelligent, and has a better suit than Batman. Anyway,

I'm Anisa, and I'll forgive your poor choices in comic book characters. What's your name?" She stuck out her right hand while balancing a textbook with the other against her chest.

I grinned, taking her hand--which sent a warm tingle up my arm, settling in my shoulder--and immediately knew I'd like her. I mean, not *like* her like her, but I immediately knew we'd be friends. "I'm Logan, and I suppose I expect fangirls like you to be enamored with lame, colorful characters like Iron Man and Thor."

"Careful." She squeezed my hand tighter and narrowed her eyes. "Not another word about Thor."

"You got it, *Batgirl*," I said, teasing her, knowing she'd hate the DC reference and getting the perfect scowl from her in return.

Coming back to the present, I listen to the sound of our tires on the asphalt, following her bike with mine before repeating the question. "So, are you going to tell me what your deal is? Why aren't you going to the movies with your dad and Jeena?"

"I just don't want to, okay? Can you lay off my case, nosey-pants?" Her voice sounds strangely shrill, and I wonder why she's being secretive. We've talked a lot over the summer and she's never been one to shy away from conversation with me. She's not someone I'd refer to as a social butterfly--in fact, I'd say she's sort of a loner, always doodling in her notebooks--but for some reason, she's comfortable talking to me. And generally, she does most of the talking. Sometimes I wonder if she even breathes when she gets going on a rant.

"Did you get into a fight with them or something?"

In an effort to avoid answering my question, Anisa takes off at breakneck speed on her bike, zooming across the parking lot and jumping over a small pothole in the pavement. I don't know what's gotten into her, but I hate the knot that's coiling in the pit of my stomach, like it's warning me of impending doom.

And as if I'm watching her in slow-motion, I see her get off of the saddle and turn her bike to come back toward me exactly when the look on her face falters, indicating something didn't go as she had expected. Instinctively, I pedal toward her as fast as I can, but I can only watch helplessly as she loses her balance and topples over with the bike landing heavily on her side.

"Oh, shit!" I yell as I throw my bike onto the ground and run to her.

She whimpers, the sound causing a strange pain in my chest. "Ouch!"

I take the bike off her and squat near her crumpled form on the grass. She must have slipped on the asphalt when she was turning and lost control. "Anisa! Look at me! Are you okay?" I shove her shoulder gently to turn her, but she has her knee pulled into her chest and is holding it for dear life.

Her knee is scraped badly and a layer of skin looks like it's come off, blood pooling along the edges of the white layer below. "Are you hurt anywhere else?" I ask as she continues to whimper.

A pained cry comes out of her mouth, vibrating through my bones, as streams of tears slip out of her eyes. I take her helmet off, still examining if she's hurt anywhere else. It only appears to be her knee that's banged up. "Anisa," I take off my helmet and run a frustrated hand over my hair, "tell me if there's any other place you're hurt. You're scaring me."

She shakes her head, pursing her lips and squeezing her

eyes shut. Her chest quickly rises and falls under her bent knee. "Nowhere else."

I sigh in relief. "Okay. Okay. Well, it doesn't look too bad. Just need to get you cleaned up. Let's get you home."

"No!" she wails, louder this time. "I don't want to go home. I don't give a shit about my knee."

Confused, I lean over and swipe a tear from her face with my thumb, tucking a wet strand of hair stuck to her cheek behind her ear. "Then why are you crying? You barely even said *ouch* when you broke your wrist on the trampoline."

She shakes her head again, sobbing. Letting her knee go, she places her palms against her eyelids. "I'm not crying about my knee, Logan. I'm . . .."

I wrap my hand around one of her wrists, mentally shielding myself for what she's about to say. *This was the impending doom my body was preparing me for.* "Then, what?" My voice feels like it's grating against my throat and my gut tells me I'm not going to like what she's about to say. Even in the short time I've known her, I've felt connected to her in an unnatural way. Like we're more than friends. Like we're . . ..

"I don't want to go. I like it here."

"Okay, so we'll stay here. Just look at me, will you?"

She removes her hands from her eyes and I help her sit up. I swipe the hair matted over her forehead, feeling a thin layer of sweat that's formed over her brow, and meet her caramel gaze. I've never seen them look so glassy, so defeated. And now that my hands have touched her face, it's as if they don't want to come back to my sides. I wipe another stray tear from her cheek, letting my thumb rest on her skin longer than I should, as she sniffles. "I don't want to go."

"I hear you, *Batgirl*. We won't go, but you need to clean that scrape soon."

She shakes her head as fresh tears pool in her eyes. "Lo, you're not getting it! I'm not talking about going back home."

"Okay. Then what are you talking about?" I chuckle a little, remembering something Wayland had said to me about girls being confusing. I assume he was talking about Jeena, but I'm getting a first-hand account of it myself.

My smile slips off my face as soon as the next words leave her mouth and she puts a gash in my heart. "I'm moving at the end of the month."

1

ANISA
PRESENT DAY

J wiggle the key into the lock and turn it a couple of times before I feel the bolt slide. "Ah, home sweet home!" I sing, walking into my new apartment in downtown Austin.

"Where are the light switches?" Jeena asks, carrying the new bedding we just bought and setting it down near the entryway.

We've been traveling from San Francisco to Austin all day. After getting the keys to the apartment I secured online, Jeena and I went to the local department store and purchased a few essentials we needed for the night. I tried to tell my sister that I didn't need help moving in since I was just taking a couple of bags of clothes and some personal items, but between her and Dad, I knew I wasn't going to win the argument. I'm only a year younger than Jeena but I swear, she acts like she's my second mom--*more like a second layer of skin*--sometimes. It doesn't help that Dad still treats me like I'm the same kid who didn't listen when he told her not to try stunts on the trampoline.

It was one time, and I learned my lesson the hard way.

After turning on the lights, we do a cursory run-through of my furnished apartment--one large bedroom with an en-suite bathroom, an alley-style kitchen with white appliances, and a small living room with a balcony that has a great view of the University of Texas clock tower. It's not the most luxurious apartment--definitely not on the same level Dad would have gotten for me in San Francisco--but it's close to my new job and affordable enough with my new salary that Dad doesn't feel inclined to help me with it.

That doesn't mean he didn't try, though. Once we moved past the initial battle of me moving back to Austin, he insisted on buying me a condo here, but I refused, knowing that any place he bought for me would come with strings attached. It wouldn't *really* be mine. I wanted to prove I could make it on my own without his help, that I'd finally grown up and didn't need him to supervise me on life's proverbial trampoline.

Don't get me wrong, I love my dad and my somewhat-overbearing family, but a girl needs to breathe outside the bubble she's been raised in. With every luxury at my disposal in a matter of a call to my dad, I know how fortunate I am that there will always be a safety net to catch me in case I fall. I just want to be able to walk the tightrope if I so choose.

After putting my bags down in my room, I find Jeena going through each drawer in the kitchen with a grimace, as if merely touching them will require her to sanitize her hands. Her light brown eyes--a copy of my own--scour the area as if she's looking for rats or roaches. Of the two of us, she's definitely the more high-brow and persnickety one. I still remember our trips to India when we visited our grandparents and cousins. While I could sleep in any old sleeping bag on the floor, Jeena would curl up between Mom and

Dad in their small guest bed, claiming the floor smelled dusty.

Knowing that her train of thought is probably about to lead her to cleaning my entire apartment with bleach, I distract her with what I know she'll be excited about. "So, we can go shopping for groceries tomorrow, but you know where we absolutely need to go tonight?" I'm sure my ear-to-ear smile leaves no room for guessing.

"*Chuy's!*" She claps her hands, her face lighting up with shared excitement, and her thoughts of cleaning my place already long-forgotten.

"Yes!" We haven't been back in Austin since we moved ten years ago, but neither of us have forgotten the best TexMex food in the world. San Francisco may be the home to world-class cuisine and restaurants, but good TexMex can only be found in Texas.

"Alright, let's freshen up, then we can take an Uber to the nearest *Chuy's* to celebrate." Jeena unzips her overpacked designer roller bag to take out her toiletries and makeup while I change into shorts and a tank top since evenings in May are way warmer in Austin than they are in San Francisco.

Thirty minutes later, Jeena and I are sitting in a familiar green vinyl booth, reacquainting ourselves with the eclectic decor and the fresh salsa and chips reminiscent of our youth. It's not surprising the restaurant is so busy on a Friday night, and I happily inhale the scent of fresh tortillas and mouthwatering adobo chili sauce, reigniting the memories of when Mom and Dad used to bring us here for dinner.

Even though we grew up mainly on Mom's home-cooked Indian food, my parents would always take us out to eat on Friday nights. And since we could all find something to eat at a TexMex restaurant, we'd usually end up at the *Chuy's* near our home. Mom and Dad would always share a vegetable enchilada plate--since Mom was vegetarian-- while Jeena and I would get chicken quesadillas with fresh guacamole. Dad was still trying to pitch his startup idea to investors at that time, and I recall Mom being careful with expenses, though she'd always make an exception for Friday night dinners.

The waitress comes over to our table, her blonde hair secured in a high ponytail, wearing a half-apron around her dress. "What can I get you ladies to drink?" she asks, her Texas accent accentuating the vowels in her question.

Jeena and I look at each other and smile broadly before Jeena orders for the both of us. "We'll take Texas martinis with salt, please."

Now that's something we never had as kids, but I remember watching Mom moan over it when she ordered a glass.

The waitress nods her approval. "Two martinis, coming right up!"

I can't help but feel giddy about the start of my new life, especially after the past few months I've had. It was always my dream to come back to Austin one day. And even though I have plenty of childhood memories growing up in San Francisco, the sweetest ones still come from Austin. The sweetest ones are filled with *him*. If it wasn't for Dad convincing me to go to Berkeley because of their specialized animation and graphic design program, I probably would have ended up going to college here, too.

But let's be honest, whether the program was better or not, going to Berkeley was just another way for Dad to ensure I stayed a stone's throw away from our house in the East Bay so he could keep his eyes and ears on his *choti beti--*

his little girl. It's only by sheer miracle that I was able to escape the guilt trip he plastered on me for not taking the higher title and compensation he offered me to work at his company.

Dad always had it in his head that both his daughters would work at his company and eventually take over one day. And while Jeena, being the dutiful, rule-following daughter she is, made that a reality for him--becoming his deputy general counsel--I had other dreams. Namely, finding my independence and working for a leading online gaming company.

I scoop up some salsa with my chip before popping it into my mouth. "So, because you're always complaining that I don't tell you about plans ahead of time, I um . . .." I steel myself for the rebuke that will inevitably be launched my way as soon as I complete my sentence. "I may have made an appointment at the local animal shelter tomorrow after-noon to bring home my new fur-baby."

My sister's eyes become saucers, even though I know she's not that surprised. "Are you serious? Anisa, you just got your apartment. You don't even know what your work hours will be yet. How are you going to take care of a pet when you're living alone for the first time?"

I let her words slide over me like raindrops on glass. Jeena's concerns are valid, but I love the idea of starting a new life with a companion. We'll figure it out together. Thankfully, the waitress comes back with our drinks, giving me a chance to collect my thoughts. "Cheers!" I say, lifting my glass to my sister's. Taking a sip, I let the cold, tart liquid wash over my tongue. "God, this is so good."

Jeena nods before licking a little salt off the rim of her glass. "Cheers, and happy early birthday!"

"It's crazy, isn't it? I can't believe I'll be turning twenty-two tomorrow and starting a new job in a new city on my own on Monday. You'd think I was growing up!"

"Let's not get ahead of ourselves," she deadpans. "But I am proud of you for growing into an incredibly gifted animator, web designer . . ." she waves her hand as if to catch all the different things she thinks I do, "and computer badass, who takes life by the horns and paves her own path!"

We clink our glasses again but I don't miss a flutter of something--wistfulness, perhaps--cross over her face before she schools it. I know she's genuinely happy for me, but I sometimes wonder if she's happy, too. My sister has always done what my parents have expected of her. She's stayed on the straight and narrow, following the path they laid out. And even though the past couple of years have tested her strength unfairly, she's never complained. In fact, she stands taller and more self-assured than ever before.

I know I won't get away with not answering her previous question about the animal shelter. After taking another sip of my martini, I fold my hands on the table and look at her. "I know you're concerned about me getting a dog, and I agree that it's going to be a little challenging managing everything, plus a new job. But--"

"But you're doing it anyway." She cocks her head, giving me a look that reminds me of our mom.

I continue unperturbed, "I just happened to be looking on the Austin animal shelter website a couple of weeks ago and saw there was a thirteen-year-old Australian shepherd mix, who apparently had been given up by his previous family. I called them and they told me he was really sweet but had a few health issues. They said he just needed a home where he could be comfortable. He's been there for almost three months and keeps getting passed up for the younger dogs." My shoulders deflate, thinking about the sweet little guy waiting for his family to come back for him. Poor thing is probably so heartbroken. "Jeena, I can't just let him live out the rest of his life in a shelter. I can't."

Jeena shakes her head, knowing there's no use trying to change my mind. This isn't the first time I've brought home a pet who no one wanted. I still remember how Mom had to promise she'd let me get a new pet if I stopped being so upset about moving to San Francisco.

The sadness of leaving Austin--of leaving my best friend, possibly the only person aside from Jeena who accepted me for *me*--wasn't lessened by the prospect of getting another pet, but I was going to have to move anyway, so I'd decided I might as well get something out of it.

So, a week after we moved into our new house, I made sure Mom made good on her promise and brought home our fourteen-year-old, one-eyed cat, Madrid. He lived for two more years, and I cried for two weeks after his death, but it helped knowing that he died being loved as part of our family.

"I assume I can't change your mind about this and that you've already signed the paperwork online, so now all you have to do is pay the fees and pick him up." My sister might be an amazing lawyer, but even she knows that once I've made up my mind, it's hard to get me to change it.

I smile broadly. "Yup! His name is Lynx, and he has the cutest face!" I take out my phone to show her the picture I'd downloaded from their website. "Look at his eyes, Jeena! One is blue and the other is brown. Isn't he gorgeous?"

Glancing at Lynx's picture, Jeena takes a sip of her cocktail, then looks at me pointedly. "You've always had a thing for blue-eyed boys."

I shrug, putting the phone back into my purse, knowing

who she's alluding to and feeling a familiar discomfort in my chest. "Yeah, I suppose I have."

"So, how long did you and Logan stay in touch after we moved?"

I bite my lip, trying not to show the way his name still makes my heart throb. "Like a year, on and off. We played video games together online for a while but . . . I don't know." My throat tightens a little, thinking about the last few times we talked, and I force down another gulp of my drink. "We just sort of stopped talking as much and then after a while, we completely lost touch."

I realize now that we didn't know exactly how to tell each other how much we missed the physical closeness we'd developed and how not being able to see each other every day was torturous for the both of us. Around the same time, he started hanging out with a new group of friends and instead of video games, he became more interested in music. I still remember the last time I heard his boyish voice, telling me we'd talk again soon but never fulfilling the promise.

The waitress comes back to our table to ask if we've decided on our entrees. Both Jeena and I give her our orders and drink in silence for a minute after she leaves.

"Do you ever wonder where he is or what he's doing now?"

A tiny fissure opens inside my chest, one I'd sealed ten years ago when I had to leave my best friend, knowing that we'd become distant over time but hopeful we wouldn't lose touch. "I have wondered but . . .. You'll be surprised to know that I've never looked him up."

"Really? Why?"

I lift a shoulder, moving my index finger to draw a swirl on the layer of condensation around the cocktail shaker. "I suppose I never wanted to see him grow up without me in his life, and looking him up would mean seeing him through pictures and through someone else's eyes instead of my own. It would have just reminded me of what I was missing."

Jeena reaches out to grab my hand. Neither my parents nor Jeena have asked about Logan in years, knowing how much talking about him hurt me. "Oh, Nees, I know how much you missed him. I still remember the way your face would light up when he called or how it wilted when he didn't. He wasn't just a boy you were friends with . . .. I think you loved him."

Did I? Did I even know what love was back then? Do I now?

I don't think I've been in love before. At least, not since I started dating in college. My longest relationship was with Naveen, and I'd rather pull my fingernails out with pliers than relive the last six months with him. Six months that disintegrated twenty-one years of trying to feel comfortable in my own skin. Six months that shouldn't have lasted more than six minutes.

Roughly the time he lasted during sex.

Six months that will probably take me the next six years to flush out of my system.

"I guess that's why, besides you and Nelly, I don't really have a best friend or a tight group of friends. The move didn't affect you in the same way, but for me, it changed the way I thought of friendships, of relationships." I didn't get too attached to anyone. I kept people at arms-length because I never wanted to miss anyone the way I missed Logan.

Of course, I made friends over the years, in both high school and in college, but I'd never been that social of a person. Instead of talking about boys or fashion like some of the girls my age, I preferred to stick my nose in my sketch pad and draw fantastical characters or play video games online with people who were more like me. Instead of going to school dances or college football games, I spent my time building 2D designs of worlds I'd created online.

Second only to Jeena, my friend Nelly is my closest friend from college, but even she doesn't know me the way Jeena does--like only a sister can. Nelly is the type of person you go out with, having no expectations that she won't disappear in the middle of the night with some hot guy she found. She's the life of any party and has a way of making you laugh and do crazy things that you'll regret the next day, but she's not the friend you bare your soul to. She's not the friend who'll hold you while you cry because of a broken heart or because you don't know why you feel lonely some-times. She's the friend who'll accompany you with a bottle of tequila and tell you to douse your heart with it because boys suck and alcohol cures loneliness. That didn't mean she was heartless. She had a rougher childhood than we did, and she didn't give away her heart as easily.

Every tender-hearted introvert should have a friend like Nelly to toughen them up and drag them out of their comfort zone, because while she wasn't a big listener, Nelly *was* a doer. She wouldn't entertain you whining about your woes; instead, she'd get you off your ass so you could stop thinking about them for a night.

"Do you . . .." Jeena pauses before restarting again, "Do you think that's why things didn't work out with you and Naveen?"

I laugh bitterly. "Things didn't work out with Naveen because he was a condescending prick, but yes, I think some of my issues with him were related to the difficulty I've always had opening up to just anyone, but he also didn't do anything to earn my trust."

"I still can't believe some of the things he said to you. He was such an asshole. Has he tried to call you recently?"

I think about the text message he sent me yesterday, telling me how I was making a mistake by moving. How there was still time to cancel, take a job at my dad's company, and get back together with him. I'd just rolled my eyes and scrolled past it. "He's called, but I haven't picked up."

Our food arrives and my mouth waters at the smell of the chicken tacos and Mexican rice. Shoving aside the bitter memories of Naveen, I feast my eyes on my plate. It's way more food than I'll be able to eat, but I can't wait to dive in.

Jeena and I take a mouthful from our plates before I catch her eyes. There's a rare gleam in them that I only see when she decides to stray away from that straight line she generally walks. It doesn't happen often but when it does, it's usually something we talk about for years--like the time she decided the two of us should skip school and get on the BART train to tour the city on our own, and our parents organized a search party after not finding us for hours. Or the time in high school when she decided to change her hair color, except she used me as her test subject and bleached my hair blonde. But these are stories for another time . . ..

Already nervous about what she has on her mind, I circle my index finger in the air around her face. "Why do you have that look on your face? The one that gets us into trouble from time to time."

She chews around the bite of stuffed serrano pepper in her mouth. She'll finish every morsel of food on that over-loaded plate and not even feel an ounce of guilt, guaranteed.

"I was thinking . . . maybe you should look Logan up. See what he's been up to."

My heart thumps in my chest. *Say what, now?* Something tells me this conversation hasn't been just a walk down memory lane. "Why?"

She shrugs, her lips tilting up at the corners, similar to that of a villain in a Disney film. "Just look him up."

Thump thump. "Why do I feel like you *have* looked him up?"

Jeena's face lights up and she reaches for her drink again. "Well . . ." she clears her throat, "I *may* have done a little research. Logan Miller, right?"

I try to keep my voice casual. "Yeah."

"So, we both must be living under a rock, Nees, because Logan Miller is a huge, Grammy-winning DJ."

It takes a moment for me to process what she's said but when I do, I throw my head back, barking out a laugh. She's got the wrong person. "Right. Logan is a famous DJ, and I'm Daenerys Targaryen."

"No, I'm serious. Have you heard of DJ Access? He remixes EDM and techno. Probably why we haven't heard of him since we mainly listen to pop or whatever else is on the radio." She swipes a napkin over her mouth before lifting up her phone, punching something in, and shoving it in my direction. "Look! That's him!"

I almost close my eyes. Call it a reflex reaction, call it self-preservation. It doesn't matter. I don't want to see him. I don't *want* to know what he's like or that he's a famous DJ. I don't want to open up the locked box of feelings. I know I was only a kid at the time, but connections like the one Logan and I shared don't just go away without leaving a mark somewhere deep.

But between all the feelings swirling inside of me,

curiosity prevails. Giving in, I reluctantly reach for her phone, steadying the tremor in my hand.

What I see doesn't compute with the boy whose image I'd entombed in my head. This *man* looks nothing like my Logan, though there are irrefutable similarities. He's standing behind what looks like a turntable, one tattooed arm in the air as if he's riling up the crowd and the other hand on his ear, over his headphones. There's a huge lit screen behind him, casting him in a glow like he's untouchable, inhuman. He's looking into a crowd of thousands as they cheer him on. This man looks nothing like the shy, subdued Logan I knew.

I slide the picture and instinctively press my palm to my chest as if to ensure my heart stays inside. The next picture is attached to a short article: *Logan Miller, DJ Access - The Man Behind the Music.*

What the hell?

I skim the article that talks about how Logan has been DJing for the past five years and has gained fans all around the globe. Clubs and festivals sell out based on his name alone. It even lists his net worth to be a ridiculous number where I have to count all the zeros.

How could I have not known any of this?

I stare at the picture of the man, trying to reconcile him with the boy I knew. The boy who gently picked me up when I fell off the trampoline. The boy who wiped away my tears when I skinned my knee. The boy who made fun of my superhero crush.

Suddenly, I'm not hungry for anything on my plate.

This man . . . he's stunning. There are no other words to describe what I'm seeing, really. His light blue eyes are exactly how I remember them, perhaps sharper, rimmed with a circle of gray, making them look like infinite wells.

His hair has grown darker over the years. While there are still streaks of blonde mixed in, it's mostly light brown, cut short around the sides and longer on top. He's the perfect combination of lean and athletic, his muscles evident even under his shirt.

He isn't smiling--at least, not in any of the pictures I've looked through--though his pink lips look like they were meant for it. They look like they were meant for a lot of things . . ..

And, God, his scruff--perfectly trimmed down his delicious creamy neck, right above his Adam's apple--makes the area between my thighs clench. How can scruff look so sexy?

I swipe picture after picture, skimming over headlines and building a new image of my old best friend. There's a hardness to him--from his eyes to the set in his jaw--as if his features have been etched into stone. Gone are the traces of tenderness that used to pull me toward him like a moth to a blaze. And if I'm not completely off base, he even seems a little sad.

Who is this man? Is the Logan I remember even in there?

Jeena reaches over to cover the phone and I startle, jolted out of hypnosis. "I know." She nods. "I looked at those pictures with the same shock. But it's him, Nees. It's Logan. He even has his own record label and has worked with a number of famous singers. Apparently, some of his music has even hit the Billboard charts, and he's won a couple of Grammys." When I just look at her in a state of dumbfounded silence, she continues, chomping on her bottom lip, "And . . . don't get mad . . .." She gives me a pointed look, worrying me. "For your birthday . . . I secured a VIP table for us at the club he'll be performing in tonight."

Yup, that straight line she walks? It's more like a squiggle.

The fork I was apparently holding in my other hand clatters to the table, akin to the way my stomach clatters to the ground. "Y-you, what?"

"Apparently, he lives in New York and Austin, and he performs here once in a while. I called the club last week after finding out he'd be here. They were completely booked, but I told them I'd pay triple for the table and they made it work."

My breath hitches and I wonder if maybe I'm so exhausted from the day that I've fallen asleep somewhere and this is all part of an elaborate dream. "We've been trav-eling--sitting next to each other on the plane--all day, and you just *now* decided to tell me this?"

She winces, an apologetic expression crossing her face. "Surprise!" she whisper-yells, holding both hands up and wiggling her fingers. "Happy twenty-second birthday, little sis!"

2

ANISA

*P*anic sets in somewhere between the time I step into my apartment and the time I've mindlessly walked into my room, making me repeat what I've learned over the past half hour. My old best friend is now a famous DJ, and he's going to be at the club Jeena is dragging me to. When did Jeena and Nelly decide to switch personalities? Nelly is the one who does the dragging.

Oh, God. Please tell me I'm being punked.

"Breathe, Anisa," I encourage myself, trying to force oxygen into my lungs.

No, I'm not going.

I'm not ready.

I haven't seen Logan in a decade, and I sure as hell am *not* prepared to see him tonight. I open the bag with my bedding and start to cover my bed. I'll just tell Jeena that the rice and beans aren't sitting well in my stomach and I need to sleep it off.

Yup. Good plan. When everything else fails, blame it on gas.

"What are you doing?" Jeena walks in as I'm running through the excuse again in my head.

"Hmm?" I stall. "Oh, just making the bed. I'm kind of tired from the whole day. I think I'm going to stay in tonight."

I glance at Jeena, who's now squinting at me. "For all your tough-guy act, you're really kind of a big baby. Maybe I need to tell Dad that you're not ready to live on your own after all."

"What?" I scoff. I hate when she gets like this-- connecting disassociated events to make some weird point. "What does being tired have to do with me living alone?"

She levels me with a stare. "I can smell bullshit from a mile away, and you reek of it. You might be tired, but that's not the reason you want to stay home. You're scared you'll see Logan, whom you've never stopped crushing on since middle school."

My right eye twitches as I face off with my sister. "That is simply not true."

She steps forward, challenging me with a quirked eyebrow. "Isn't it?"

"I'm also gassy . . ." I mumble under my breath, losing steam, but hoping to dissuade her.

Jeena rolls her eyes. "You're going to the club with me, Nees, gassy or not. So, take some *Gas-Ex*, make yourself look less . . ." she waves her hand, motioning to all of me, "bloated, and get yourself together."

"Get out of my apartment," I growl, bunching up a pillowcase and throwing it at her as she giggles, dodging it and heading to the bathroom.

"That's not hard to do," she shouts from behind the door. "It's like, what, twelve square feet. You're practically living outside, anyway."

"Little witch," I mumble under my breath while I look through the clothes in my bag. I don't own anything appropriate for a club. I take out a few T-shirts and ripped jean shorts before spotting my Captain Marvel tank top. I guess I can pair it with dark jeans. I eye said jeans, wondering if I'll still be able to fit into them. *They'll definitely be on the tighter side . . ..*

So maybe I gained a few pounds over the past few months. Sue me. I needed the extra weight to help me make it through the brutal San Francisco winter! Or maybe I needed them to cushion the verbal punches from Naveen. In any case, I needed them. Plus, I don't mind the extra curves around my hips and ass. I don't have the biggest breasts, but my waist is still cinched, making my body look like a nice figure eight. Besides, my clothes may fit snugger than they used to, but at least I feel renewed and free.

There's no point in trying to find slinky shoes in my bag--I don't own any--so I'll have to borrow some heels from Jeena. From the size of her suitcase, she's obviously packed her entire closet to come here for the weekend.

About an hour later, Jeena and I are in the back of another Uber heading toward downtown Austin. She looks perfectly put together as always, in a short, black halter dress and a pair of nude heels with her hair in a low ponytail. I, on the other hand, look like her grungy sidekick in heels, my long dark hair falling in waves down my back, and the slightest bit of lipgloss and mascara accentuating my features. It's surprisingly a pretty accurate representation of who we are as people, too.

I haven't stopped biting the inside of my cheek--a nervous habit since I was younger. Why did I agree to this? It's a crazy idea and borderline stalkerish. My only hope now is that Logan doesn't remember me. Then, I can go back to my previously scheduled life without him.

Will that even be possible if I see him again?

I imagine passing by him at this club without him even sparing me a glance. Just the thought sends sharp pain shooting through my chest. Why are both scenarios--him recognizing me or not--so nerve-wracking? Wouldn't it be better if he doesn't remember me? Then I won't have to make any awkward conversation with him or ask what he's been up to for the past decade.

Or why he stopped talking to me.

Plus, I wouldn't even fit into his life now. He's a famous DJ, probably with a posse that follows him around, and I'm a computer nerd who prefers to live in animated fantasy worlds rather than real ones. The only people who follow me around are my overbearing family. *Case in point, Exhibit A, sitting to my left.*

I'm probably being presumptuous. This club is going to be so packed that coming face to face with the DJ will be an impossibility. Anyway, I'm sure he'll be off-limits in the DJ booth with federal armed guards securing access to him or something.

Stop being ridiculous, I chide myself. I don't even need to worry about any of this. I'm just going to go for a little while to appease Jeena, especially since she's shelled out enough money to buy a small island rather than a table. She's sweet to celebrate my birthday, and I just need to put my big girl pants on and be grateful.

I've already got the big girl pants covered.

My cheek biting becomes more frantic and my palms sweat as we exit the highway. The positive self-talk I gave myself a moment ago turns into an agitated internal rant as I think about what I'm being dragged into.

I don't even like clubs or club patrons overcrowding the bar, gyrating to loud music, slinging sweat on anyone within a four foot radius. It's unhygienic, really, and I'm surprised

Jeena is even okay with it. She knows me well enough to know that even without the threat of happenstancing with the hot DJ, a club would be the last place I'd want to celebrate my birthday. Why couldn't she have chosen something less people-y to do, like listen to a podcast together in the comfort of my new apartment.

It's not like I haven't been clubbing before. Nelly guilted me into going with her in college a few times, forcing me to get out of my comfortable sweats and into microscopic clothes she'd made me pick out from her closet. She said I needed to join the rest of the human race from time to time.

Let me tell you, I was not a fan.

Through the entire excruciating experience, I'd sit at the bar, feigning interest while some random guy invaded my personal space with his pearly teeth and expensive cologne, blathering on about the newest Tesla his dad bought for him. Meanwhile, I'd think about how much additional storage I'd need to upload my latest designs onto the cloud.

"I can hear the neurons firing around that head of yours. Stop thinking so much or they're going to cause a fire." Jeena pulls me out of my reflections as we get to the light near Fourth Street. I watch from the window as a group of women in form-fitting dresses and tall heels walk from one bar to the next, waving to a group of guys leering at them like they'd go well served with mustard and mayo. "Look, we're probably not even going to see him. Just think of this as us celebrating your birthday and your new job."

She grabs my hand and I scowl at her. "This doesn't feel celebratory. It feels like I'm being forced on stage for a performance I'm ill-prepared for."

She tilts her head and blinks at me. "With all that drama, I think you're well-prepared."

"I'm going to kill you for this."

She smiles, squeezing my hand. "You can't. You'll need me to get you out of legal troubles and to be the good daughter so you don't have to be."

"That's true."

We giggle and a few of the tangled wires in my stomach relax. Our driver lets us off near *Club Vex* and we make our way toward the long line of people waiting to get in. Jeena pulls my elbow and takes us toward a secondary line where only one other couple is waiting. I assume that's the line for people like Jeena who paid for the island.

After checking our IDs, the bouncer scans his list and confirms our names before we make our way into a darkened entryway with another pair of large men guarding the door. Geez, this place has more security detail than a military base. They both look us up and down before opening the large doors leading into the club.

While the music could be heard with the doors closed, I'm immediately struck by the bass when the doors open. The vibration streams through my veins like a liquid drug, trying to take over. A hostess greets us in the front, verifying Jeena's name and motioning us toward the stairs. Walking behind her and Jeena, I examine my surroundings.

The dance floor is packed with bodies bouncing and shaking to the music. Some have their hands up, holding a glass in the air, while others swivel their way sexily down someone else's body, trying to find friction. I can't see anyone's face, but the strobe lights illuminate the mixture of mainly black, white, and silver outfits on the floor.

My gaze finally lands on what must be the DJ booth, upstairs in a glass enclosure. I see a few people moving inside, but it's too hard to tell who they are. My heart picks up again at the thought of Logan being in there, but I keep moving up the stairs.

We make our way upstairs and the hostess seats us at our island--uh, table. Within minutes, two women--one blonde and one brunette--in identical short silver dresses walk over to us with large containers of what looks to be mixers and carafes of alcohol. "Hi, ladies!" They lean over to greet us. "We'll be your bartenders tonight. This is cranberry juice and this is pineapple juice," the brunette yells above the music, pointing to each colorful decanter. "What can we get for you?"

After my sister and I order our mixed drinks, I continue my perusal of the floor as the music thrums inside my chest. My nerves are standing on end as if preparing my body to either fight or flight. Right now, it's leaning toward flight. I know Jeena can tell because she leans over and tells me to calm down.

"It's my sister's birthday!" Jeena yells to our bartenders.

The blonde girl throws her hands up and hoots as if it's the most incredible thing she's heard all night. "Happy birthday, beautiful!" she yells at me while the brunette pours us all shots. "Let's celebrate!"

I resign myself to the fact that I'm going to regret this in the morning and throw the shot back, cringing slightly as it burns through my esophagus. The brunette slams her shot glass onto the table before her eyes light up. "I've got an idea!" *Uh oh. Nothing good has ever come from those words, especially after slamming a shot.* "Let's get DJ Access to wish you a happy birthday! He's about to start his set in a few minutes."

I forcefully shake my head while my sister nods with equal vigor. "No, I don't think so," I yell while Jeena claps her hands and squeals, "Yes! Best idea *ever*! Let's have him wish her a happy birthday!"

I get a vision of wrapping my hands around my sister's

throat. Giving her a meaningful look, I try to catch her attention. "Jeena."

She ignores me--of course, she does--and motions to the brunette to come closer so she can whisper something in her ear. *Freaking traitor sister.* The brunette's eyes gleam while she looks at me over Jeena's shoulder and screeches, "Oh my God! This is going to be epic!"

I squint at Jeena and try to catch the brunette but she's already moving away from us, disappearing into the crowd. "Jeena! What the hell? Whatever you said to her, it's not a good idea. I'm not ready!"

The blonde bartender throws me a confused look. "It's not a big deal, honey. They wish VIPs happy birthdays all the time. Consider it part of your package!"

"Yeah," my sister mocks, smiling wildly. "Consider it part of your package!"

I wish smacking my sister was part of the package.

I growl, slumping back in my seat, wishing I could get off this overpriced island. My heart hammers against my chest as if to say, "*If you don't get out of here, I will!*" When the music changes, the blonde shrieks, wiggling and dancing to the rhythm, "That's *him*! You can always tell when he takes over the turntable!"

"What's up, what's up, Austin?" the most gloriously deep voice I've ever heard says through the microphone. The velvety baritone around his words crawl down my spine, warming me from the inside out like hot chocolate on a cold day. Immediately, I know I'll never forget this voice for as long as I live. "You been waiting for me?"

Yes . . . for so long.

The crowd on both floors respond with eardrum-shattering consent as the music picks up to match the speed of my heart. The beat gets faster, mixed with a hypnotic synthesized melody, making the crowd go wild. I can't believe this is *my* Logan performing. It's as if I'm hearing him for the first time. And though I can't deny that I'm curious about meeting him again, fear is still the reigning sentiment at the moment.

As we wait for the other bartender to return, a couple of guys lingering near our table make eye contact with my sister. One of them smiles at her, taking his cue to come over when she flashes him her sultry smile. Astute as she is, she knows exactly how she comes across, and not many can resist even the tiniest attention she spares them. Both men are incredibly handsome and I chuckle to myself, knowing that neither will have a real shot with Jeena--not that they would have a shot with me either, given my current hiatus from men.

If I've been called a social hermit, Jeena's been told she's emotionally unavailable. I don't blame her, not after what she's been through. She'll have fun for a night and hookup here and there with a guy--Lord knows she gets enough offers--but she'll never invest more of herself with any of them.

"Hey, ladies," the gorgeous black guy yells over the music. He has the prettiest smile I've ever seen; his perfect white teeth surrounded by the softest, plump lips. "Mind if we join you or would either of you like to dance?"

Jeena shakes her head, her ponytail swaying delicately. "We're waiting for a particular song and if that comes on, I'll dance with you!"

We're waiting for a particular song?

After a few seconds, Jeena invites them to sit with us, and the two guys slide into either side of the table, next to both of us. I tell the man sitting next to me, Adam, that this is our first night in Austin and that I moved here for a new job. He tells me he also works for a startup in the area, and we start talking about the city's startup scene. I notice that he leans in close to my ear, even though I'm sure I could hear him just fine with how close he's sitting.

The blonde bartender notices that I've finished my drink and asks if she can make me another. *Oh, why the hell not?* Maybe getting wasted will calm my nerves.

I glance at Adam as I take a sip of my fresh new cocktail. He's watching me, his hazel eyes growing darker as they zone in on my lips. I've often been told I have beautiful lips. I suppose aside from my light-colored eyes--a rarity with Indian genes--my full lips are what stand out on my face.

"You're really beautiful, but I'm sure you know that." Adam's breath ghosts over my ear, creating a flutter in my stomach. "You might have the most beautiful lips I've ever seen."

He really is a good-looking guy--tall and well-built, but not over the top. His reddish-brown hair sticks out over his ears and he has a casual look about him, like he just uses his fingers to comb through the perfectly disheveled mess. For a moment I almost forget that I'm taking a break from men or that I'm nervous about potentially meeting someone else entirely.

"Thanks." I take another sip of my drink to wash away the heat rising to my cheeks. Both Jeena and I have received enough compliments about our appearance over the years to know we're attractive, but where she's able to move past them like they're commonplace observations, I've always felt awkward about receiving them, as if the giver was just doing me a favor.

Adam's hand slips to my thigh while the alcohol in my system convinces my brain that I'm fine, that I'm completely in control. It's only when I hear that same deep voice on the microphone again that I jolt back to full consciousness and remove Adam's hand as if it were a hot coal against my skin.

"This song is for a *Batgirl* turning twenty-two this weekend. If she can hear me, I have a message for her . . .. Come find me, *Batgirl*."

My heart stops and my wide eyes connect with Jeena's. Her mouth drops to the floor as she realizes who he's talking about. I'm not quite sure which one of us says, "Holy shit."

The music changes with another fast beat, mixing with the familiar guitar and drum beats as the song *Kryptonite* by *3 Doors Down* comes on. The hypnotic rhythm rouses the crowd while my brain tells me this song is no coincidence. It's a veiled message of our friendship--lyrics containing words like *Superman* and *kryptonite*--Morse code meant only for me to decipher.

I guess he still has poor choices in superheroes.

I don't even know when I pick up my purse, motioning for Adam to scoot so I can slide out of the booth. *I have to leave. I have to get out of here. I can't go find him, I'm not ready.* Adam moves over while Jeena scans me, knowing I'm ready to bolt. But before I can go any farther, the brunette bartender who'd left our table earlier rushes back with a frenzied look in her eyes. She scans me from head to toe as if seeing me for the first time.

Speaking loud enough for the table to hear, she says, "You've got to come with me. Access wants to see you."

3

LOGAN

"You look like roadkill." Luckily for me, Wayland never pulls punches when it comes to telling me like it is, but I could do with a little less of that today. He may be my manager but he's one of my closest-- and unfortunately, most brutally honest--friends first.

"If you don't want me looking like roadkill, then get me off the fucking road," I growl back at him as I close the door to the DJ booth behind me. Between the jet lag and the long nights, I'm in dire need of some time off.

Wayland has had me booked solid for the past month to the point where I don't even remember which city I'm in until I'm behind the damn turntable. I've woken up in seven different cities on three different continents in the past four weeks, and my body is reeling from the lack of sleep--and my moods aren't any better.

I'm sorry for being an ass. I send an apology text to my mom for snapping at her earlier before slipping my phone back into my pocket. She didn't deserve it. She's done more than her share of what any mom would be expected to, and she hasn't complained once about it. She doesn't deserve her MIA son yelling at her for making decisions on his behalf when he's not there to make them himself.

After bumping fists with the DJ completing the previous set, I get a quick read on the crowd. He lists off a few mixes he's played so we don't overlap and gives me a rundown on some new equipment that came in last week.

Within a couple of minutes, I've connected to my playlists and I'm behind the table at the club I started my career in. It was five years ago when this club, *Club Vex*, gave me a chance to show off my skills. I played off-peak, either getting the early crowd warmed up or close up the club, but it was enough to hone my talent and get discovered. I owe it to this club and the owner for giving me that chance. Now, whenever I'm back in Austin--which is usually every couple of weeks, though with how much Wayland has had me booked, this is the first time in a month--and if I have any energy left, I only charge them half my normal rate for a short set.

With the way I'm feeling today though, I should have canceled. But I also know how much these clubs invest in terms of marketing, and it would be shitty of me to cancel so last-minute, unless it was an emergency. Plus, I've worked hard at building my brand--foregone spending more time with the most important person in my life--I need to rally and get through the night. Thankfully, I don't have to fly out again until Tuesday night, so I'll get most of the weekend to spend with her.

The only one this is all for. The only one who matters.

As if Wayland is reading my mind, he says, "Take it easy this weekend 'cause you'll need all your energy for Paris next week."

I grunt a response, putting on my headphones and

turning a knob on the controller. I hold up a finger, letting him know I'm about to unmute the microphone before speaking into it, greeting the crowd with my standard line. "What's up, what's up, Austin? You been waiting for me?"

The increase in volume from below lets me know they're ready to dance, so I start the new sequence I worked on a couple of nights ago, beat matching a couple of songs first. Sometimes I use this crowd to gauge how a new mix will be received in bigger venues.

Wayland answers a knock on the door, opening it with his standard gruff greeting. "What?"

"Hey, Wayland," comes the high-pitched voice of some girl I'm sure he's intimately familiar with, "I didn't realize you were going to be here tonight, too. I saw you come in and thought I'd say hi." I glance over at her, briefly taking in her short silver dress and flushed cheeks. I vaguely recognize her as one of the hosts for the VIPs section.

"Great. Hi. I'm busy," he growls, shutting the door on her when she holds up her hand, pushing against it.

"Actually, I'm not here to bother you. We got a VIP who'd love for Access to give her a shout-out."

"He doesn't do that shit anymore. Ask the closing DJ to serenade her if that's what she needs."

I adjust the crossfader, barely paying attention to their conversation. I'm tempted to tell them to take their lovers' quarrel outside so I can focus when I hear the last thing the brunette at the door says, "Her name is Anisa. Her sister says she knows Access."

Every hair on my neck rises as I turn to catch Wayland's eyes, but they're frozen on the brunette's face as if he's trying to read her lips.

"Anisa?" he repeats, glancing at me before looking back at her. "What's her sister's name?"

She makes a face like she's trying to remember it. "Jenna or Gina or something. They're sitting in the VIP section, celebrating a birthday. I told them Access would give her a shout-out. Can he do it just this once?"

A whoosh of air rushes out of me as a cyclone of memories hit me square in the chest. Memories I've often turned to in cold hotel bedrooms and long international flights. Memories that have inspired both my music and my creativity in more ways than I can count. Me and Anisa sitting side-by-side, eating plain jelly sandwiches in the field behind our school because she didn't like peanut butter and thought no one else did, either.

Thoughts of us putting our palms flat against each other to compare hand sizes and doing the same with our shoes, surface to top. I remember having to hide my smile whenever she gawked at how much larger my hands and feet were compared to hers. Even at that age, I felt this strange need to take care of her, to protect her. She showed everyone a tough exterior to balance out whatever internal insecurities she harbored, but I knew she still needed armor. And I was happy to be that for her.

"You're a freaking mutant!" she'd scream. "How do you have such big hands and feet? You should apply to the *Justice League*."

"Are you saying I'm your superhero, *Batgirl*?"

"Pshh, you wish!" she'd respond, making a face of disgust and bumping her shoulder against mine.

The brunette at the door says something else to Wayland, bringing me back to the present, before he starts to close the door on her again. I'm surprised he didn't ask more about Jeena. It took him a whole year to get over her after they moved, though he'll never admit it aloud.

"Wait," I say, taking my headphones off. "Tell her I want to see her."

Her face twists. "Which one? Anisa or her sister?"

I look at Wayland and see the slight lift at the corner of his lips. "Anisa." I test out the name again on my tongue as if it's a flavor I haven't tasted in ages. And it feels deliciously familiar.

Turning back toward the equipment, I unmute the mic again, letting the brunette know my door is open, before adding a song to the playlist, beat matching it with the previous one and pulling it to the foreground. It's a change from the set I'd prepared, and it's a song that I haven't listened to since the summer I remixed it, but it's a song that means more than just its lyrics when it comes to her.

A song that's *her*.

4

LOGAN

BEGINNING OF SUMMER, TEN YEARS AGO

"*H*i, Mrs. Singh. Can Anisa come out?" I look past Anisa's mom after she opens the door to see if I can catch a glimpse of *Batgirl* in the hallway, but she isn't there. Instead, Scooter waddles over to get the treat I've been bringing for him every time I come over--a little piece of jerky. I get the feeling that he's set this as the price I pay for letting me see his girl.

"Sure. Let me get--"

"Can Jeena come, too?" Wayland huffs up next to me, skateboard in hand and a little perspiration lining his dark brow.

Mrs. Singh smiles at the both of us. She has the same eyes as Anisa and Jeena's--light brown and kind. Hers have tiny lines around them, reflecting her age, but they're just as clear and bright. "Jeena just started summer camp so she can't join, but I'll get Anisa." She leaves the door open and walks toward Anisa's room.

Wayland kicks his skateboard in frustration, making it slip out of his hand. I mask a smile. I feel bad for the guy, but he's convinced that Jeena just hasn't come to terms with her feelings for him.

On the last day of school last week, some girl slid a note into his locker and Wayland was sure it was Jeena. He had no proof but I played along, knowing he just needed someone to believe him.

I suppose there are worse qualities than overconfidence.

I hear Anisa's voice come from her living room before I hear the refrigerator door close. "Don't slam the fridge, Neesu!" her mom scolds as Anisa rushes down the hallway, ignoring her mom and stuffing something into her backpack.

She's still messing with her backpack as she walks toward us, and I watch every move like some creeper. Her hair is in a messy ponytail, some locks hanging out of it loosely. She's wearing an X-Men tank top and another pair of psychedelic tights. Now, I don't know much about girls' fashion, but I get the feeling she's not a trendsetter. But I love that she owns it and couldn't care less about what others think.

As soon as she looks up, I quickly avert my gaze and pretend to look at my skateboard on the ground as if I just noticed it was there.

"Hey!" she breathes as soon as she's at the door.

"Hey, yourself."

Wayland is already carving his skateboard around her cul-de-sac when Anisa picks hers up from her front porch and closes the door. "Let's go." She motions to me with her head.

We ride to the school parking lot, Wayland leading the charge with Anisa between us. It's a typical summer day in Austin, where one gust of warm wind feels like a reprieve in the desert. In classic Anisa style, she tries to act like a professional skateboarder, jumping the curb and zig-zagging past Wayland. I cringe internally, trying not to visualize her falling.

"It's the first week of summer and Jeena's already in summer camp?" Wayland asks, holding back his agitation by a thread. I know the real question he's dying to ask, why is Jeena even *in* summer camp when she should be here with us?

"Yup. My parents made her go."

"Why didn't they make *you* go?"

"Because Jeena does what my parents ask her to do. It's some sort of debate camp. They asked me to go too, but I told them the only person I like to debate with lives two doors away from us and I've already kicked his ass in every worthwhile argument, so I'd rather not waste their money." Anisa gives me a pointed look and I shake my head, knowing she's referring to me.

Please. I could whoop her ass in every debate. I just choose not to.

"Debate camp? Does she want to be a lawyer or something?" Wayland presses on casually, slowing a little so he won't miss a single word out of Anisa's mouth.

"She wants to be whatever my dad wants her to be. So, yeah, a lawyer."

"And what do you want to be?" I ask as we turn past the stop sign and into the school drop-off area. I don't know why I have a pressing need to find out what she dreams about, what she imagines for her life. Maybe if I'm lucky, I'll see it happen one day, too.

She does another zig-zag but stays close enough for me to hear. "Probably an artist or a government spy."

"Let's get back to Jeena for a minute," Wayland carries

on as Anisa side-eyes him. "Will she be in this camp all summer? Is it every day of the week?"

Anisa sighs as we ride into the parking lot. "No, it's only for three weeks, Monday through Thursday. But she starts a public speaking camp after that. And in case you're wondering, her favorite flavor of ice cream is pistachio--which I think is gross, by the way--she loves *Fruit Loops* a little too much, she sleeps with a nightlight on because she's scared of the dark, she's a lefty and we buy her special notebooks with the spiral on the other side, and no, she doesn't have a boyfriend." She looks pointedly at Wayland, who has turned the same shade of red as his shirt. "Any other questions?"

He narrows his eyes at her, looking over at me when I can no longer hold in my laughter. "Yeah, laugh it up, asshole," he says and takes off with his board to ride around the parking lot, probably still mumbling profanities at us.

"What did I say?" Anisa calls after him, acting innocent as he flips her off.

After another half an hour of trying out different stunts and tiring ourselves out, Wayland waves to the two of us and heads back home while Anisa and I plop onto a patch of dry summer grass. She opens her bag and hands me a small bottle of water before twisting the cap off one for herself. Then, she takes out what I already know will be grape jelly sandwiches. She's made them almost every day this week. She thinks I like them, but I don't have the heart to tell her how much I hate grape jelly, so I just power through them.

"I made a sandwich for Wayland, but since he left . . . do you want it?"

"No," I respond quickly.

She shrugs and puts the sandwich away and takes out her notebook. "I drew something new. Want to see?"

I always do, but I give her a shrug like it's no big deal. I don't want to seem overeager. When she turns to the page and shows it to me, my head jerks back a little. "Wow! You drew that? That's some good shit, *Batgirl*!"

She lifts a shoulder, taking a bite of her sandwich, but I know she's happy that I like it. And why wouldn't I? The pterodactyl picking up a human with his talons looks more realistic than if it was created digitally. And she drew it by hand!

"Thanks." She blushes a little, the dimple on her left cheek becoming more prominent. "Do you want it?"

"Yeah." I don't even need to think twice about it.

She rips out the drawing, folds it, and hands it to me. I put the paper in my pocket but remember I have something to show her, too. Taking out my phone and the headphone wires, I hand one earbud to her. "Remember I told you I've been messing around with mixing music lately?"

Her eyes brighten and I look away, not completely understanding why my face feels hot. She plugs one of the headphones into her ear and leaves the other for me. "Yes! Are you going to let me listen to something you mixed?"

I tamper down any of her high expectations. "It's not that good, but I had fun messing around with all the sounds."

She wiggles excitedly. "Well, hurry up then! I want to listen."

I chuckle, scrolling to the song. I don't know what made me choose it--*or maybe it's not hard to guess*--since it's kind of an old song now. Putting the other bud in my ear, I start the music and watch her face.

A smile creeps onto her lips as she stares into my eyes, listening to the beat and tapping her foot against the grass. I want to look away but the heat of her stare keeps me frozen in place. She's looking *at* me, but she's looking *inside* me too, making me feel exposed. "Lo, this is so good! I can't believe you mixed this."

"It's a song called *Kryptonite* by a band named *3 Doors Down*."

She listens intently for another few seconds. "I think you were thinking of me when you mixed this," she declares as if she knows me better than I know myself. *And she probably does.*

I scoff, "And why would I be thinking of you?"

My eyes attach to the smile she beams at me and I can't help but think how cute that dimple is. "Because," she giggles, "I'm your kryptonite."

5

ANISA

"*W*e're leaving. *Now*." I give my sister the look that says I'm going to wash all her undergarments with bleach if she doesn't listen to me.

"You are being such a wimp," she whines, slurring as she gets out of her seat. *Clearly, she's not feeling those drinks at all.* She can think I'm being a wimp all she wants; she doesn't have to deal with my internal turmoil. What if he thinks I'm *boring* or *socially stunted* like Naveen said? Being a famous DJ, I'm sure he has tons of gorgeous, stick-thin women hanging off his arm. What if he finds me unattractive?

With my panic soaring, I'm just pulling her by her elbow while she hugs the guy who was sitting next to her--taking her sweet time and ignoring my strife--when I hear our two bartenders gasp behind me. It's as if my body knows there's impending doom lurking nearby. My nerves stand on end, and I consider abandoning my sister and gunning it for the exit. When their heightened squeals become unbearable, I look over my shoulder to follow their line of sight, immediately wishing I'd followed my gut and left earlier.

Gulp.

My eyes land on a man who looks like the live-cutout from the pictures I saw earlier tonight. Over six feet tall, broad-chested, covered in a fitted black tee that stretches from shoulder to shoulder, and a full sleeve of tattoos visible over his lean muscular arm. He's stalking toward me like a lion in the Serengeti, eyes locked on its prey. They shift imperceptibly to Adam standing next to me before coming back to mine, his jaw tightening just a touch.

Thinking through this objectively, if I ever thought Adam was attractive, he's a mere mortal compared to the god striding toward me with single-focus. As if following his silent order, I step forward, offering myself as bait and dismissing any thought of self-preservation.

Here, kitty kitty . . ..

Sometime during the past ten seconds, my heart rate has gone from elevated to lightning speed, making me pant like an eighty-year-old smoker pulling oxygen into her lungs. At the sight of the mouthwatering man coming to a stop in front of me, a sound somewhere between a bray--like I'm a damn horse--and a groan escapes my lips. This man will undoubtedly be the star of all my fantasies--effectively replacing the Hemsworth brothers--from now on.

The cut of his jaw, the winter in his eyes, and the muscles pulsing under his sleeves are so sharp, he should be outlawed.

He barely leaves an inch of space between us as I look up into familiar blue eyes with gray rims, scorching my skin in their perusal. Tilting his face to look at me under a hooded gaze, he drawls, "You weren't planning on leaving without seeing me, were you, *Batgirl*?"

"Yes, she totally--" my sister yells, somewhere behind me right as I counter with, "No! Of course not!"

I am totally bleaching her underpants!

While I'm aware that we have an audience and a few have taken photos as well, Logan's face gives nothing away as to if he even notices. We stand there for nearly a decade, close enough to feel the heat from our bodies. Close enough for me to pick up the smell of cloves and soap. Close enough to see a vein pulse in his neck to the beat of the music--a vein I find myself fixating on like some sort of blood-deprived vampire.

His focus slowly crawls to my lips and I swallow, fighting against my body's desire to launch myself at him. Exhaling to give the heat building inside me an outlet and trying to start over, I squeak, "Hey."

"Hey, yourself." His voice, like warm butter, seeps into my stomach before dropping somewhere lower into my core and pooling in my panties. His arms wrap around me in the warmest embrace, holding me tight against him like he's afraid I might slip away again. His warm breath fans over my ear. "Happy early birthday, Anisa. It's . . . it's good to see you."

As if I'd been waiting for those words--to hear my name on his lips again--all the tension in my body releases and I melt into his arms. My throat tightens as I feel him around me and I ask myself if this is just a dream. *It has to be a dream, right?* Everything about him seems familiar and foreign, like visiting your childhood home after someone else has moved in. I'd forgotten how protective and warm his arms always felt wrapped around me. The last time I'd been buried in them was over ten years ago.

We'd ridden to the school for the last time that summer since I was moving to San Francisco later that day. I'd even packed him a jelly sandwich, knowing he loved them so much. But we didn't ride around on our skateboards in the parking lot like we usually did. That day, we just held each other, letting our embrace say all the things we couldn't say aloud, words we didn't even understand ourselves. We hugged for so long, I thought the summer sun would melt us together.

I remember thinking how unfair it was that I was moving right when I'd finally found a friend who liked me for me, who laughed at my jokes and had the same interests as I did. As I stood enfolded in his arms, my throat felt tight, like there was a rough-edged stone lodged inside, threatening to break the dam of tears I was barely holding at bay.

Not wanting to tarnish my tomboy reputation with dramatic tears, I finally broke away from his embrace and got back on my skateboard without saying a word. I couldn't find enough courage to look back, even though he was still standing there. I knew my heart would break in two if I did. Barely managing to keep myself upright until I got home, I fell into Jeena's arms, finally releasing the tears I'd forbidden to shed in his presence.

And now, as I breathe in his spicy cologne, nuzzling my face in the space between his shoulder and neck, those same tears make an unwelcomed reappearance. Undoubtedly feeling the wetness soaking through the collar of his shirt, Logan pulls us apart to look at my face. He surveys my tears before his large hands wrap around my neck and his thumbs wipe both of my cheeks. I see his soft lips quirk up from under my wet lashes. "It looks like you missed me, *Batgirl*."

"You wish." I giggle against the sob ready to break free. "I was just crying because you still have bad taste in music."

He laughs, the vibration from his chest connecting with mine. Over the years, I'd often wondered what he looked like--though I was always too scared to look him up. Never in my wildest dreams did I imagine him to turn out as gorgeous as he did. His hair looks like it's been kissed by the sun in the most mouthwatering way. His lips are exactly how I'd seen them online--plump . . . kissable.

Wait, no. Not kissable because you're taking a break from kissing anyone these days.

"You're . . . beautiful." His voice is as rough as the hand he tangles in my hair, his touch sending a flash of heat down my spine. "I can't believe how long it's been."

I'm just about to respond when my sister clears her throat next to me, effectively breaking me out of my trance. I don't have to look at her to know how smug her smile is and that she's barely holding back, taking a proud bow with how this night has turned out. "Any chance the sister responsible for this reunion can get a hug, too?"

So predictable.

My body wails when Logan takes his hands off of me and turns to hug Jeena. I watch the bartenders swoon around us, eavesdropping on everything they can pick up. Adam and the other guy--I never did catch his name--have moved to another table with a few other women, clearly put off by our display of affection over the past few minutes.

"By the way," Jeena continues, speaking louder over the beat, "you're an amazing DJ. It's incredible how much you've done in such a short time, Logan."

Even in the dim lighting, I see the slight blush that rises to his cheeks and I wonder why. I'm sure he's used to getting compliments from raving fans. "It's kind of easy when you have a muse," he says with a shrug.

Right. Because why wouldn't this smoking-hot, successful artist have a real-life muse? I bet the inspiration for all his music is waiting for him at home.

It's like ice water thrown on a new spark, but I remind myself that it's a good thing that Logan is taken. I should just be happy to have reconnected with him. Pasting a smile back on my face, I continue to listen as Jeena tells him how I moved here today and will be starting a new job on Monday.

She's just telling him which apartment complex I moved into--not failing to mention how small it is, either-- when she stops mid-sentence, her eyes widening as another man comes to stand next to Logan. He says something in Logan's ear before turning to smile at me. His gaze lingers on Jeena momentarily and a strange sense of déjà vu grips me. I know those grayish eyes and that scar on his eyebrow where the hair doesn't grow. "Wayland?" Even though it comes out as a question, I know for sure it's him. He's maybe an inch shorter than Logan, but he's still over six feet tall and towers over my five-foot-seven and Jeena's five-foot-five frame.

"Hey, Anisa." He leans in to give me a hug before he and Jeena exchange a strangely wooden wave. "Been a long time. How are you?"

"I'm good! God, I can't believe I'm finally seeing both of you after so long. You guys look so . . .." My gaze idles on Logan. He's so captivating, I almost forget what I want to say. In fact, every word I want to use--*gorgeous, happy, grown up*-- all sound inadequate in my head and I land on "Incredible," not feeling any further assured.

"You both do, too," Wayland says, trying to catch Jeena's eyes. I look over at my sister but she appears overly occu- pied, stirring the drink in her hand as if she's trying to find lost treasure in the cup. "So, what brings you back to Austin?"

"Anisa just found a job here," Logan responds for me, his eyes affixed to mine. I know if I let myself get entangled in the heavy eye contact again, I'll probably forget my own name, so I draw my focus away to look at Wayland. *It's safer there.*

"Welcome back to Austin, ladies!" Wayland smiles, looking from me to Jeena.

"Actually, it's just me," I correct him. "Jeena is going back to San Francisco in a couple of days."

Wayland nods but I see something flicker in his expression--disappointment, maybe?--while Jeena remains mute.

"So, do you still live here?" I ask Logan, trying to bury the awkward silence between Jeena and Wayland.

The timber in his chuckle fires off goosebumps along my arms. "Theoretically, yes. Here and New York. But most weeks, I live where Wayland tells me to." He swivels his head toward Wayland, who just shrugs. "And that's generally in a hotel room."

"Wow," I breathe. "That must get exhausting. Do your parents still live here?"

"My dad passed away a couple of years ago, but my mom and--" He stops himself before continuing, "My mom's still here."

I feel instant regret not knowing about Logan's dad's passing. He was much older than Logan's mom and a really sweet man. I remember meeting him for the first time at an art fair in school and thinking Logan looked like a mini version of him. "I'm sorry to hear about Mr. Miller. That must have been tough for you."

Before Logan can respond, Wayland leans over to say something to him but the music is so loud I don't catch it. Logan's attention comes back to me, a little resigned. "I've gotta get back, Anisa. Will you both be sticking around for a bit longer?"

I look over at Jeena, who just shrugs, and I make a mental note to strangle her later. All night I couldn't get her to shut up but all of a sudden, she has nothing to contribute? "Actually, we've been traveling all day and have a lot going on tomorrow. We'll probably be heading out shortly."

Logan nods, though he seems to be struggling for words and a sudden awkwardness lingers in the air between us. "Well, now that you're in town . . . don't be a stranger."

"Yeah," I say, feeling a sense of unease crawl back as if I've left the front door unlocked or the garage door open. Should I ask for his number? Would that be weird? What if he has a girlfriend? It kind of sounded that way with the vague "muse" comment he made earlier. At the end, I settle for, "You, too."

Leaning in, he holds me against him once more and I breathe easy in his arms, feeling his solid chest against mine. Inhaling his delicious scent, I tighten my hold around him and hope he can feel how much I've loved seeing him again. He cups my head before placing a small kiss on my forehead, then he turns away to walk back with Wayland.

This time, it's me who's left standing there wondering when I'll see him again.

"*W*ant to tell me why you could only communicate in sign language after you saw Wayland last night?" I step in front of Jeena to give passersby room on the sidewalk as we make our way to the grocery store a couple of blocks from my apartment.

"Hmm?" Jeena hums, likely trying to buy time. "What are you talking about?" She pulls her hair into a ponytail and fans her neck with her hand. Even at ten in the morning, the sun is blaring down on us, and I'm positive there will be a puddle of sweat under my breasts by the time we get to the store.

I side-eye her. "You're not the only one who can smell bullshit. Do you and Wayland have some history I don't know about?"

"How much history can someone have in middle school, Nees? You're trying to find a story where there isn't one."

My bullshit meter would disagree, but I don't push further. It's unlike my sister to keep things from me. We've been each other's confidants since we learned to talk, so if she is holding something back, it must be because she hasn't come to terms with it. I'm positive I saw something--like a secret only they shared--between her and Wayland last night. People don't just get awkwardly silent like that without a reason.

"God, I shouldn't have drank so much last night. My head's still pounding. How do you have so much energy this morning?" Jeena asks as she pulls a grocery cart from the corral.

I shrug, hurrying into the store to feel the cool AC against my skin. "I didn't drink as much as you did." The truth is even though I seem energetic this morning, I barely slept last night. I might be running on the adrenaline coursing through me, incited by all the changes in my life over the past couple of weeks--from breaking up with my ex-boyfriend, to my move here, to reacquainting with a boy . . . a man I now can't stop thinking about.

Every time I tossed in my bed last night--unworried about Jeena since she sleeps like she's been knocked out with horse tranquilizers--I saw Logan. I felt the weight of his arms around my waist, the breeze of his breath near my neck, his fingers inside my hair. I was so turned-on, I felt my underwear get damp. Never in my life have I felt a hunger so intense and painful as when I saw him last night, as if I'd been left starving for years.

I suppose I have.

What would happen now? Would I ever see him again or would I go on fantasizing about him for the rest of my life? Neither one of us has a way of getting in contact with the other, and I'm not about to hunt him down at the club again. I'm certain he no longer lives in the middle-class neighborhood we grew up in now that he has the means to live somewhere more upscale.

In a way, I wish I hadn't seen him again. At least then I

could go on living without the smell of cloves and soap lingering in my senses. At least then I wouldn't feel this visceral need in my most hidden parts at just the sound of his husky voice replaying in my head. How can a man's voice make someone wet? It makes no sense. Seeing him last night was like being sprinkled with a sporadic rain shower in the desert--quick enough to feel the droplets on your face but not enough to quench your thirst. And I need more.

Within an hour, Jeena and I have loaded up the cart with everything I need for the next couple of weeks. I even got a dog bed and food for Lynx since I'll be picking him up this afternoon. I'm dying to meet him and bring him home. It'll be fun to start this new adventure with him.

Once we get home, Jeena tells me she'll put away groceries and clean my apartment--though it looked plenty clean to me--while I'm at the shelter picking up Lynx. So, after a quick entry of the address into my Uber app, I'm on my way to meet the guy I'll be living with.

"He's over here on this side of the building," Tammy, an elderly lady with short gray hair, says. She leads me to a kennel toward the back of the large room separated into two with kennels lining each wall. Each enclosure houses dogs of different sizes and colors, awaiting a familiar face. A few look resigned to their uncomfortable mats akin to their fates, barely sparing me a glance as I walk by, while others alert their neighbors with a bark. A pang of guilt stabs my chest as I pass them, wishing I could be the bearer of hope in all their lives.

Tammy comes to a stop in front of the very last kennel and calls out to Lynx in a sweet, but high-pitched voice, "Hey, buddy, look who's here to meet you!"

The old dog lifts his head to briefly survey me before sighing and curling further into himself on his tattered dog bed. Even from a distance, I can see his tri-colored fur is matted in various places.

Tammy opens up the kennel door and waves for me to follow. "He's really friendly but like I told you on the phone, he's old and has arthritis in his back legs. We have a little bit of the joint pain medication left for him that you can take if you decide to adopt him today, but you'll need to get it refilled soon."

The constriction in my chest increases as I lean down to scratch Lynx behind his ear. "Hey, big guy. Are you ready to go home?"

At my use of the word *home*, Lynx wags his tail once, his bi-colored blue and brown gaze surveying me dubiously. Noticing the positive response, Tammy and I smile at each other. "Do you want to take him into the courtyard in the back and get to know him a little? You don't have to decide anything today."

"Sure, I can do that." I take the leash from Tammy's hand and attach it to Lynx's collar. "But I already know I'm going to take him home with me."

"Well, we're thankful for that, but I've got to ask, why an older dog? Why didn't you want one of the younger ones like everyone else?"

Mom had asked me the same thing once when I was younger, so it doesn't take me long to answer while I help Lynx to his feet and get down on my knees to rake my fingers through his long, knotted fur. He struggles to lift out of his position but appears stable once he's on his feet. "I feel a kinship with older dogs. We're alike in a lot of ways-- both looking for someone to accept us exactly the way we are, wishing they'd see that we're a lot more than the sum of our tattered parts and give us a second chance." I shrug, looking up at Tammy from where I'm crouching next to

Lynx. "I want to restore his faith in us, and maybe he and I will heal each other along the way."

Tammy gives me a sympathetic smile. "I wish more people thought that way."

Out in the courtyard, I let Lynx dictate our meet-and-greet. He smells along the edges of the wire fence, seemingly ignoring my presence even though I'm still holding his leash. I can relate to his stance on this whole situation--somewhat standoffish, unsure if it's worth investing his heart only to be disappointed or abandoned in the end.

Taking out a bag of dog treats from my purse, I gingerly sit on a nearby bench. At the crinkling sound of the bag, Lynx momentarily halts his sniffing but pretends not to be interested. "These *treats* look pretty yummy!" I enunciate 'treats' to see if I can get a reaction. His ears perk up, but he keeps his focus on sniffing around the fence.

After thoroughly investigating the edges of the courtyard for almost fifteen minutes, Lynx slowly makes his way over to me. Still avoiding eye contact with me, he sniffs the air a bit, then cautiously strolls over when I hold out a treat for him. "Come get it, big guy."

Once he's comfortably inspected the treat in my hand, he gently takes it from me and I feel the feather-light touch of his tongue on my fingertips. I'm not sure why, but I feel like we've just crossed a little milestone in our relationship and this is going to work out just fine.

"Happy birthday to me," I mutter to myself. "You're exactly the birthday present I was waiting for, Lynx."

"Happy birthday!" my parents chant in unison, big smiles lighting up their faces.

"Thank you!" I return.

"Now, walk me through the apartment." Dad gets right down to business during our FaceTime call Sunday morning. It's not easy for him to take off the CEO hat, even when he's not at work. Mom sits next to him with her hand on his shoulder and a forced smile on her face. She begged me not to move so far away and hates my mulishness on finding my own way. I know she's trying to be as supportive as possible, but still, I know when her smile is forced.

"There's not much to walk through, Dad." Jeena purses her lips to stop from laughing, avoiding the daggers I'm throwing at her with my eyes.

"There's enough room for one person. I don't need any more." I take the phone from Jeena's hand and flip the camera around using the touchscreen, walking my parents through the apartment.

"How's the kitchen?" Mom asks while I'm showing them the view from my small balcony. "Maybe you can finally try cooking on your own. It's not hard to make a simple *daal* and *sabzi*. I packed you a small box with the Indian spices you'll need, and I'm sure you can go to an Indian store to get more."

Not wanting to argue with her for the hundredth time that cultivating culinary skills was as high on my list of priorities as learning how to weave a rug, I hum a non-verbal response before proceeding to show them the kitchen.

"Wait. What was that moving around near the cabinets?" I hear the admonishment in Dad's voice before he even gives it. "Was that a--"

"Dad, now don't freak out . . .." I flip the camera to me so he can no longer see Lynx lapping from his water bowl in the adjoining laundry room. I might as well rip off the band-aid. Giving Jeena the stink-eye for snorting, I continue, "Look, I know what you're going to say, so don't waste your breath. I got a dog yester--"

"A dog!" Both Mom and Dad have their own unique looks of astonishment. Honestly, I don't really understand their surprise. They know I've never lived without a pet, and getting one as soon as I moved here isn't *that* far off the mark of something I would do. "You've only been there two days and you already have a dog? You haven't even started work! Where's Jeena?"

Oh, right. My babysitter.

I grind my molars, tamping down my desire to growl. "Yeah, Dad, I know I haven't started work. It's not like people can't own pets before they start a new job." I take a long inhale and walk over to the couch where Jeena is sitting with her knees up, sipping from her coffee cup, and giving me her best *I-told-you-so* look.

Once she's in the camera frame, Dad starts again, directing his next question at her as if I'm a five-year-old entrusted to my six-year-old sister. "You let her get a *dog* the first weekend she moved there?"

"Dad, do you think I have the ability to control Anisa?" Jeena says incredulously. "She did most of the paperwork online before we even got here."

"Neesu, how are you going to manage all this on your own? You don't even have a car yet." Mom presses a hand to her temple as if she's exasperated. *Yeah, you and me both, lady.*

"Firstly, you guys really need to stop treating me like a child. I'm taking responsibility for my dog, and I'll figure it out. Secondly, my car is on a truck and will be here in a couple of days. I'm perfectly capable of managing without it until then. Can you guys just chill out?"

A collective sigh emits from them as if they know there's no point arguing with me. Which, there isn't. After a moment, Mom changes the subject, asking about my neighborhood and whether I've figured out where my company is located yet. I'm more than happy to move past the previous conversation, and I assure her that yes, I'm in a great neighborhood and yes, I can manage taking an Uber to my job for a couple of days until my car arrives.

"I still think you could have found everything you were looking for working at *Techsess*." It's the fourth or maybe the ninety-fifth time--I've lost count at this point--that Dad has mentioned me working for his company--a play on the word 'Texas' that he always thought was clever for a software startup. "I would have let you lead a small team of developers, and you could have worked under Rob, who's one of the best managers at the company."

"I know, Dad. And I appreciate it." I offer my standard response. "But like I've said before, I just need to do this for myself. I need to start at the bottom somewhere without you being there to catch me with every fumble. I wouldn't have earned my place at *Techsess*."

"I could have put you in with the developers, and you could have started like they did with an entry-level job!"

"Dad." I don't have the energy to argue about this yet again.

He sees the resolution in my face. "Fine, have it your way, but call me the minute you change your mind. You always have a job with me."

My heart warms, knowing how much this man has done to make my sister and me feel loved and secure. He's always been the best balance of strict and doting. "I know, Daddy."

Getting right back to business, he continues, "Have you

spoken to Naveen recently? He was asking about you yesterday."

Of course, he was. Ever since he'd gotten a position at my dad's company, Naveen has made sure to 'casually' ask about me . . . a lot.

"He texted me this morning to wish me a happy birthday, but I haven't had the chance to respond." *And if I can help it, that chance will never present itself.*

My parents know about my recent breakup with Naveen, but they aren't aware of the real reason. Using the excuse of me moving to Austin, I'd told them that it made sense for us to take a break. I think my dad still secretly--or maybe not-so-secretly--wishes Naveen and I will make up. Though, I'm not sure he'd wish that if he knew how Naveen treated me during the last few months of our relationship after I got him the job at my dad's company.

In fact, I'm pretty sure Naveen would be out looking for another job if Dad knew. Which is exactly what I'd threatened my ex with during our last phone call when he told me I needed to get off this "dumb kick" of seeking independence and realize when something good was right in front of me--meaning him. I laughed so hard, I was in stitches.

It was hard for Naveen to find a job after college because of a DUI he'd received during our senior year. One where he also hit and injured someone, landing him a felony on his record before he even graduated. After being rejected by several companies, despite his good grades, Naveen had little hope left of finding a job. In an effort to help him, I'd pleaded with my dad to hire Naveen, promising he'd be a hard worker. And after seeing Naveen's strong academic record--and multiple degrees--Dad had given in to my request.

What I never expected in return from my then-boyfriend was loathing and resentment. Instead of feeling relieved about the chance to work at a well-known company, he used his bruised ego as a reason to verbally bludgeon me. At first, it started with small resentful jabs about my dad's wealth and my so-called entitlement. Then it turned harsher, with remarks about my body and introverted personality. Toward the end-- when I'd finally had enough--he'd enhanced his vocabulary with words like "stuck-up bitch" and "spoiled brat."

My new job in Austin could not have come fast enough. I used the employment contract as a one-way ticket to get away from it all.

And I have no desire to return.

I hear my dad continue with his thoughts about Naveen. "He's a nice boy and you're of the age where you should think about marr--"

"Dad, I'm not thinking about marriage right now." Especially not with my sociopathic ex. "This isn't nineteenth-century India. Plus, you clearly have an older, more responsible daughter you need to worry about first."

Jeena squints at me and pinches my bicep, making me yelp, and I can't help giggling. The laughter eclipses the bitter turn my thoughts had just taken. Jeena takes the phone from me. "Guess what? Anisa and I met Logan last night," she says to our parents, hoping it'll take the impending focus off her.

"Really? Logan, as in Anisa's childhood friend?" Mom perks up. She'd always liked Logan, saying he was adorable and respectful. I bet she wouldn't use the word "adorable" to describe him now, more like hot, sexy, and delectable. I quickly shove away thoughts of my mom using any such words for Logan.

"Yup. He's a famous DJ, actually. We went to the club he was playing at."

"DJ?" Dad's eyebrows furrow. "So, what . . . he just mixes music?"

Jeena and I exchange a glance, hearing the judgment in Dad's tone. "Dad, he's done really well for himself. He's traveling all around the world and makes a shitload of money."

"Language," Mom reprimands.

Dad still looks dubious. "Anyone can be a DJ. Sure, he may have gotten lucky and is doing well now, but these are not skills you can make a living on long-term. Once a better DJ comes along, Logan will be forgotten."

I'm not sure why the need to defend my childhood best friend rises inside me, but I won't sit here and let my dad dismiss the raw talent I heard last night--the talent people around the world pay to see. Even though I try to suppress the anger bubbling in my voice, my words still come out sharp. "That can be said for anything, Dad. A better competitor could surface and rub *Techsess* into the dirt. The board could decide there's a better CEO to run your company and--"

"Anisa!" Mom's glare glitters through the screen, barely concealing the edge in her voice. It's a look I've received several times in my life and a look I hate being the recipient of. My parents may not have the perfect marriage, but if there's one thing they've perfected, it's mutual respect for one another. They're like a two-person army, and neither will stand for an insult to the other.

I immediately feel like shit. Sure, my dad passed a quick judgment on Logan, but he's also given me nothing but love and support. He didn't deserve my biting words. "I'm sorry, Dad. That was rude of me." I look down at my hands, feeling my throat tighten. This entire weekend has been confusing. Old wounds I'd patched up, albeit weakly, feel like they've reopened. My parents haven't shown an ounce of happiness about my new life, and I can't stop thinking about a man who's probably already forgotten about me. Again.

Gah!

"Look at me, *beta*." My dad only uses the term of endearment when he can see I'm at my wit's end. "It's okay. I judged too quickly. I know you've always had a soft spot for Logan. Did you find out more? Does he still live in Austin?"

I nod, feeling the tightness in my throat dissipate. "He lives here part-time. His mom still lives here though, so he's here relatively often."

"Maybe you'll run into him again." Mom gives me a hopeful shrug. "Did you exchange numbers?"

"No! They just stood there like awkward doofuses!" Jeena scoffs, shaking her head.

I look over at her incredulously. *Better get your gloves on, sis, because you're about to go down.* "I'm sorry, Jeena, did you just say *we* stood there like 'awkward doofuses'?" Before she can respond, I grab her phone and make a dash for my bedroom to tell my parents about Jeena's little *Silence of the Lambs* stunt on Friday night.

She runs after me with an *oh-shit* look on her face. *That's right, sis. Payback's a biatch.* "Nees, don't you dare! Come back here!"

I run to my room, giggling while trying to close the door behind me. "You guys have no idea who else we met on Fri--" I can barely finish my sentence, pushing the door against Jeena. She's freakishly strong for a dainty-looking person. It must be from all the sugary cereal she consumes. "Do you remember Wayland?"

Before I can finish the rest of the story, Jeena pushes her

way in and grabs the phone from my hands while I try unsuccessfully to swipe it back from her, laughing hysterically. She turns to my parents' confused faces. "Bye, Mom and Dad. I'll see you guys at the airport tomorrow."

No sooner has she pressed the end button and turned her narrowed glare at me that I'm running into the safety of my bathroom, squealing.

Maybe I'll stay here until she leaves for the airport tomorrow.

7

LOGAN

*S*ome of my favorite memories growing up--besides the ones with Anisa in them--are of fishing with my dad. He worked long hours, often leaving the house around four in the morning to meet his crew at one of their construction sites, but whenever he had a day off, we'd spend hours at the lake.

"Fishing can teach you a lot about life, son," he'd say in his deep Southern drawl, hemmed by his hoarse voice from years of smoking. "It teaches you to be patient and to persevere, but it also teaches you to hang on tight when you catch something good . . . something that'll give meaning to this whole thing. Don't let go when you catch something good. That's the key."

I'd nod my head earnestly, my eight-year-old brain not knowing what he meant by "this whole thing" but soaking up all the wisdom nonetheless. But that wasn't why I was there with him--for his wisdom or even to fish, really--I was there just to be with my dad. Hell, I'd sit and watch paint dry all day if it meant he was sitting next to me. But it wasn't until I was older when I realized that sometimes you don't have as many chances to *sit* with a person you love as you think you do.

It's because of the time I spent on the lake with my dad that I bought the house I live in now--a sprawling, ranch-style estate, complete with six bedrooms, including a separate fully-equipped house for my mom in the back. The estate boasts Italian marble floors, manicured lawns, and an outdoor pool area fit for a Hollywood-style party. But it's the private beach and entrance to the lake that sealed the deal for me. It's the only place I can turn off all the chatter and noise--the entire world--just for a couple of hours.

Except, there's one person I'd never tire of chattering to me all fucking day.

"We gonna catch white crap again, Daddy?"

I chuckle, sweeping my glance against the blonde pigtails Mom put in my four-year-old's hair this morning. "They're called *white crappie*, lazy-pants, not white crap. And careful saying that word around Grams. She'll make you brush your tongue again, and we know how much you hate that."

Still holding on to her fishing rod and looking over her shoulder, she squints at me. "My name is *not* lazy-pants, it's *Lainey*-pants!"

I purse my lips apologetically. "Oh, my bad. I don't know how I got those mixed up."

She continues to stare at me, her blues picking up the sunlight and her eyebrows arch high on her forehead. Her expression reminds me so much of my mom's, it's a little unnerving. I guess body language is a learned behavior.

"What?" I ask, grinning.

"Aren't you going to apollo-gize?"

"I thought I did! Do you have too much wax in your ears again?"

She scrunches her nose, probably reeling from the recent memory of going to the pediatrician to get her ears cleaned. "Grams said 'my bad' is not an apollo-gy, Daddy. Now, say it properly. It won't make you shorter."

I should call her bossy-pants instead, but then we'd be rehashing this whole conversation with me apologizing for yet another thing. "Fine. I'm sorry. Is that better?"

She nods, looking back toward the lake, her pigtails swooshing over the life jacket around her shoulders.

This kid could ask me to find a goddamn mermaid in this lake, and I swear I'd jump in without a question and give it my best try. She knows it too, the stinker.

"I think you need more sunscreen on your nose and shoulders, baby girl. Get up carefully and come over here so I can put it on."

She affixes her fishing rod into a groove on the boat and gingerly walks toward me. She's only four, but I swear sometimes I feel like she's wiser than most forty-year-olds. Between my mom and her, I have enough unsolicited advice to last a lifetime.

I've always hated surprises, good or bad, but when Lainey came into my life unexpectedly, I felt like my lungs expanded as if I hadn't actually been breathing during those past nineteen years. She changed my stance on some surprises.

Mandy and I had broken up before she told me she was pregnant. We were together for almost five months, but between the number of hours I spent on the road and Mandy trying to figure out how to manage some of her mental issues, time together became sparse. She'd been diagnosed with bi-polar disorder and depression around the same time, and we'd both decided it was better for her to focus on herself and getting healthy. I'd promised her I would be there in any way I could to support her.

A month later, Mandy showed up at my doorstep with a positive pregnancy test and tears streaking down her cheeks. I hadn't questioned whether the baby was mine--she wasn't that kind of girl. While I'd met plenty of women in my line of work who were money hungry or just plain bitchy, Mandy had never been anything but kind and caring, and I knew she had a good heart.

We'd met while I was playing at a club she managed and somehow, we had hit it off. She had the same dark hair and features that reminded me of someone else, and I was lonely.

Goddamn, traveling makes you lonely.

We started dating but within a few weeks, I started seeing cracks in our newly-laid foundation. Her unhappiness with her life--even though she seemed to have a decent one--her insecurities with me traveling all the time, and her sudden mood changes--warm one minute to cold and bitter the next--put a lot of stress on our relationship. So, after telling Mandy that I really wanted her to focus on figuring her life out, I'd broken it off with her and she'd agreed it was for the best.

Until a month later, when focusing solely on herself was no longer an option for her.

Lainey was born eight months later, her eyes the same shade as mine, bright and observant from day one. It took me less than ten seconds to realize I was going to be putty in this girl's hands and she could mold me in any which way she wanted.

But that wasn't the case for Mandy. At first, I thought it was postpartum blues, but I knew something was very wrong when months went by and, aside from keeping the baby fed and safe, Mandy felt nothing for her.

My suspicion was confirmed when she dropped Lainey off with my mom one day while I was on tour in Seoul, telling her she'd be back when she felt better.

That was over three years ago.

"Are you done, Daddy?" Lainey shakes me out of my musings as I apply more sunscreen to her shoulders.

"Yup, you're all set, although . . . is that . . .? Oh God! Is that a frog inside your life jacket?" I try to keep my laugh from bubbling up.

"What! How . . .? Get it out, Daddy!" Lainey shrieks, her eyes bulging while her face tenses with fear. I'm a sick bastard for being amused with her being scared and relying on me for help. "Get it out!"

I pretend to put my hand in between her shoulder blades and her jacket and get something out, throwing a flat rock I'd found earlier into the water and making it splash. Lainey turns to see if she can spot the supposed frog below the surface and a tiny tinge of guilt--though mostly laughter--hits my chest. "There. Did you see how big that thing was?"

"Thank you, Daddy!" She throws her tiny, sweaty arms around my neck as I pat her back. Suddenly, she stills and pulls away, looking at me. "Daddy, you weren't playing tricksies on me, were you?"

Constructing my face with shock, I scoff, "I would never!"

MOM AND LAINEY walk into the entryway of my house on Monday afternoon, and Lainey drops her preschool bag right on the floor and runs toward the kitchen. "Grams said I could have a popsicle!"

"Not so fast, young lady." My mom's voice feigns displeasure. In reality, my mom is even more of a pushover than I am when it comes to her granddaughter. "Put your school bag where it belongs, wash your hands, and then you can have a popsicle."

"Yeah, and give your dad a hug, too," I add, watching Lainey come back with her shoulders slumped as if she's just received bad news. She wraps her arms around my legs and I bend to pick her up, placing a kiss on her cheek before letting her finish up her chores.

"What time is your flight tomorrow?" Mom asks as I bend down to give her a hug, too.

"Pretty early in the morning. It's an eleven-hour flight, so I'm hoping to get there with some time to prepare for the show the next day."

Mom nods, but I see the grimace across her mouth. "Are you going to be on the road a lot this month, too? I feel like you're wearing yourself thin."

"I'll be back from Paris on Friday, and I'll be home for about ten days after that. Then I'm on a two-week tour around the West Coast." I already feel a growl emerge, thinking about not seeing Lainey for so long. If it wasn't for my mom's fear of flying, I'd have them fly over to see me wherever I was once in a while, but as it stands, I'm usually the one who has to come back home. Anyway, I like that my little girl has a stable life here and it makes sense to not disrupt her routine any more than necessary.

"Okay, as long as you feel like you're getting the rest you need in the middle of these tours. I just don't want you turning into your dad where he never took enough time to rest. He died too early because of it, and I won't see that happen to my son."

Dad died early because he smoked like it was an Olympic sport, but I'll refrain from reminding my mom of that. "I get it, Mom. I already told Wayland he needs to ease up on my schedule a bit, especially with summer coming up." Lainey would be done with preschool for the summer, and I'd promised her a trip to Disney World.

Mom seems satisfied with my response. "I'm making lasagna if you're around for dinner again tonight," she says, watching me sort through the mail in the entryway mail bin.

Thinking about what I'm planning on doing this evening--something that's been rolling around in the back of my mind for the past couple of days--I give her a noncommittal response. "Uh . . . my plans are a little up in the air tonight. But leave me a slice in case they fall through."

Maybe I shouldn't even be making these plans. Maybe I should stick to the original plan I made after Mandy left and focus on my job and on raising my kid. Maybe I don't need any other complications in my life, and moving forward with these new plans will do just that--complicate shit.

But if I was so hellbent on saying no to crazy plans, I'd leave no room for maybes.

Anisa Singh has taken over my every thought ever since I saw her again, like ink in water. I still can't believe I ran into her so randomly on Friday night. And though I can't be sure, I could swear she was trying to weasel her way out of the club without seeing me, even though I'd sent her a clear message to come find me. I'm glad I went looking for her.

It didn't take long to find her in the crowd, even though I hadn't seen her in a decade. Truth be told, I probably would have found her with my eyes closed. I felt like a magnet being pulled by raw metal--a force so strong, I wasn't in control.

She looked the same--light brown eyes surrounded by a thicket of black lashes, pert little nose, and an adorable indentation from the dimple on her left cheek--yet so different. The little girl I used to know was replaced by this gorgeous, curvy enchantress, a beacon for desire I couldn't help move toward.

Even as a teenager, I thought she was cute, but I'd never imagined she'd become a fucking knockout. Her dark, wavy hair was splayed down her back as I ogled her curves in her jeans and tank top. Only the tiniest sliver of skin showed around her waist and I swear, I hardened to a steel rod inside my pants. What would that skin feel like beneath my fingertips?

Raking my gaze over her body, I knew her small breasts would be perky and perfect in my hands. But it was her beautiful face and that deer-in-the-headlights look that had me itching to get to her. I felt like a man on a fucking mission, programmed to find my target at all cost.

My hands moved on their own accord as I pulled her toward me and buried my nose in her hair, inhaling the scent of magnolias and pineapples, and diffusing the awkwardness I thought I'd feel seeing her again. She was so warm and pliable in my arms, I felt like I was holding sunshine. My heart thudded inside my chest when I saw her tears. She'd missed me just as much as I'd missed her. I felt both relieved and guilt-stricken at the thought. Why hadn't I kept in touch?

God knows I'd thought about her enough over the years. Before Lainey--and even after--Anisa was the sole inspiration for so much of my music. She'd always believed in me and encouraged me when I was just a kid messing around.

I'd actually looked her up on social media a time or two but since I wasn't part of her network of friends, all I could view was her most recent profile picture. And unfortunately for me, most of her pictures were of her pets. The rest of her account was locked, and I told myself she probably didn't remember me anymore so I never connected. Looking back, I was an idiot for doing that.

And now that she was back in town, I'd be an even bigger idiot not to rekindle our friendship. Or maybe I'd be an idiot *to* rekindle it.

Key word: Friendship.

Because anything more and I'd lose focus on my number one priority--Lainey. With my tour schedule, I'd already been spending less time with her than I wanted. I didn't have room in my life for anything more than a friend--someone who would expect nothing more than a phone call or an impromptu drink. Someone who wouldn't need extravagant dates and weekends away. Someone who wouldn't demand priority in my already busy life or take me away from the little girl I'd promised to put first.

It's with those thoughts running through my head that I assemble a few things from my fridge and place them inside a paper bag. Giving Lainey and my mom a kiss on the cheek, I head out the door to try to beat the evening rush.

8

ANISA

"Team, I'd like you to welcome our newest member, Anisa Singh. She'll be working closely with you on our upcoming *Fantastical Fantasies* game as an animator and developer," my boss, Travis, addresses the group during the Monday morning meeting. Some of my team members wave in my direction while a couple murmur hello. "Anisa, would you like to tell us a little about yourself?"

Not really.

Public speaking or any kind of attention for that matter isn't something I look forward to. Trying to work past the unease in my stomach, I make my voice sound as even as possible. "Sure. Like Travis said, I'm Anisa. I moved here from San Francisco this past weekend. I've always wanted to work for a world-famous gaming company like *Escapade Games*, and I'm fortunate to have the chance." I find the smiling face of a woman with blonde hair, who looks to be about my age. "I'm looking forward to working with all of you."

"As a rule," one of the guys sitting across from me says,

"we ask all newcomers to name their favorite online game. What's yours?"

"I love games with really immersive environments and where characters have innate super powers, so I'd say my favorite would be *League of Legends*."

"Nice!" he replies with an impressed look. He has a short, dark goatee which matches his dark hair and eyes. "I'm leading the project to create a new character and scene for *Fantastical Fantasies*." As he continues to speak, I notice another team member covertly roll his eyes. "Since you're interested in immersive environments, I'd love to have you on that project."

"That sounds like a great place to start, Blake!" Travis nods at the man with the goatee--Blake, who looks exceedingly pleased with himself for the suggestion--and then turns to me. "Anisa, what do you think?"

The fact that I'm getting to live out my dream of being a game developer is exciting enough, so even if they tell me to design a tree for the game, I'll work on making the best damn tree there is. "That sounds great!"

After the meeting, I walk through the open workspace to find my desk. It's a simple space with a chair and multiple large monitors in between a row of similar-looking workspaces. The large, sprightly-colored room is functional, with both similar rows of workspaces and meeting areas with low-backed orange couches. There's even a foosball table and a large TV for playing video games on one end of the room.

I'm seated next to the friendly-looking blonde from this morning's meeting. She looks up as I take my seat. "Hey, Anisa, welcome to the team! I'm Sydney, another animator on Travis's team." She sticks out her right hand for me to shake after sweeping her blonde bangs to the side above her blue-green eyes.

I smile after releasing her hand and settle into my designated desk. "Thanks." I've never felt comfortable breaking the ice after introductions, but I'd promised Jeena yesterday that I'd do my best to meet new people and be more social. "Have you been at *Escapade* for a while?"

"About two years. It's a great place to learn, and Travis is one hell of a manager, which is rare to find." She waves to someone passing by, and I notice my teammates are back at their desks with headphones on, diligently working on their projects. "Is this your first job out of college?"

"Yeah, I just graduated from Berkeley."

"Cool! I went to UT Austin, but we have people here from all different colleges." When I nod, she continues, "Do you have any plans for lunch? I could show you the cafeteria downstairs or we can go out."

"No plans, but I need to run home for a few minutes and let my senior dog out. I live pretty close by. Do you want to come with me, and then we can grab something to eat on our way back?" I haven't figured out how I'll be managing Lynx every day while working. With him being an older dog, he needs to be let out relatively often, and I know it'll just get worse with time. The dog service I called was pretty pricey but if I don't find another option, I'll have to book with them.

"That's perfect!"

The day until lunch progresses fast with my first one-on-one meeting with Travis where he tells me about the projects he'd like me involved in, and my meeting with Blake to talk about splitting up the work for the new scene in the game. I've been charged with animating the new character, a warrior goddess.

"Now, don't hesitate to ask if you have any questions about anything at all, Anisa. I'm the most senior person on the team here, so if I don't know the answer then . . . well," Blake chuckles like he's about to make a really funny joke, "we're in quite a lot of trouble. Anyway, most of the code is written in Java or Javascript, which I'm sure you're somewhat familiar with, yes?"

While it sounds like an innocent enough question, I sense an undercurrent of condescension. During the interview, I was asked to develop a game using both coding languages, and the HR recruiter had told me I'd done better than any of their other candidates so yes, I was *familiar*. I decide to forgo thinking too much about Blake's cockiness. "Yes, I should be able to manage."

"Great! Well, I've let Travis know that I'll be happy to mentor you, so don't hesitate at all." His gaze falls below my chin and lingers right above my breasts, but I tell myself I'm probably just overthinking it.

I'm just walking back to my desk from the meeting room--getting lost only briefly--when my phone vibrates with an incoming call. *Naveen*. I puff out a breath before hitting the *End* button, sending him to voicemail. I honestly don't understand where I was unclear with him.

I recall our last phone conversation. I had just finished my finals and received a C-plus in an elective macroeconomics course. I'd lost sight of the class with the heavy course load during my last semester and hadn't studied enough for the final exam.

Already disappointed, I was trying to console myself that at least I'd still graduate with a very respectable GPA. Luckily for me, I didn't have those typical Indian parents who would only make me feel worse about getting a bad grade. But where I didn't have *those* kinds of parents, I did have *that* kind of a boyfriend.

"Are you fucking serious? You fucked-up macro-econ? That's the easiest shit in the world. Why didn't you ask me if you were struggling?" This was how Naveen started with most conversations where I was the subject--or rather, the object--of his belittling, which was often. He would ask a series of questions, not necessarily looking for me to answer, before moving on to the next round, somehow making himself the victim. "Oh wait, that's right, you wouldn't ask me because God forbid you ever talk to me! Do you even know how to communicate?" He chuckled disgustedly. "You know, I wouldn't be surprised if you were a robot. In fact, that would explain the way you just lay there, unresponsive, when we're fuc--"

"That's it, Naveen. We're done." Straightening my spine and grasping the phone hard enough to turn to dust, I repeated myself as calmly as possible, "Let me *communicate* this super clearly to you in case assholery is blocking your hearing. You and I are finished. Lose my number because you're totally right about one thing, I don't want to talk to y---."

"Anisa. B-babe." I heard the panic in his voice as he tried to mollify me. "You're overreacting."

I continued as if I hadn't heard him, "Oh, and I accepted a job in Austin. I'm moving in a couple of weeks so . . . perfect timing!" With that, I ended the call and threw my phone so hard, the screen cracked. I should have sent the prick the repair bill. In fact, I should have asked him for a full refund for the past six months of my life, but I wanted nothing more to do with him.

Pushing aside my frustration with him calling me again today, I fabricate a smile on my face when I see Sydney.

She's waiting for us near our desks to go to lunch. It's been a great day so far, and I'm not letting my asshole ex ruin it.

"So, have you lived in San Francisco most of your life?" Sydney asks as we carry our burritos to an empty table in the middle of the restaurant. Thankfully, Lynx hadn't had any accidents, so letting him out for a break only took a few minutes while Sydney waited in her car. Still, I felt a little guilty that I was leaving him again after he'd had only a day to adjust to his new home. I reassured myself that he'd get used to it in time.

I lay the paper napkin on my lap. "Sort of. I was born in Austin and we lived here until I was in middle school, then we moved to San Francisco for my dad's work."

Sydney's brows pull up. "Oh, wow! So this must sort of feel like being back home in some ways."

I laugh. "Things have changed a lot since then, or maybe I don't remember the details as well, but yeah, it all feels familiar." *Like being in the arms of a guy you used to know.* "What about you? Are you from Austin?"

Sydney chews around the bite in her mouth and shakes her head. "No, I actually grew up in Dallas and moved here for college. But I love it here."

We continue to talk more about living in Austin and working at *Escapade Games*. She tells me about a couple of people at work whom she's formed a great relationship with and a couple to avoid. "Don't get me wrong," she takes a sip of her soda, "Blake's a smart guy, but he's also a little singularly-focused. Even though Travis hasn't made him an official team-lead, Blake constantly tries to take over high-visibility projects and pretends that he's the smartest one in the room. He's also misogynistic and conceited, so don't be surprised if he starts man-splaining everything while you work with him."

Yeah, I already got that from the half-hour meeting with him today. *Maybe Blake should meet my ex.* "Thanks for the heads-up."

"So, I know you're just getting settled in your apartment and the job and everything, but my boyfriend and I are going to this wine and food festival near *Zilker Park* next weekend. We went last year and it was really fun. Would you like to join?"

I think about it as I finish the bite in my mouth. Socializing isn't my jam. I prefer the company of my pets or immersing myself in my sketches over having to make small talk with strangers. But, remembering my promise to Jeena and putting on the best upbeat face I can muster, I say, "Sure, that sounds fun!"

The rest of the day at the office goes by in a flash. Between a spontaneous meeting spurred on by a bug in the game, to new employee paperwork that I need to fill out, to setting up my computer with the digital tools I need, it's one thing after another and before I know it, people are disappearing from the office like flies in the winter.

A quarter after five, Travis comes over to ask if I need anything and tells me to not stay too long. He's an older man, maybe in his mid-fifties, but extremely fit and well-groomed. His kind, dark eyes and trimmed beard reminds me of my dad, and I even get a warm fatherly feeling from him. I can see why Sydney likes working for him.

I'm in the Uber when my phone vibrates in my hand. "Hey, Mom."

"Hi, Neesu. How was your first day?"

I yawn, thinking about how fast and furiously the first day went. I'm sure I'll have to ask some of my teammates for their names again, but I really liked meeting them. It was also exciting that I'll be working on a high-stakes project. "It was tiring but really great. I'm just on my way home."

"That's good. When is your car getting there?"

"Tomorrow evening, so I should have more mobility starting Wednesday." Then I can finally take Lynx to the vet and get some things I still need, like new sketch pads and coloring supplies. Even though most of my designs have been digital in recent years, drawing by hand is therapeutic for me. There's just something meditative about sketching, seeing the picture clear in my mind before actually creating the strokes with my pencil.

"Good. Now, I texted you a recipe for *rajma*," my mom continues, pretending not to hear me groan. "I even snuck a can of kidney beans into your suitcase before you left." I recalled finding said beans in my suitcase when I opened it this weekend. Honestly, the woman was relentless when it came to something she wanted me to do. For someone who was a pretty non-traditional parent in many ways, making sure her girls knew how to cook Indian food was something she didn't budge on. "You just need tomatoes, onions, and the spices I packed you. Jeena told me you got a decent amount of things from the grocery store, so you should be all set."

"So, there is this service called *food delivery*, Mom. People use it in the twenty-first century. In fact, I was planning on utilizing it tonight." I hold in a chuckle, knowing I'm going to get a verbal smackdown for my snark.

"Anisa," Mom only uses my given name with her stern voice, "don't be smart with me. You can't eat out for every meal. Anyway, you need to learn these things as you get older. One day, you'll have a family of your own, kids you'll want to make a meal for--"

Whoa, whoa, whoa! "One thing at a time, Mom. And who says I want kids?"

That earns me a pause on the other line, and I lift the phone from my ear to see if maybe it has disconnected. *I wouldn't mind if it did . . ..*

I haven't really considered whether I want children or not. I'm new to living completely on my own, finally untethered from having to meet the expectations of everyone else. Maybe one day I'd be ready to have kids, but right now I'm enjoying living independently too much. Plus, I don't even think I'd be good with kids.

"Don't be ridiculous. Of course, you'll want kids. Anyway, you're too young to know what you want."

Getting out of the Uber, I swing my crossbody purse across my chest. First, she said I was getting older, now I'm too young. I swear, the woman changes my age with the direction of the wind. "Okay, Mom, I just got back to my apartment. Let me talk to you later."

"Okay, try making the *rajma*." She tries once more.

But as I'm walking away from the parking lot toward my building, I notice a familiar tall and imposing figure wearing a black cap leaning against a very expensive black car. His tattooed arm flexes under his fitted black T-shirt as he puts his phone back into his jeans pocket and lifts off the car to stride toward me, his sapphire gaze locked with mine.

"Bye, Mom," I barely get out before ending the call. My throat feels dry against my forced swallow as I look up at him and my heart picks up speed. "W-what are you doing here?"

9

ANISA

*T*he side of Logan's mouth tips up into a lazy smile, reminding me of warm summer days, the clunky sounds of skateboard wheels on sidewalks, and fresh-cut grass. "I thought, uh . . .." Despite his towering frame and broad shoulders, there's a vulnerable look in his eyes, as if he's second-guessing himself. "I thought I'd see if you were hungry." He holds up a brown paper bag.

"I . . .." I'm so bewildered by seeing him here, the words feel jumbled in my head. "How did you know where I lived? How long have you been waiting?" I glance back at his car before I meet his gaze again.

He chuckles, the rumble of it collecting at the bottom of my stomach, dancing between my thighs. Dear God, why does everything about his voice make me feel like I'm coming apart? "Your sister told me where you lived that night at the club, remember?"

My brows furrow. "She did?" I don't recall that, but she was quite the blabbermouth that night--until Wayland somehow hit her mute button. Speaking of, I need to find out how he did that for my own benefit one day.

Logan nods, his cornflower-blue eyes dancing in mirth. "You want to eat out here or . . .?"

"Oh!" I shake myself out of my weird daze. "No, come on! Though . . ." I bite my bottom lip, trying to conceal my smile and realize his gaze has followed the movement, "should I be worried you're stalking me?"

His eyes slowly lift back to connect with my own, igniting a blaze and charging the air between us. Suddenly I feel like I've asked the wrong question. His jaw ticks and my heart feels like it's doing the work to support an army, thudding in my chest hard enough that I'm sure he can hear it.

"I wouldn't trust me if I were you." His voice is gruff, and I can't comprehend the meaning behind those words. Feeling breathless, I try to focus on keeping myself steady on my feet. But before the electricity can intensify any further between us, Logan squeezes his eyelids shut as if trying to shake himself out of a trance.

He clears his throat and I take that as my cue to cover the awkwardness or whatever *that* was. "Um, I'm just right around here." I walk ahead of him, putting distance between us fast. Looking over my shoulder, I repeat my previous question, "How long have you been waiting?"

"About forty-five minutes." His voice booms in the small alleyway as we make our way to the back of the building. Noticing my saucer-like eyes, he continues, "I didn't know which apartment you were in or if you were already home." He chuckles again, almost like he's embarrassed. "Honestly, I hadn't quite thought through the what-ifs. I figured if you didn't show in the next hour, I'd head back. Anyway, I was getting some work done while I wait--"

Before he can even finish his sentence, I stop abruptly and turn to face him. Getting on my tiptoes, I wrap my arms around his neck. I don't know why, but my chest feels warm thinking about him waiting for me for so long, for coming out to find me. For being here with a damn paper bag with food. Burrowing my nose into his neck, I breathe in his scent of cloves and soap, the same way I had a couple of nights ago. "I'm so glad you're here," I murmur against his neck.

He hesitates only for a second before wrapping his arms around my back and pulling me tight against his body. There's not even space for air to travel between us. The tip of his nose grazes against my temple and every hair on my arms stands on end. His hand moves up my back and around my nape when he whispers in my ear, "I should have gotten your number that night."

"Why didn't you?" I mumble back, my lips moving against the soft skin near his collar. It's warm and scented, and it takes everything in me to stop from tasting it.

As if knowing my internal predicament, he growls, pulling my hair so I'm forced to look up at him. His eyes blaze, as blue as the hottest part of a fire, and my nipples tighten against the fabric of my shirt. Every response from my body feels attuned to him and the rock-hard bulge I feel heavy against my belly.

Oh God, it feels like it's still growing.

A mixture of emotions flicker across his face. "So many reasons."

I swallow thickly before licking my lips again. I'm not entirely sure what that means, and I'm afraid to ask. I need to get back some semblance of control, but my voice comes out as a pant. "Let's go inside."

We unwrap from each other and I hear Logan curse under his breath, something that sounds a lot like "bad idea," but he follows behind me as I unlock my door and step inside my apartment.

He shuts the door behind us, and I hear the jingle of a

collar along with the clicking of nails on my linoleum kitchen floor. "Lynx?" I call out to my new roommate, who slowly walks toward us, giving Logan a hesitant glance.

"You brought a dog with you?" I feel Logan's chest at my back and I have the urge to fall into him. *Think semblance. Think control. Think about breathing.*

Taking a step forward to put my purse on the side table near the couch and getting some distance between us again, I crouch to hug Lynx. Smiling at Logan, I wonder if he'll be surprised by my admission. "I just got him from the shelter this weekend."

Logan walks toward the bar in my kitchen, setting the paper bag down as Lynx comes to sniff his leg. Bending down to scratch him behind his ear, Logan looks over at me, a knowing smile tipping up his lips. "Of course, you did."

The air feels a lot less tense between us and I take in a few lungfuls. Pulling the leash off the hook in the coat closet, I attach it to Lynx's collar. "Let me just take him out to do his business. I'll be right back."

"Do you want me to come with you?"

I shrug my shoulder and smile. "Sure."

Luckily there's a nice patch of grass just a few feet from my apartment for Lynx to sniff around before he picks a spot. The sun is still pulsing down on our skin and it doesn't help that the man standing next to me radiates the same amount of heat. I turn toward Logan to see him already looking at me with a dubious expression. "So, you moved all the way back to Austin for a job in software, even though there are way more jobs in San Francisco for that kind of thing?"

I watch Lynx sniff around the grass some more. "I guess I needed a change of scenery to truly live on my own."

He smiles, lifting his chin toward Lynx. "You're not

completely on your own. You have your trusty guard with you."

I chuckle. "True. He's about the only one I can be responsible for aside from myself."

The smile that was previously on Logan's face slightly falters, but he doesn't say more. I want to ask what he's thinking, but I decide to stay quiet until I call out to Lynx to come back in.

Once we're back inside and I've poured some kibble into Lynx's bowl, I nod toward the bag Logan brought. "So, whatchu got in there?"

Getting on one of the barstools, he smirks that lazy smile that's probably melted thousands of panties. *Ugh, I could do without the visuals of other women's panties . . . especially when my own seem to have disintegrated.* I stand there ogling his gorgeous face, his curled dark lashes around light blue eyes, the shadow of scruff against his jaw. What would that feel like against my tongue? Against my thigh? Between my thighs . . ..

Logan clears his throat and I almost jump out of my skin. The tiny smirk he's trying to mask tells me I've been caught staring. "Got anything to drink?" He lifts his chin to where I'm standing near my fridge.

Opening it to give my hands something to do, I bow behind the fridge door to hide my face and proceed with my humiliation in private. Relishing the crisp air, I breathe in and out several times, tempering my nerves. I can't hide behind here forever. "Sprite, beer, a half bottle of red wine, a quarter bottle of white, a full bottle of vodka . . .." I peek over and find him smirking at me. "Hey, don't judge."

"I wouldn't dare." But his mischievous eyes say something different.

I squint at him. "I feel like you are and just for that, I'm giving you warm tap water."

He laughs, the timbre of his voice doing that thing it always does to me--sending butterflies soaring into my ovaries. "You haven't changed a bit, *Batgirl*."

Warmth collects in my chest at hearing my childhood nickname again. "So, what's it going to be?"

"I'll take a beer." He pulls out a few sandwich bags from the brown bag, laying them on the counter. My gaze narrows, examining them as I carry our beers, getting onto the barstool next to him. He pushes a bag toward me and takes out his sandwich, completely oblivious to the heat radiating from my chest. "I didn't know if you liked potato chips or corn chips, so I brought both," he says, looking at his sandwich.

He takes a bite and turns toward me, stopping abruptly when he notices I haven't moved. How can I when all I'm trying to do is not throw myself at him? "You made--" I can't even finish the thought because now my chest feels like a furnace.

"Do you not like them anymore? I'm sorry, I only had strawberry . . . I know you used to make them with grape jelly."

My nose tingles before my eyes pool, and I slowly slide them up to meet his inquiring gaze. He swallows his bite and his thumb lifts to my cheek as a tear slips past the barrier, igniting a fire inside the furnace of my chest. One side of his mouth turns up into a half-smile. "You're crying a lot more than I remember."

Sob-laughing, I shove his shoulder with my finger and gingerly take my sandwich out of it's bag, biting into the soft bread and jelly. A frenzy of emotions swim around inside of me, but I focus on the sweetness of the sandwich instead of the sweetness of its maker to keep myself from turning into a puddle. I haven't eaten a jelly sandwich in a decade. I couldn't get myself to eat them after we left Austin because it was something that felt sacred to being with Logan.

"So, what have I missed these past years?" he asks after taking a swig of his beer. I notice he's only taken a couple bites of his sandwich. Maybe he doesn't love them as much as he used to.

I work around my bite. "Well, it's unfortunate, but you missed my purple-mascara and fuchsia-lips stage in high school. That came as a preamble to a year in my life where all I wore were oversized button-down shirts and black eyeshadow."

He laughs, his ocean-colored gaze washing over me. "Damn, I would have liked to see that. How are your parents?"

"They're good. Still overprotective, overbearing, and overwhelming as ever, but they mean well." I think about my last conversation with my mom. I'm positive she's going to ask me if I made the *rajma* when we talk again, and I'm already coming up with excuses in my head. If I tell her Logan visited, she'll just make assumptions and add that to yet another thing to nag me about. *The life of a twenty-two year old, ladies and gentlemen!* "What about you? How is your mom?"

"She's good. She keeps herself busy with . . . things."

Watching him carefully, I take a sip of my beer. I get the distinct feeling a shutter has fallen over his face and I wonder what that's about. "What happened with your dad? How did he pass?"

Logan shrugs. "He loved the poison stick too much. Heart attack."

"I'm sorry, Loga--" My voice breaks off when I see my

phone light up on the counter, buzzing with a call. *Fucking Naveen again.*

Logan regards the screen, and I don't miss the sharpness around his voice. "Do you need to get that?"

"No." I roll my eyes, hitting the red *End* button again. I need to block this asshole. "Some people can't take a hint. Or, in this case, they can't take very clear requests."

"I'm assuming we're talking about a boyfriend?" The edge hasn't softened in his voice.

"*Ex*. Ex-boyfriend." I finish the last bite of my sandwich. "Anyway, forget about him. Tell me more about you, mister world-famous DJ! Honestly, I'm not surprised since you were already good at mixing music when we were kids. Though, I have to admit, I'd never looked you up and had no idea how famous you were until Jeena told me."

Logan shrugs again and I can truly see he hasn't let the fame get to his head. "It's a job, just like any other. I travel a lot for it." A grimace crosses over his face, and I get the feeling there's more to that statement than he's letting on. I store that in the back of my mind to ask him about later.

"I've heard your music, Lo, and it sounds like more than just a *job*. You put so much of your heart into it."

He gets a wistful look on his face. "I almost go into a trance when I'm working, whether it be in the recording studio or in the booth at a club. It's where I feel the most free, if that makes sense. When I'm matching beats or writing music, it's the only time I can *speak* openly . . . I can be one hundred percent *me*."

I nod in understanding, knowing exactly what he means because that's how I feel when I'm sketching. It's medicinal and therapeutic, but it's also liberating.

Moving over to the couch, he sits next to me and pulls my legs over his knees so my back rests against the armrest.

It feels comfortable between us, like the adult version of our childhood friendship. We talk some more, catching up on the past few years as Lynx settles onto his dog bed. Logan tells me about his journey to becoming a DJ, and how Wayland started managing him. He tells me how he alternates between living in his Manhattan condo and the house in Austin, but that his life is way more hectic when he's in New York. "I work too much when I'm there, doing a gig almost every night. It can get exhausting."

"Is that why you come here every couple of weeks? To take a break and see your mom?"

I don't miss the hesitation on his face again. "You could say that."

"And what about a significant other? Do you have one of those?" My throat clenches at the thought of him with someone, but I ask anyway. Call me a masochist.

He shakes his head, watching me with hooded eyes. "No."

"Is it because your life is so crazy with all the travel?" It's bold of me to pry, but I figure he asked about Naveen when my phone rang earlier, so it's not completely inappropriate.

He sighs, running a hand over my bare foot. The contact feels so intimate, I almost moan. "Partly, yes."

His aloof answers keep me from giving into the haze. He's being guarded, and I see that shutter descend on his gaze again. I know I'm missing something, but I don't really have the right to ask him to tell me more, either. It's not like I mean anything to him anymore. He's just here because we once knew each other and he wants to reconnect. He doesn't owe me anything more.

Maybe he can read my thoughts or maybe he sees the disappointment on my face because he reaches out and swipes his thumb across my bottom lip. Our eyes lock and I will myself not to draw his thumb into my mouth. After a few seconds, I can't help but pull in my bottom lip to wet it and my tongue makes the slightest contact with his thumb.

All movement comes to a standstill between us before I hear Logan's breathing get labored. My gaze fastens to his neck as a vein pulses right under his skin. He swallows thickly before speaking. "When I saw you at the club that night . . . I honestly thought I was dreaming."

I circle my hand around his tattooed forearm, feeling it flex under my skin. I know his tattoos go all the way up to his shoulder from the pictures I saw of him on Jeena's phone, but I wonder if he has them anywhere else. What I wouldn't give to trace over each of them, memorize them. He drops his hand into my lap and I link my fingers with his long ones. My voice sounds small even to my ears. "I was scared to see you."

"Why?" His voice is soft and quiet, as if he's whispering to a lover in bed.

I shrug, braving eye contact with him momentarily before settling my gaze back on our entangled hands. My hands look so small inside his, and I recall how we used to compare the size of our hands and feet when we were kids. "I don't know. I just thought maybe you wouldn't remember me or if you did, maybe I wouldn't meet your expectations in some way."

His thumb rubs mine before his hand tightens like he's telling me what he's about to say requires my full attention. I lift my chin and watch his mouth, not wanting to meet his gaze. "You surpassed everything I ever imagined about you, Anisa."

I exhale a breath I didn't know I was holding. The tension between us, like the rhythm of my heart, keeps amplifying and I finally get the courage to meet his eyes.

They roam over me, all of me, as if he's assessing a possession that's been returned to him.

Before I lose my nerve, I decide to ask him something that's been bugging me ever since the last time we talked on an online game, years ago. "Lo?"

"Hmm?" His blue gaze leisurely makes its way to my sepia-colored one. There's a familiar warmth in them that was missing from all his pictures.

"Why did you . . .. I mean, how come we didn't keep in touch?

A tinge of color stains his fair cheeks. "Because I'm an idiot, Anisa." His hand tightens against mine and a similar tightness hits me between my legs. His eyes collide with mine in a mixture of apology, vulnerability, desire, and urgency. "I'm a *fucking* idiot."

Before I even know what's happening, Logan pulls me so I'm straddling him on the couch. His head lays back on the backrest as mine hovers over him.

My heart feels like a racehorse sprinting to the finish line inside my chest as my hands find their way into his hair. *What am I doing? Why is his hair so soft? Is every celebrity's hair this soft? They probably use shampoo made with dead seahorses. Wait, why am I thinking about dead seahorses right now?*

Logan stares at me and I can feel his heart thudding through his shirt, like he's weighing this out just as much as I am. Our heads are at war with our bodies, but our hearts are beating as one. His large, rough hands move under my silky cobalt-blue shirt and a shiver runs through me as they slide against my hot skin. My center pulses with arousal as my eyelids flutter shut and my head rolls back.

This is bad.

This is very, very bad.

This is so against my plans to stay away from men.

This is so bad.

But, God, this feels so good.

Trying to slow this high-speed train filled with lust and desire, I curl my bottom lip into my mouth, grasping it between my teeth. Logan doesn't seem to get the same memo though, because he hones in on the movement like a focused predator. His hand wraps around my neck, pulling my face so it's inches from his. "I've always loved and hated those lips."

"Why do you hate them?" My breath tangles with his.

His hips arch up and I feel heat explode in my core. "Because they've been a part of some of my filthiest fantasies."

And as if I'm no longer in charge of my body, my hands cup his cheeks before my mouth covers his. I taste the sweetest mix of strawberries and beer on his lips before his tongue demands entrance into my mouth. A moan escapes me, the sound only spurring him on further as he deepens our kiss, sucking on my tongue, kneading it with his own. An animalistic frenzy builds up inside me as I reciprocate, kissing him with everything I've got, biting his delicious bottom lip before sliding my tongue across it to salve the twinge. His tongue snakes farther into my mouth.

Digging my fingers into his scalp, I grind down on his lap, feeling his heavy, needy shaft against my center. I'm so wet, I can feel my panties slick against my skin. My hips move against him again and he groans into my mouth--throaty, manly, heady--making my nipples painfully taut inside my bra. His large palms squeeze my ass as he guides my hips to grind against him again and again, taking from me as much as I'm taking from him.

All this grinding, sliding, chasing, and rubbing is going to cause a damn fire! I don't even have insurance!

I haven't kissed many men in my twenty-two years but after this--dear God, after *this*--I don't think any others will even meet the minimum standard. The previous basic qualifications of a good kiss have been officially obliterated.

It's unlike me to be so physical, so lust-driven, so bold. It's not that I haven't enjoyed fooling around or even sex before, but with Naveen, the exchange was always one-way. He took and I gave. No hungry kissing, no foreplay, no wanton stares. It was a means to an end for him, where the end was only within *his* reach. So toward the later part of our relationship, I remember just checking out--thinking about the newest 3D printer or my latest sketch--and letting him finish.

Panting hard against Logan, I fist the bottom of his shirt, ready for him to take it off, when his hands gently land on mine. I feel him retreat under me and it's as if everything comes to a grinding halt--literally. "Anisa." It's both a plea and a warning, like he can't decide which one it should be. He's still breathing hard, but I see something that looks like remorse cross over his face.

Remorse . . . or maybe it's regret.

As if a lust-filled fog has lifted, I go still in his arms, releasing his shirt. Embarrassment cascades over me when I feel the prick of tears. "Oh God. I'm so sorr--"

Logan's hands cup my face, tilting my chin so I'll look at him. I try to turn my face away but his strong grip holds me in place. "Anisa, look at me," he urges again, and I flick my eyes at him before halting them somewhere around his shoulder. "This was not all you. I was right there with you." I nod, flushing from head to toe. I try to un-straddle him but again, his strong hands keep me against him. *Stupid, gargantuan hands.* "Anisa. Can you just listen to me for a second?"

"God, I feel like an idiot. You just came here to reconnect

and be sweet, and I just . . .." I cover my face with my hands, squeezing my eyelids shut behind them. My throat feels like it's on fire. "I *mauled* you."

His rough hands pull at my wrists so I'm forced to meet his creased brows. "You didn't *maul* me. I was the one who pulled you over to me because I've been wanting to kiss you since the night I saw you again."

Breathless, I don't know if I'm hearing him right. "What?"

He lays his head back on the couch and holds on to my wrists. "Fuck, Anisa, I've thought about kissing you so many times, not just in the past couple of days, but over the past decade. Why do you think I didn't keep in touch?"

"I don't . . .. Why?"

"Because in the year after you left, I realized that the feelings I'd had for you were not as platonic as I'd originally thought. And . . . fuck." He runs a hand through his hair, frustrated. "I had no means of seeing you or being with you, so I decided I needed to get away." He pauses, letting me absorb his admission. "It wasn't the right way for me to handle it, I know that now. But I was a hormonal teen who couldn't work through his feelings and just took the easiest path." He releases a frustrated breath. "So, if there's an idiot here, it's me."

Silently thinking about the years where I thought maybe I'd done something wrong or I'd become boring--one of my many characteristics, as per my ex boyfriend--I stay in Logan's lap staring at him. Before I can ask him where we go from here, a resolution seems to take over his features.

"But my job, my life situation . . . it's complicated, Anisa. I can't . . . we can't do this again because it wouldn't be fair to you."

I'm nodding before I've even heard the rest of what he

has to say. I get it, I really do. Anything more would be complicated and messy. A completely crazy idea. If it ended, it would ruin our friendship--this new one we're forging. Plus, it's as far away from my plan to be detached as the moon. *I'm supposed to be finding myself, living on my own, not being tethered to anyone, remember?* Dating isn't part of my plan. *Logan* isn't part of my plan.

So, if it's all so sensible in my head, why isn't my heart getting the damn memo? And why, God, *why* am I crying again? Haven't I embarrassed myself enough for one day?

I lift off Logan's lap--he lets me this time--swiping the back of my hand against my cheek and forcing up a laugh to contradict my emerging sob.

"Anisa." A flicker of pain sweeps across his face as he reaches for my hand.

"No, it's fine." I pull away, trying to plaster on a smile. "I mean, you're totally right. We would be such a bad idea and it would be so unfair to me." There's nothing that can be done about the mess I've made today, so I continue with the only thing I can to try to amend it. "I mean, who even thinks strawberry jelly is a good substitute for grape on their sandwiches?"

Logan rises to his feet, grimacing. My joke clearly hasn't diffused the situation as I'd hoped. "Come here." He pulls me into his warm chest and holds me so all my senses are once again replaced with him.

10

LOGAN

*a*t first, touring was all I looked forward to--the buzz to get my set ready, the excitement of getting on a private plane with my entourage and flying to the next metropolitan city or music festival, and the adrenaline raging through my veins when the crowd cheered and swayed to the beat I'd created. Every performance and tour meant I was getting closer to my goal of making it big.

And I did.

Week after week, month after month, I'd pack my bags and head to the next venue. The travel and gigs would center me, keep me aligned to my goal of having my name beamed on Vegas casinos or plastered on billboards world-wide. I'd feed off the crowd's energy just as much as they'd feed off of mine in a mutually-beneficial, co-dependent rela-tionship.

Once the gig finished for the night, I'd head to the after-party or throw one of my own where the biggest names in the industry would attend. No matter how much I tried to convince myself that I was having the time of my life, I couldn't get rid of the emptiness inside my bones. I might be in the entertainment business, but I didn't have an endless supply of myself to give like some of my colleagues. Between the crowd, the booze, and the general debauchery, my energy was usually drained before the end of the night and I'd sneak back to my hotel room alone, instead of with some random woman--or women--who'd passed me her number. I'd already seen how that life played out for a few of the artists and friends, and it never appealed to me. In the back of my mind, all of this was always a means to an end, a way for me to share my music and craft with the world.

Did that mean I'd never had a one-night-stand or an unplanned tryst to blow off some pent-up sexual energy? No. But that wasn't really my M.O. For me, it's never really been about sowing my oats or fucking the next supermodel. I prefer a deeper connection aside from a purely physical one. Call me old-fashioned that way.

Even when Mandy was pregnant and we were discussing our next steps, I'd suggested we get married. Sure, we'd only dated for a few months and still needed to get to know each other better, but I'd expected us to figure it out along the way. I wanted Lainey to grow up in a nuclear family where she saw both her parents together, just like I had. But Mandy was against it, saying she wanted to be in love with the person she was going to marry and that plenty of happy and healthy children grew up in non-traditional families.

Checking into my Paris hotel, I set my bags down and text my mom, telling her I'll FaceTime them tomorrow. The rest of the crew that traveled with me all have plans to party tonight, and they know not to ask me anymore. I'll go when I need to--usually strategically to make connections or promote a new release--but given a choice, I much prefer the quiet of my hotel room to the incessant noise of a party.

Over the past couple of years, traveling has started to feel more like a chore. Even though most of my time is spent producing and working on my own music label, I still have to tour to promote and network. It comes as part of the job but lately, the cost seems to outweigh the benefit. Mainly because it keeps me away from the people I want to be around the most.

At twenty-three, it's still too early in my career to stop touring all together, but I need to figure out how to balance it so I'll actually be around to watch Lainey grow up.

Unpacking a few of my things, I decide to shower before getting into bed. Tomorrow is going to be a packed day, meeting two different artists to record something we've been working on for a few weeks and an interview Wayland has scheduled for me with *T&T News*.

A shower will also help ease the disquiet that's made a home in my body ever since I left Anisa's apartment. I haven't been able to steady my mind. All I do is think about her, the smell of her, the taste of her, the feel of her. Hell, maybe I should make it a cold shower instead. Maybe that'll finally rid me of the massive hard-on I've been dealing with for the past twenty-four hours as well. After multiple attempts to *manage* it on the flight here, I have to consider whether I'm having some sort of reverse erectile dysfunction.

I need a reprieve from my thoughts that have done nothing but keep me awake and twitchy like some sort of junkie after getting home yesterday. Even when I tried to throw myself into work on the flight here, they kept popping up like weeds in a meadow. *Clarification: They took over the damn meadow like it was their little bitch.*

So what are these thoughts? They're of delicious, full lips that taste like fucking raindrops from heaven. Of drawn-out, thirsty sighs, breathing carnal desires against my mouth. Of hands scraping my scalp and gripping my shirt like they'd destroy anything in their path to get to me. Of breasts and hard nipples rubbing against my chest, begging to be nipped, licked, and savored.

I run a hand through my hair, pulling it, hoping it'll somehow pull out my lewd thoughts of Anisa as well. It would have been so convenient if she hadn't turned out so fucking sweet and gorgeous. The curve of her hips, the shape of her ass, the plush of her lips . . . none of it is convenient. And now, Anisa Singh is making me imagine the unimaginable, consider the unconsidered, and bid the forbidden. I feel like I'm coming apart at the seams.

I'd cursed myself all through the drive back home from her place yesterday. What the hell was I thinking showing up at her apartment uninvited? And why the hell did I tell her how much I'd thought about her over the years? It was like that damn jelly sandwich had truth serum in it. I was blurting out things, knowing the consequences would be exactly opposite to my plans.

Plans I'd made to stay focused on my kid and my career. Plans she was ruining by showing back up in my life.

I wanted her then and I want her now. I wanted her hands all over me, her body hot and needy on my lap, grinding against me. I wanted her moans and her palm-sized breasts. I wanted it all. How I managed to tear away from her last night, I don't know. I should honestly be given a Good Samaritan Award. I'm not exaggerating when I say that it took herculean strength on my part to take my hands off her when all I wanted to do was tear off her pants and get inside. If the skin on her back and torso felt so velvety soft, what would her most secret skin feel like?

Yeah, time for that cold shower . . ..

Aside from my body revolting against me for not doing what it really wanted, there was another reason I felt like a total jackass last night. After I'd reluctantly pulled away from our kiss, I'd unintentionally made Anisa feel like shit. I hated seeing her mortification as if she'd misjudged our explosive chemistry. What had changed that overconfident, shit-talking girl I once knew into someone so unsure of the effect she had on people? The effect she had on me?

I wanted to convince her that it wasn't all her, that she hadn't mistaken it. But my words did little to assuage her embarrassment. And to truly show her how I really felt would mean giving in to what my body wanted.

But I couldn't--I can't do that ever again--because we were going to remain just friends.

After jacking off for the third time today--because being friends with someone doesn't mean you can't think about them when masturbating--I get out of the shower and pull on a pair of pajama bottoms. I'm just looking through the changes to a contract I'm signing with a country artist when my phone vibrates with a text from Tessa.

I heard you're in town and I doubt you accompanied the others to whatever party they went to. Want to meet for a drink?

I frown, thinking about the last media onslaught after being seen with Tessa. I need to finish up some work. Plus, I saw a couple paps lingering outside the hotel when I checked-in. I'm too tired to get into a high-speed chase around the city with them on my tail.

Her reply comes after a few seconds. Is DJ Access

```
scared of a couple paps? Fine. How about I
come meet you at your hotel for a drink?
I'll get in through the back exit. And I
promise to let you get your beauty sleep by
a decent hour. It's been too long since I
saw you.
```

Tessa is nothing if not persistent. Sounds good, I type, along with the name of my hotel and try to ignore the ominous feeling in my gut.

```
See you in a half hour.
```

I'd recently--as in, two months ago--taken Tessa London, heiress to the *London-Bridge Organic Foods* company, with me to The Grammys. We'd met at a charity event prior to that, and I immediately liked how spirited, unreserved, and honest she seemed. We'd hit it off, chatting about our pasts and the state of our present. She told me about a string of bad relationships she was coming out of and how she was really looking to be unattached for a while. Somehow, I knew that wouldn't last as long as she hoped, but I didn't dampen her denial.

Tessa reveled in a life without rules, being in the public eye, and having enough money to buy the planet. She was feisty and fiery but somehow took a liking to me. While we were complete opposites, it was refreshing to see someone so unguarded and free.

Since neither one of us were looking to date anyone at the time and we enjoyed each other's company, we'd decided to accompany each other to The Grammys.

But nothing in this business was ever private, and the media always decided how something was perceived.

Showing up with Tessa to the awards and meeting with her for a drink a few weeks afterward had titillated celebrity gossip news everywhere. *Does Tessa London Have Exclusive 'Access' to Logan Miller? Read More About Who the Hottest Celebrity Single Dad Is Dating Now!*

It took Wayland and my publicist an entire week to manage the misinformation, with both me and Tessa giving formal statements refuting the implications. No sooner had the false news made headlines that my mom, my aunt Beth, and even Lainey were questioning me about it. And while Lainey couldn't read yet, there was no telling what she'd conclude from a picture of me--especially alongside a female--on a magazine cover at the grocery store.

I'm well-aware that Lainey wanted a mom like most of her friends, and I hate that these types of pictures made her hopeful. Even though she spends most of her days with her grandma and has no lack of female figures in her life--between my aunt Beth, my cousin Ana, and her preschool teacher--she still misses the presence of her mom.

On more than one occasion, Lainey has asked me about Mandy and why she hasn't come back. I've always responded with what I know--that her mom is still trying to recover and that hopefully one day, she'll feel well enough to visit. Still, Lainey is optimistic that even if her mom never returns, I'll find someone to "complete our family." Which is why such pictures and stories, taken out of context, further spur her hopes and worry me.

Lainey is too young to understand the things that keep me up at night, and I hope she never has to. I've often felt guilty about the bubble I've had to raise her in. Most children her age don't worry about being photographed without their knowledge or taken advantage of because their dad is famous. Regardless of the security around me and my home, there is always a looming threat to my privacy. I've had to fight hard to preserve any semblance of control but privacy has been transitory. Thankfully, I've succeeded so far in concealing Mandy's identity, but Lainey has been photographed multiple times without my consent.

Aside from the lack of privacy and its ramifications when you're trying to get to know someone genuinely, I worry about bringing someone into my life who could change my family dynamic or my relationship with my daughter. For me, Lainey will always be my first priority and anyone I'm with will need to come to terms with that. She'll need to love Lainey as much as me and unfortunately, I haven't found anyone like that.

I've never made it a secret that I have a daughter and that I take my job as her father seriously. Unfortunately, there weren't many women my age who understood or even accepted that. Most were more concerned about which designer they were going to wear or which plastic surgeon could give them a new nose.

In the handful of dates I'd been on, most women never even asked me a single thing about Lainey, as if she was an unflattering and inconvenient part of my life. And if I couldn't trust someone to take genuine interest in the most important person in my life, then how could I bring them into hers?

Which is why I'd decided I was better off alone than dealing with the additional stress of fitting someone else into my life. I'd do my best to be both the mom and dad that Lainey needed. And if that meant being single until Lainey was an adult, then so be it. It was a small price to pay to stay on my plan.

That is, until I saw Anisa again and couldn't remember what that plan actually was.

"*H*ey, lazy-pants! Are you getting ready for school?"

Lainey purses her lips dramatically and crosses her arms over her chest. "Daddy, you're doing it on purpose. It's not lazy-pants, it's *Lainey*-pants."

I laugh, happy to see her finally get on the camera. We went through a phase a few months ago where Lainey refused to get on the phone with me. I thought about talking to a therapist but thankfully, her reluctance was resolved before I needed to. "Right, my bad. I keep doing that." When her blue gaze moves from her grandma back to me with her eyebrows suspended high on her forehead, I add, "Oh, I mean, I'm sorry."

"Will you go to the *I Fall Tower* again on this trip? Can you bring me another snow globe from there?"

"I wasn't planning on going to the Eiffel Tower this trip, but I promise to bring you another snow globe."

Her resulting smile tightens my chest momentarily. "Thanks, Daddy. Are you coming back Friday?"

I nod, watching my mom brush and tie Lainey's hair,

getting her ready for school. "Yup. It'll probably be past your bedtime, but I'll see you on Saturday morning."

"Ooh, are you coming to the fair with us?" Her smile stretches across her face and her eyes gleam.

I furrow my eyebrows, looking at my mom for help. "The fair?"

My mom leans forward to chime in, "Beth has a booth at the food and wine festival on Saturday, and I promised her that Lainey and I would come support her--even if that meant just hanging around and taste-testing the items she was making."

My aunt Beth--my mom's fraternal twin sister--and her husband Oliver owned a bakery in Austin for the past fifteen years. Aunt Beth is a world-class baker and my favorite aunt. *She's also my only aunt, but that's besides the point.* Her bakery did really well and usually was booked months ahead of time with big events like weddings and large parties. In fact, every time I'd hosted a party at my house, all the desserts and cake had always come from *Beth's Bakery*.

"How long are you guys planning to go for?" I ask, a little bummed that I wouldn't get to take Lainey fishing like I was hoping to on Saturday.

"Just for a few hours," my mom says, moving Lainey to her lap so they're both in front of the camera. "I know you don't like being at these public events, but maybe you can consider coming with us for a bit?"

"Yeah, Daddy! We can wear hats and glasses again so no one knows it's us!" In her effort to contain her anticipation of me coming along, Lainey wraps her arms around my mom and hugs her tight, bouncing on her lap. "And Grams said there's even gonna be cotton candy there!"

How the hell do I say no to that? "Oh, alright. I'll come

with you guys for a bit, but only if you promise to share half the cotton candy with me."

She thinks about it for a beat. "Deal!"

The rest of the call lasts another ten minutes with Lainey showing me her freshly painted fingers and toes, and my mom giving me some updates from Lainey's preschool teacher and reminding me to book the private swimming instructor over the summer for Lainey.

After the call, I meet up with Wayland for a drink at the hotel's private lounge.

"How was last night?" I ask him after we order our drinks. It never ceases to amaze me how alert and coherent Wayland always seems, regardless of the jet lag and the late-night partying. In the five years we've been working together, he never once missed an important meeting because he couldn't wake up on time.

He shrugs. "A few people asked about you. They weren't surprised when I told them you decided to stay in. I believe the vernacular floating around about you was 'chump.'"

I chuckle and take a sip of the scotch I'd ordered. I wasn't a heavy drinker but having a drink prior to an event always helped me loosen up on stage. "I needed to get some rest," I respond, deciding not to tell him about having a drink with Tessa last night. After the media fiasco we had to fend off recently, it's not worth having Wayland worry about anything more. As it was, the evening didn't quite go the way I had expected.

"Yeah, and have some alone time with your thoughts." He air-quotes 'alone time' with his first two fingers.

I side-eye him because he's caught me off-guard. "I don't know what you're talking about."

Wayland takes a swig of his beer before releasing a soft laugh. "Please. As if I didn't see the way you ogled Anisa that night. There were literal heart shapes dancing in your eyes."

I shake my head. "Shut the fuck u--"

"Seriously! I thought I'd have to call the paramedics."

"You're an asshole." I turn toward him. If he could dish it, he'd better be ready to take it. "As if you were any better with her sister! You both practically started miming because neither one could get out a word."

To my surprise, Wayland doesn't defend himself. Instead, he lets out a mixture of a huff and a sigh. "Seeing her after all this time . . .." He shakes his head as if he's trying to clear away a vision of Jeena from his mental *Etch-A-Sketch*.

Though he doesn't disclose any more as he looks pensively at his beer, I know exactly what he means. "Yeah," I say without prompting him for more. I haven't told him about my unannounced visit to Anisa's place on Monday night. It's not that he would care, but something about it feels like it just needs to be left between me and her.

He sighs, seemingly acquiescing to his unrequited feelings for Jeena before turning to me. "How did the recordings go this morning?"

I nod. "I think they went well. The mix with the country song is going to be legit. I cut the bass using the EQ at one point and the song just came to life."

"Nice. I got the updated contracts. Both bands have agreed to the terms of co-producing the album with you."

Wayland and I clink our glasses together. I'm about to ask him about some things that have been on my mind in regards to my touring schedule when he looks at his watch and takes the final swig of his beer. "Ready for the interview? The reporter should be waiting in the conference room downstairs."

I nod, deciding to talk to him about it another time. "Yup, let's go."

We're on the elevator, heading to the interview when Wayland gets a text. His eyebrows furrow as he brings the phone closer, looking intently at whatever he's been sent. "The fuck?"

I'm just about to ask him if everything is okay when the elevator doors open and I see the crowd of cameramen and lighting specialists, along with the reporter. She gives me and Wayland a bright smile as we arrive.

"We need to talk," Wayland says, keeping his face stoic. "Now."

But before I can respond, a short, curly-haired brunette sticks out her hand for me to shake. "Mr. Miller, I'm Zelda. If you'll come with me, I can show you to your designated changing room. We have an array of clothes you can choose from for the photoshoot." Since this interview would be for a magazine, they also wanted me to pose for a few pictures.

I look over at Wayland, who's glaring at me as if I'd just killed his pet goldfish. I turn to Zelda. "Can you give me a few minutes?"

"We'll run behind if you take more than five, so please just keep that in mind."

I give her a tight smile and then tilt my chin letting Wayland know I'm ready to follow him. We find a relatively private spot near the exit in the back. "Is there anything you want to tell me, Lo?"

I meet Wayland's hard glare. He knows I don't answer vague and esoteric questions. "Get to the point."

He lifts his phone and shows me the photograph that I assume he was looking at in the elevator. "Marcus just sent it to me. He says it's already too late to squelch it, so you need to come up with how you're going to address it before this interview. And if the shark-like sneer on that reporter's face is any indication, she's going to rip you apart."

I squint at the image. It's fuzzy and there's definitely a glare from the glass window it was taken from, but there's no mistaking it. It's a picture of me and Tessa at the private lounge last night with her mouth firmly pressed to mine. "This isn't what it looks like." I shake my head at the picture.

"Yeah? Well, you better start talking about what it *is*, then."

My stomach turns. "Shit."

ANISA

"*T*his is really great work, Anisa!" One of the scene designers, a Latin-American woman named Rosa, who has blue streaks in her uneven bangs, watches over my shoulder as I demo the first version of the new warrior goddess, Eterna. Rosa created the basic character design and I added the animation this week to make her come to life. At the moment, Eterna is bent on one knee, holding a spear, and heaving at the ground. Her jet-black hair flutters in the wind, along with her fitted moss-green hooded dress. "You've made a lot of progress in just one week!"

"Thanks!" I turn toward her with a smile. "Your design storyboards were really clear, so that helped."

"What do we have here?" Blake sidles up behind Rosa, leaning toward my computer screen but I don't miss the way Rosa flinches, then distances herself away from him. "Ah, nice work, Anisa. Although . . ." he puts his index finger on his lips, as if he's thinking profoundly, "her waist needs to be a bit more cinched and maybe her breasts be more pronounced."

Rosa and I both startle. "Excuse me?" I ask, which really should be interpreted as, *"Excuse me, did you just make the world's most sexist comment to two females right in front of you?"*

Blake looks between the two of us as if we're imbeciles. "Oh, come on!" he scoffs. "Over seventy percent of our players in this game are hormonal teenage *boys*. In case you're not aware, these testosterone-producing juveniles are the reason we stay in business. Enticing them with curvaceous characters will continue to persuade them to play the game."

"It also continues to feed a culture of sexualizing women and propelling self-objectification by sending out a message that women must adhere to a certain body image in order to be beautiful. That isn't what our games should promo--"

"It's not up to you and me to decide what the game needs to promote, Anisa. The gaming market has been this way for years, and our job is to meet the requirements set forth by our biggest market--teenage boys."

I'm about to say something in rebuttal--though I don't like the idea of butting heads with my project lead on the first week--when Rosa beats me to it. Her chestnut eyes flash and I get the distinct feeling this hasn't been the first time she's had to deal with Blake or his comments. "It seems like you have a lot in common with these hormonal teenage boys, Blake."

He shakes his head, huffing out an unaffected laugh. "I'm leading this project, Rosa. Let me do my job. I don't have time to explain the gamer market to you both at almost five on a Friday evening." Then, looking at me as he moves toward his desk, he continues, "I'll be sure to tell Travis how well you're progressing this week, Anisa. But make the changes I've requested first."

If I'm not mistaken, his words of praise are tinged with a threat. He'll tell Travis that I'm doing well *if* I make the changes he's requested. Rosa and I exchange a glance before I decide how to respond. "Once Rosa gives me the story-board update, I can make the changes." I see Blake getting ready to launch a counterstatement, so I continue, "That will ensure that when the quality assurance team tests out the scene and the new character movements, we all stay in sync with the requirements."

Rosa gives me a small satisfied smile before looking at Blake. "And since Travis is the head creative director for this project, I'll run the changes by him *before* updating the storyboard."

For the first time all week, I see a spark of something menacing cross over Blake's face before he schools it. "Do as you please. Travis knows the market better than anyone." With that, he packs up and heads out the door.

Exhaling the breath I feel like I've been holding for five minutes, I look at Rosa. "Is he always like that?"

She hasn't stopped glaring at the door. Her jaw tightens at my question, and I get the feeling she's forcing herself to recompose. "Oh, that was nothing."

I consider asking her more about what she means by that remark, but she's already packing up to leave for the evening. Something in her grimace tells me she wouldn't want to tell me anything more anyway.

I've always known sexism and the objectification of women was rampant in the video game industry--I'd grown up playing the same games that the so-called 'hormonal teenage boys' played--but it was unnerving to see it so overtly displayed today. Most companies, including *Escapade Games*, have made respectable strides in penalizing displays of sexism that used to be excessive in the workplace, but there were always misogynists like Blake who'd discreetly use their power to sabotage the effort.

Reflecting on the past few minutes, I decide to finish up the last touches to Eterna's outfit. I'd prefer not to work over the weekend and get some sketching done since I now had new supplies, courtesy of my car.

I'm just tweaking the last changes on the graphic when Sydney walks back to her desk, head down, scrolling through something on her phone. "I didn't realize you were still here," I say to her, closing my laptop.

She looks up at me, almost like she's surprised to see me, too. "Oh, hey! Yeah, just got done with a meeting." She watches me pack up. "Give me a sec, I'll head out with you."

"Sounds good."

"How was your first week?" she asks, putting her laptop inside her backpack.

I consider telling her about the strange encounter with Blake, but I decide to mull on it before telling anyone. I don't want to stir up gossip. If it's still bothering me next week, I'll talk to Rosa or Travis. "It was good! I'm loving it."

"Good!" She pulls her purse out of her desk drawer. "You're still coming to the food festival tomorrow, right?"

I'd forgotten about that but I suppose aside from sketching, I don't have anything better to do. I had promised my friend Nelly that we would have a FaceTime date, but I can move it. "Sure, I'll see you there."

Sydney gives me a genuine smile as we make our way to the elevator. "Yay! I'll be there with my boyfriend Ken, but just text me when you get there and we'll come find you."

"Sounds good."

Sydney goes back to reading something on her phone again as we descend in the elevator. She shakes her head. "Celebrities, man. They're so predictable."

My eyebrows furrow and I'm curious about what she's talking about. "What do you mean?"

She chuckles. "Oh, nothing. I know it's stupid, but I like to keep up with celebrity gossip. It's one of my guilty pleasures." She gives me an embarrassed look to see if I'm judging her. I'm not, considering one of my guilty pleasures is watching reruns of *Friends or* re-watching the Avengers movies. Really, Chris Hemsworth wielding a hammer is too sexy to only be watched once. And yes, I realize that I just mentioned sexism in the gaming industry and now I'm drooling over a man with miles of muscles, brandishing his . . . *tool,* but I'll argue that there's a difference between objectifying and appreciating.

We exit the elevators and walk into the parking garage. "Anything interesting?"

"So, you know DJ Access, right? He's pretty famous and even lives here in Austin, from what I've heard."

Oh God. My stomach flip-flops at the mention of Logan's name and I consider telling her not to continue.

I've managed to do a decent job of enclosing my memories of our kiss--and my subsequent mortification--from Monday night into a nice, neat box in my brain this entire week, immersing myself in work and errands.

Who am I kidding? It has been next to impossible to do anything but think about his strong, rough fingers digging into my torso, igniting a fire traveling up my entire back. More than once--a lot more . . . like, *a lot* more--I've indulged in the memory of his tongue against mine, ravaging me and giving me a glimpse into the promise it could deliver in other places.

Heat rises to my chest and face as I think about how foolish I must have seemed to him, jumping into his lap and then lapping at his face like a dog with a bone. Ugh! Why didn't a heavenly bolt of lightning just strike me down right then?

And even though he told me multiple times that it wasn't all my fault, that he's thought about kissing me before, I can't seem to believe it. How can I when he promised to text me from Paris to figure out a time for us to meet up again but hasn't all week? Maybe he just said that to be nice and help me save face.

It doesn't surprise me in the least. He's always been a good guy, a nice guy. But now Logan Miller was also one of the hottest, most wanted bachelors in the entire world-- potentially the entire universe--and I'm not foolish enough to think he'd be waiting around, pining for me when he's had the world's hottest women begging to be on his arm.

He's just a really great guy who came to visit an old friend with a jelly sandwich as a sweet gesture, and that friend totally ruined it by grinding on him like she was in heat!

My mortification haveth no end!

I haven't responded to Sydney in the time we've been walking to our cars, but she continues, ignoring my silent mental breakdown, "Anyway, he's been dating Tessa London, who's this fake and bitchy celebrity known just because her father has a shitload of money. Just a few weeks ago, they both made public statements that they were never together and were just friends, but now there's this picture floating around of them from this past Tuesday night."

Tuesday night. The night after he and I kissed. Or rather, the night after *I mauled him.*

But didn't he tell me he didn't have a girlfriend? If he's the same Logan I knew years ago, he's not one to lie. But maybe this Tessa lady and him were "taking a break" like

Ross and Rachel on *Friends,* and maybe I became the Chloe who Ross kissed in this whole situation.

Oh God! I don't want to be Chloe!

Sydney turns her phone toward me and my stomach bottoms out as I look at the picture on her screen. A woman with platinum blonde hair has her arms wrapped around Logan's neck and her face plastered to his. She honestly looks like she's sucking out his soul through his mouth like a dementor from *Harry Potter*. Her perfect, lithe figure and tiny waist between his hands are accentuated by low hanging jeans and a top that barely covers her breasts, showing off a flat, bare torso. She's what wet dreams of teenage boys--and Blake--everywhere are made of.

I don't mean to recoil so visibly, but Sydney doesn't miss it. "I know," she scoffs, clicking off her phone and opening her car door. "Doesn't look like they're just friends." She curls two fingers, air-quoting 'just friends'. "Oh, well. I'll see you tomorrow, okay?"

"Yeah, tomorrow," I repeat robotically, walking back to my car and trying to repress the urge to hurl.

I finally pull myself out of bed early Saturday morning, giving up on trying to sleep in. Truth be told, between all my tossing and turning, I probably only slept four hours. Even Lynx got off my bed at some point and moved to another spot. I could swear I heard him grumble a few expletives under his breath.

Throughout the night, my mind buzzed with images of Logan and the blonde kissing, his hands resting on her hips. Every time I pictured it, I felt like throwing off the comforter and punching my pillow or the wall or something. The image and my own reaction to it made me sick and angry. We'd kissed not even a day before, and he already had his tongue down someone else's throat! But maybe *I* was the 'someone else'. Maybe *I* was the one who had complicated his perfect life by launching myself at him that night. The thought kept spinning inside me like yarn and in the end, I just felt like a knotted mess.

Getting to my feet, I shuffle groggily to the bathroom to brush my teeth and wash my bleary eyes. Running my fingers through my matted hair, I pull it into a low ponytail before trudging to the kitchen and turning on the coffee maker.

After taking Lynx out, I sit with my coffee at my breakfast table where I'd laid out my sketches this week. I've been working on a scene inside the Catacombs of Paris. My main character, a short-haired assassin who prefers her skateboard to any other mode of transportation, strolls through the scene, observing the wall of human remains and skulls.

The scene reminds me of Logan. Not because of the human remains, but because it makes me wonder if he's back from Paris. He still hasn't called or texted like he said he would, and I try to swallow the disappointment down with a sip of coffee.

After rinsing out my cup, I get to work sketching out the scene some more, shading in the wall and the cobblestone pathway. I've been working on it for about an hour when my phone chimes with a text from Nelly.

Hey! Are we still on to FaceTime later? I ask because it directly impacts me taking a shower and putting on clothes today.

In my morose haze getting back home last night, I'd forgotten to let her know that I wasn't going to be able to FaceTime today at the time we'd set. Unfortunately I'm being 'encouraged' to go to a food and wine festival with some co-workers at the same time today. Can we reschedule?

Her reply comes a few moments later. You're really taking this 'being social' promise to Jeena seriously. I'm proud of you! Yeah, what about tomorrow?

I text her back and we settle on a time that works for both of us. After graduation, Nelly moved to the East Coast to work as a business analyst for a company near her mom. Her mom has been sick on and off for the past couple of years, and Nelly wanted to be near her so she could take care of her. Under that hard outer shell and the laissez-faire demeanor, Nelly has a heart of gold. She doesn't hand over said heart to anyone often, and I consider myself as one of the lucky ones.

No sooner have I finished texting with Nelly, my phone rings. This time it's Jeena.

"Why are you up so early on a Saturday?" I ask, looking over at my clock and reading the time. It isn't even six in California.

"I don't know. I got hungry and then couldn't sleep because all I could think about was food," Jeena answers through yawn.

"You're always hungry," I tease my sister with our ongoing joke. Ever since we were little, Jeena has had an extraordinary appetite and metabolism--the kind that makes you want to throat-punch her. The girl can eat a horse and the hay it was feeding on and still *lose* weight in the process. Even though she's shorter than me by a couple of inches, her thin and leggy frame, pert nose, and perfectly unblemished face has always made her look like a runway model--a constantly hungry model who could eat pretty much anything and not even show a food-baby. See what I mean? Throat-punch.

Meanwhile, I'll eat a salad without any dressing and still manage to gain weight. I'm not a large woman by any means. In fact, I'm average for my height, but I've had to work hard to maintain that. Even as a kid, I struggled with my "baby fat" as Mom referred to it. She never made me feel anything but beautiful, but she also put me in more sports than Jeena, which I suspect was to combat said "baby fat."

I still remember one of Mom's friends--a woman who was part of the *No-Filter Indian Aunty Squad*, as Jeena and I referred to them--giving me a backhanded compliment during my high school graduation party. *"You're looking quite healthy and happy, Anisa! You've put on a few, no? That's okay. You'll burn it off in no time if you stop eating all the carbs."*

Mom had told me to ignore *Asshole Aunty* and reminded me that I was beautiful no matter my size, and I'd shrugged it off, pretending the comment hadn't even fazed me. But it took months to subdue the sting. And even now, when I gain a couple of pounds or don't stay on my exercise regime, I hear *Asshole Aunty* in my ear. *"A moment on the lips, forever on the hips!"*

"What do you have going on today?" I can hear Jeena crunching on something, probably one of her favorite cereals. The girl eats multiple bowls of the stuff a day.

I secure the phone between my shoulder and ear so I can have both hands free to wash Lynx's bowls. "'You'll be proud of me. I'm going to a food and wine festival with my new friend from work today."

"Ooh! Good for you, little sis! That sounds fun. How's work? Are you showing them your animation skills?"

I think about how much fun I had creating Eterna this week and getting to know Sydney. "Yeah, it's been really good. I really like my manager and the team seems great, too." Minus Blake, but I don't need to get into all that with her.

She hums around another bite, and I know she's biding time to ask what's really on her mind. "That's good. So, did you ever hear from Logan after last weekend?"

Yeah, heard, tasted, grinded on. You know . . . friend stuff.

Since Jeena and I have been playing phone tag all week, I hadn't had a chance to tell her about how he showed up to my apartment on Monday night. It was for the best really, because I needed a few days to go through the various stages of embarrassment on my own. You know the ones. *Awkwardness. Shame. Mortification. Acceptance.* I'm currently in the acceptance stage and therefore, feeling more open to sharing. "Well, I need to fill you in."

She stops crunching. "Okay, tell me."

"He surprised me on Monday night at my apartment. He was holding dinner, so I couldn't really shoo him away. You know how I get about food . . .."

My sister squeals, "He came over? How long did you guys hang out?"

I groan, "Jeena, it didn't end well."

"What? What do you mean it didn't end well? Did something even *start* for it to *end*?"

Sighing, I proceed to tell Jeena about most of the night, cutting out the parts about me grinding on his erection, but I'm sure I paint a colorful enough picture. Then I tell her about the picture Sydney referred to at work yesterday that's all over the internet. "So, yeah, I became Chloe."

"What? Who's Chloe?"

"Never mind." I lay on my couch with my head on the armrest, similar to the way patients do at a therapist's office. At least, that's how they show them in the movies. "Basically, I ruined any chance of us being friends again, I think."

"But you said he was the one to pull you on his lap and he kept staring at your lips. That doesn't sound like he was wanting to be purely *friendly* in the first place. I don't think this was all your fault."

I groan, knowing that she's probably right but still

feeling no better about it. "Yeah, maybe. But it doesn't matter anyway. He's with someone else."

"Just because there is some picture of him floating around the internet doesn't mean he's with her. Have you looked any of this up yourself to see if he's confirmed their relationship?"

"No. You know I don't keep up with that stuff--"

"But shouldn't you at least *keep up* with Logan? Aren't you at all curious?"

I shift against the cushion. Should I be looking up Logan's life, invading his privacy and hunting through every media article about him? It's not something I'd want if the situation were reversed, especially not by a so-called friend. If I want to know something, shouldn't I just ask him directly? "Not really. He might be a famous celebrity, but I don't want to be just another obsessed fan."

I hear a distant sounding "uh huh" from her along with soft clicking noises. Looking at my phone screen to make sure I haven't lost connection, I say, "Jeena, you there?"

A few seconds later, her voice is clearer. "Sorry, I was looking this whole thing up." *Clearly, she has no such reservations on invading someone's privacy.* "So, Tessa London is this socialite and model who has been linked to like, a hundred other celebrities. I can see how the picture you're talking about doesn't look good, but I don't know, Nees . . .. Something about the way he looked at you that night at the club and then what you're telling me about Monday just doesn't add up."

"Yeah, well, it's not like he owes me an explanation or anything. Anyway, can we just talk about something else? I don't really want to waste any more energy on someone who hasn't given me a second thought."

I hear more faint clicking and then a sudden gasp on the

phone. "Nees! Holy crap! I don't know how I missed this before!" Clearly, Jeena's not ready to change the subject. "Did you know he has a--"

A beep cuts Jeena off when I receive another call. I lift the phone to see that it's from an "Unknown" caller. What if it's from work? Travis mentioned he'd be adding me to the on-call list for high-priority bugs and that the number shows up as "Unknown" when coming from our corporate office. Maybe the weekend support team needs someone and isn't able to get hold of another developer. "Hey, Jeens, I think I'm getting a call from work. Let me call you later."

"Okay, but did you hear what I just said?" She sounds frazzled, but I need to put a pin in the Logan conversation until I resolve this other call.

"No, but I need to go. Call you later." I don't wait for her response. Sitting up on the sofa, I click to the other line. "Hello?"

"Nees?"

Just hearing his voice again sends a stream of acid down my esophagus. Acrimony tinges my voice. "Why are you calling me, Naveen?" I had blocked his number after he'd called when Logan was here on Monday, and I hoped-- prayed--that he'd gotten the message. Clearly, my prayers are being left unanswered.

He chuckles as one would at a toddler fighting against nap time. "I'm doing fine, babe. How kind of you to ask," he mocks. "You've been avoiding my calls and I wanted to hear your voice."

"There's a reason people avoid calls and don't respond to texts," I bite out.

"I get it, Nees. This is your big show of independence. You wanted to prove to daddy that you were employable outside of his company. That you weren't the naive and infantile daughter he's always taken you for. Well, bravo! You did it. Now, cut the shit and get your ass back over here."

A storm brews inside of me as I grip the phone hard enough to crack it. I think about the last phone I sacrificed on him and loosen my grip. "Screw you, Naveen. Firstly, you and I are *over*. You don't get to tell me what to do, ever. Secondly, at least I *am* employable outside of my dad's company; you don't even have that going for you." It's not my finest moment, I know. I hate that he brings this hostility out of me, but I refuse to be a doormat just because his ego is bruised.

Naveen laughs, venom coating his next words. "Yes, yes, I have you to thank for your *generosity* and *compassion*. Where would I be without you?"

I feel like I've gone back months through a time warp. For a hot minute there, I thought that maybe the frequent texts and phone calls the past couple of weeks were an indication that he was regretful of the way he treated me and that he wanted to apologize. I haven't been ready to hear it, though part of me felt guilty for blocking his number and not giving him a chance to express his remorse. But he hasn't changed a bit. It's the same resentful remarks and twisted perception making him seem like the victim.

"If you hate my generosity so much, why don't you quit? Or better yet, maybe I can help you with that, too. I'm more than happy to give my dad a briefing of the past few months of your 'model' behavior."

Silence follows my statement and I know reality has just struck him. A kitten in lion garb. "You know I need this job, Anisa. It would be pretty shitty and entitled of you to take our personal relationship issues to your dad. In any case, you'd just be proving to him that you need him to clean up your messes."

"Then leave me the fuck alone!" I yell and startle Lynx from his nap. "Stop calling me and stop texting me. We've been over for a while now, Naveen. Get it through your head!"

"Don't you fucking get it, Anisa?" he yells back, loud enough that I have to hold the phone away from my ear. "I fucking love you! I miss you! I'm acting this way *because* of you. Because I hate that you left. I hate that you didn't give us a chance when we had something good. We could have worked through our issues, but you ran like a fucking coward!"

Is he in some other dysfunctional dimension? "Nothing about the last six months of my life with you would be classified as '*something good.*' I'm actually ashamed of myself for taking so long to come to the realization, for giving you so many chances. If I'm a coward for taking my life into my own hands and trying to find my own way, then so be it. I couldn't care less what you think. Goodbye, Naveen. If you call me again, I won't hesitate to involve my dad, and I don't think I need to remind you again what that would cost you."

Without listening to another word from him and with my heart almost squeezing itself through my throat, I end the call. It takes me a half hour to get the jitters out of my system so my arms no longer tremble, but I finally get up to shower and get ready for the day.

Little do I know that the day is just about to get a little more interesting.

14

LOGAN

"*Y*ou need to be low-key for a while, stay inside." Wayland uses his manager-voice on the phone with me to get me to change my mind.

"I promised Lainey I'd go with them for a bit, and I'm doing just that. I'll try not to stand out."

He huffs his frustration. "Once one person recognizes you, it'll be a swarm. Just sayin'."

"Not like I haven't dealt with it before."

"Tell Jason to stay close to you." Wayland refers to my bodyguard.

"He has the day off today. It's fine, I'm good." I know it's Wayland's job to worry but sometimes I just need a fucking iota of normalcy.

We hang up before I shuffle out of my room to find Lainey and my mom playing *Go Fish* on the family room floor. "You guys ready to go?"

"I win!" Lainey claps her hands, standing up, causing her cards to flutter around her. "Good game, Grams!"

My mom gives her a bewildered look. "We haven't finished! You did not win, miss!"

"Well, I was closest to winning. Don't be a sore loser, Grams," Lainey chides my mom before looking over at me. "We're ready, Daddy."

I can't help but laugh while my mom shakes her head, mumbling something under her breath. There's not many people who can hold sway over my mom, but I think she's found her match.

At the festival, we finally manage to find Aunt Beth's booth amongst the hundreds that have taken over the park. Even though we're here before the afternoon crowd gets in, there's already a long line forming for doughnuts and pastries. It's almost a hundred degrees and even the slight warm breeze feels like a cold gust of air under the sun. I adjust my white cap lower on my forehead, dying inside my long white shirt--to cover my tattoos--and jeans. I'm fucking burning up, but it's a small price to pay to fulfill my promise to my little girl.

Lainey, also wearing a hat, heads straight to my aunt and uncle when she sees them. "Aunt Beth!" She wraps her little arms around my aunt's legs, then looks up. "Did you make me a sprinkled jelly doughnut like you said you would?"

"Now how could I make all these yummy treats for everyone else and forget my little Lainey-pants? Of course, I made jelly doughnuts for you." My aunt's eyes warm at the sight of my daughter and she glides her hand down one of her silky blonde pigtails.

"With grape jelly?"

"Of course. I know you don't like the other kinds."

As if controlled by Freud himself, my brain immediately conjures an image of Anisa biting into her jelly sandwich, her tongue peeking out to lick up the extra jelly on her lip. I haven't been able to rid myself of the picture of her large, glistening eyes when she saw that I still remembered the sandwiches from our childhood. Her chin wobbled and I remembered the way it did the same the day she told me she was moving to fucking San Francisco. I've never hated a day or a city more.

I'd promised her that I'd call or text all week but ever since Tuesday night's debacle with Tessa, I haven't been able to get a free moment to do either. If I wasn't dealing with the PR to get new statements out then I was working until late. A trip that was meant to be pretty straightforward in my line of work ended up becoming an enormous headache instead.

I give my aunt and uncle a hug, keeping my head low and avoiding making eye contact with people standing around the booth. "Want a slice of this lemon meringue pie?" my aunt asks, pointing to one of the many desserts inside the plexiglass shelf she has propped up on a picnic table.

"I'll never refuse a dessert you've made, Aunt Beth."

My mom decides to put on an apron and help out while Lainey and I find a couple of plastic chairs to sit on to eat our pastries.

"So how's life at *Beautiful Day Preschool*?" I ask Lainey, who's licking sticky sugar off her fingers.

"Mmm, it's good." She shrugs, though I don't miss the little grimace that sets on her face.

"What's up, Lainey-pants? Something bothering you?"

She looks at her dangling feet as if she's thinking about whether to tell me. "Well, I know you'll just tell me to ignore the poop-heads that sometimes make me feel bad. And I'm already doing that, so it's okay, Daddy, I've got it covered."

Taken aback by the maturity of my four-year-old, I put my plastic fork down on my plate and look her pointedly.

"Hey, listen to me. Just because you think you know what I'm going to say, doesn't mean you don't need to tell me what's bothering you, okay? If there are poop-heads at school who are being mean to you, I need to know about them."

She slumps in her chair, as if resigning to tell me. "Sienna and Maggie said I had fat legs. They said they couldn't believe my leggings didn't just rip right off."

What the fuck? What is wrong with these kids? Shoving down the ire building in my body, I struggle to take a calming breath and refrain from using expletives. "You know what you should tell them? You should tell them that they *do* rip right off when you're angry. Like when The Hulk gets angry and tears through his clothes. That's what happens to you. So, they better be careful not to make you mad."

She giggles. "That doesn't happen to me, Daddy. I don't want to lie."

"Well, a tiny little white lie never hurt anyone."

She giggles again, her voice a little jingle in the warm wind, and the two of us sit in silence finishing up. By lunchtime, the crowd appears to be getting bigger and I'm about to tell Lainey that I'll see her back at the house when she stops me. "Daddy! You said you'd get me cotton candy. I see other people walking around with bags. Can we go find the booth?"

My mom looks over from where she's plating a dessert for a customer. "You've had a doughnut, a brownie, and now you want cotton candy? Lainey, that's a lot of sugar in the span of a few hours."

Lainey's face drops. "But he said we would get some."

I look at my mom apologetically. While I'm Lainey's

parent and could totally overrule her, I also recognize how much my mom does for her. If Lainey's had some semblance of a normal life at all, it's because of my mom's devotion in helping raise her. I don't want to disregard the rules she's set out for my daughter when she's the one who takes care of her day in and out.

"Oh, fine. But that's it, miss. No more sugar for the rest of the day."

Lainey grabs my hand, pulling me toward the crowd before my mom's even finished speaking, her face alight. "Let's go, Daddy!"

We walk around various booths, getting the smells of grilled hot dogs and wok-fried noodles. My stomach rumbles, already having digested the slice of pie from earlier. One side of the park has booths serving a variety of cuisines while the other has a row of booths serving wine and beer tastings. While most people are standing around eating, some have laid out blankets on the patches of unused grass. After stepping around more booths, we spot a few teenage girls walking toward us, carrying bags of cotton candy. One of them makes eye contact with me, and I realize I'm too late in looking away.

"Wait, is that . . .. Holy shit! Hey, are you DJ Access?" one of them squeals, drawing the rest of the group's attention.

Shit.

"Uh . . .."

"Oh-em-gee! Can we get a selfie with you?"

"Actually, I'm here with my daughter, and I'm not taking pictures today." I start walking past them, holding Lainey's hand.

I hear them collectively "aww" and squeal. Keeping Lainey in front of me to hide her, I see them in my periphery, taking photos with their cellphones. They won't get much except my profile. Thankfully, no one else seems to have noticed, or if they have, they're being kind enough to not approach me with the same request.

Usually I don't mind taking a selfie or giving an autograph--one lady recently showed me a tattoo of my name below her panty line and asked me to sign it--but today isn't the day. Once I take a selfie with one person, it becomes hard to say no to others. Anyway, the only reason I'm here is for my little girl, and I won't lose a moment of it.

We find the booth spinning the cotton candy and wait in line. I'm just checking my phone for an email confirming my next tour schedule when I hear, or rather *feel*, a familiar sound passing by me. The lilt of a laugh that I've never forgotten, one that's inspired some of the best music I've made. One that reminds me of sunny days, trampolines, and jelly sandwiches. I look toward the sound when my eyes collide with hers, her brows furrowing in silent question. She must have felt me, too. It's just how the universe works.

"Logan?" She winces before looking around quickly to see if she's drawn unwanted attention to me. Her friend comes to an astonished stop along with Anisa but then schools her features and starts chatting with the man holding her hand.

"Hey, *Batgirl*." Everything always comes to a standstill when she's around, like the world is on pause.

Her light brown gaze swivels to Lainey before she's interrupted by her friend, who's still looking at me like I've just fallen out of the sky. "Anisa, we're going to be right over there getting a beer." Her friend points toward the area serving alcohol. "Just come find us, okay?"

Anisa nods, then turns back to us. Her eyes meet with

Lainey's and instant recognition and understanding washes over them, though I don't miss the flicker of pain that betrays the smile on her face. "Hi!" She bends on both knees to Lainey's level. "I'm Anisa. What's your name?"

Lainey looks up at me as if to ask for permission and I nod. "I'm Lainey. Why does my daddy call you *Batgirl*?"

"Ah, well, unfortunately, your daddy has poor taste in superheroes and thinks DC is better than Marvel, so it's just a running joke between us."

I'm watching their exchange as if I weren't even part of their conversation. As if I'm sitting in an audience some-where, finally getting a glimpse of something I'd been waiting for to happen. It feels both surreal and perfectly natural. Two people who've never met, but who instantly feel like they should have known each other all this time.

Lainey giggles, looking up at me. "But you like The Hulk, right, Daddy? That's why you told me about him earlier? Is he from marble?"

"He *is* from Marvel," I acknowledge, then look over at Anisa. "But he's honestly the only decent one."

Anisa scoffs, looking up at me from where she's eye-level with my daughter. "Oh, are we doing this again?" One of her eyebrows rise in challenge, and I inadvertently think about sucking on those delicious, pursed lips again. "I thought we came to an agreement on this topic years ago."

The line moves forward and Anisa gets up so we can all step ahead. She tilts her head up to catch my eyes under my cap and they drink her up like cold beer on a hot day. "*You* came to an agreement on your own. Clearly, you have no idea how agreements work between multiple people, because you did not get my consent."

"Don't believe him, Lainey," she says, looking back at my four-year-old. "He has a bad memory in his old age."

Lainey looks from me to Anisa and giggles. "You guys are funny. How do you know my daddy?"

Anisa looks over at me again, silently giving me permission to answer the question. "Uh, Anisa and I were friends when we were younger."

Lainey mulls this over for a second. "Are you still friends?"

Million-dollar question, kid.

As we move a little farther up in the line, my mind instantly goes to the last "friendly" visit we had in Anisa's apartment. I'm trying to figure out how to answer that question when my eyes connect with Anisa's and a secret exchange passes between us. She's thinking about the same thing--the friendly line we crossed. The one we both want to cross again. My attention drops to her lips and a familiar insatiable hunger ignites inside me. Suddenly, nothing at this festival is satisfying enough, except for those lips. Lips that taste like rain and make me wish for thunderstorms. The tension is thick between us as I drag my gaze back upward to meet hers, dark and heavy, mirroring my own need.

"Daddy?" Lainey pulls both Anisa and I out of our trance.

"Uh . . . yeah. We're still friends."

"Can we invite her over, then?

Right as I say, "Sure," I hear Anisa respond as if she's been pinched, "Oh, no. That's okay. I actually should be getting back to my other friends."

Before I can even remark on the change in her tone, she bends down again and picks up Lainey's hand. "It was really great meeting you, Lainey."

I reach out with my hand to do something--though I'm not exactly sure what--but as if she's just realized she's about to miss her flight, she gives me a weak wave, avoiding my questioning gaze, and hurries toward the other side of the park.

15

ANISA

"*H*oly shit! You *know* DJ Access?" Sydney looks at me with the cup of beer in her hand and a renewed sense of reverie, as if I've just cured cancer or world hunger. "He's even hotter in real life!" She winces before looking at her boyfriend, who just shakes his head in a mocking display of hurt. "Sorry, babe. You're still the hottest guy I've ever seen."

"Uh huh. Want to wipe that drool off there?" Ken points to Sydney's face and she gently slaps his hand away, giggling.

I give them an evasive smile but a flutter passes over my lips. As if my lips aren't sure if they should tip up or down. Truth be told, my smile is just a cover for the emotions rolling around inside of me. My heart is inching its way to my throat, leaving a trail of pain in its ascent, and my legs feel like they're going to give out.

Logan has a daughter.

It took me all of five seconds to recognize the resemblance after seeing her beautiful light blue eyes. She's lovely, adorable, and sweet. And I could tell just from the way he looked at her that she spun his world.

But everything about seeing her broke my heart.

If I was disappointed and hurt before because of his lack of communication this week, it's a mere scratch compared to the puncture wound left there now. Not because he has a daughter or that he loves her with all his heart--as he should--but because she's another reminder of all that I've missed in his life. Because after seeing him on two separate occasions recently, he didn't trust me enough to tell me about her. Because seeing her was a stinging recognition of the chasm between us. Of how little I know about him.

I shouldn't feel entitled to know more; he owes me nothing. But I *am* entitled to my pain, nonetheless. It doesn't have to make sense but it's there with bells on.

"Anisa, are you okay?" Sydney examines me questioningly. "You look a little pale. Do you want me to get you some water? It's hot as hell out here."

"No," I mumble, feeling my chest heave. "I-I think I'm going to head back home."

"Do you need us to take you?" Ken looks at me suspiciously, as if he thinks I'll fall flat on my face at any moment.

I shake my head, unzipping my purse and hunting for my car keys inside. Even though a sense of overwhelming restlessness stirs in my gut, I try to keep my voice steady. "No, I'm good. You guys carry on. Thank you for inviting me."

Sydney leans into me for a hug, squeezing my shoulders. "Okay, can you text me to let me know you got back okay?"

I nod and wave to the both of them before making my way back to the parking lot, questioning my reaction. Questioning why I feel like crying, and why this melancholy is spreading so fast. It's not like he betrayed me or my trust.

We've both had ten years of experiences. What was I expecting? For us to get back on skateboards and compare palm sizes again?

Maybe I should have just stayed home today.

But as I think more about it, I'm proud of myself for coming out here. It was great to meet Sydney outside of a work setting. She has a bubbly, caring personality that makes everyone around her feel comfortable, and I can already tell her and I will become friends. I loved getting to see her and her boyfriend interact as well. They've only been dating for a few months, but their relationship seemed more mature and established than I'd expected. Maybe I just don't know what a true relationship should feel like because I only have Naveen to compare against.

While I'm glad I got to walk around and sample the various cuisines with them, my social quota for the day is reaching its limit. And now with the gloom that seems to be pushing past even the bright sunlight, I'm glad I didn't run into any of my other co-workers. There's only so much hobnobbing I can do in one day.

Driving back to my apartment, I think about Lainey and her adorable voice and cute little pink cheeks. She looks so much like Logan when we were kids, but she also looks like someone else entirely. Someone who I'm sure is just as beautiful and on the same level as Logan.

After parking my car and getting inside, I take Lynx for a short walk around my complex, thinking about who Lainey's mother might be. Could it be the woman that Logan's been seen with on the internet? Is she the one Logan referred to as his muse?

Getting back inside, I send Sydney a quick message letting her know I made it home and was feeling better. She replies instantly.

Good! Maybe you were dehydrated from the
heat or seeing LOGAN MILLER! I don't blame
you! Anyway, you and I clearly have a new
lunch topic for Monday.

I smile reading her text. At least someone is excited
about talking about him. At this point, I don't really feel like
I know him at all.

My mind is still a disorganized jumble of thoughts but at
least I don't feel as unsettled as I did before. If Logan didn't
think he could trust me with personal information in his
life, then as unfortunate as it is, I need to accept it. Maybe
it's for the better, anyway. It'll help me stay detached from
him and I can stay focused on my goals.

Getting to my computer, I do a quick search online to see
if I can find another dog service that could help me with
Lynx during the day. Finding the name and number of a
teenager looking to earn some extra cash walking dogs, I
text her with my needs for Lynx. She immediately responds
with a reasonable rate, saying she'd love to meet him next
week.

As soon as I finish texting with the potential dog sitter, I
get a text from my sister.

Okay. I can't wait for you to call me back
any longer. I just need to send you
something.

My phone vibrates with another text from her. This time it's
a picture of Logan and Lainey, along with another message.

He has a daughter!

I type back a quick message to her. I know. I met her

today. Will call you later to tell you
more.

I don't have the energy for a phone conversation at the moment, not even with my sister. I've always been the type who needs a chance to process and reflect on things before I come to any conclusion on them. Which is what I do for the next hour.

Busying myself with starting a new drawing in my sketchbook, I glance at the TV screen here and there. I have one of the Thor movies playing in the background while I sit at my breakfast table with all my pencils and charcoal sticks lying neatly near the sketchbook. I figure looking at Chris Hemsworth is the only cure to a shitty day.

I'm in the middle of blending a few colors into the scene when I hear a sharp knock at my front door. Lynx looks up with a bored expression, and I shuffle to the door. A gasp leaves my lips as I look through the peephole. I even consider pretending not to be home but the thought is short-lived.

"Anisa. Can we talk?" His voice sounds raspy and delicious, even with a solid wood door between us. It's truly inconvenient and inconsiderate for him to have such an affect on my heart rate.

Tamping my nerves and taking a long inhale, I do a quick swipe to get my hair in a bun on top of my head and open the door. "Hey."

His gaze traipses from my torso to over my breasts, halting momentarily on my lips before coming to my face. "Hey, yourself." He looks outright edible with his long white T-shirt and cap, his short, trimmed hair visible around the sides. The white clothing makes his eyes look vivid blue and inadvertently reminds me of the little girl I met today. The thought takes me back down the same path of jumbled sadness.

He must see my small smile falter. "Can I come in?"

"Okay," I mumble softly as I open the door wider to let him inside. His towering frame, the smell of cloves, and the heat radiating off him takes over my entryway. Moving quickly toward the living room to escape his imposing presence, I wave for him to sit. "Do you want something to drink?"

He smiles, sitting down on the same spot we were both on last time. "Why do I get the feeling that you really want to give me warm tap water this time?"

I move over to the kitchen, opening the fridge to take refuge in its cold air again, not answering his attempt to lighten the mood. "Want a beer?"

"Sure."

His fingers brush mine, sending a tremor up my arm as I hand him the bottle. I find a seat across from him this time, at a safe distance.

Removing any possibility of grinding.

Or kissing.

Or licking.

Basically, remove all possibilities.

He takes a swig of his beer and leans forward, putting his elbows on his knees and holding the bottle between his palms. He directs his next words at the bottle, though I'm pretty sure they're meant for me. "I'm sorry I didn't tell you about her."

"Who? Your daughter or your girlfriend?" I surprise myself with the sharpness in my tone. Why can I not get it in my head that I have no right to be upset, disappointed, hurt--or whatever this feeling is--with him?

His head snaps to mine, eyebrows furrowed, before realization sets in. "Anisa, I didn't lie to you. I don't have a girl-friend. I'm assuming you've seen the recent pictures. Tessa is not my--"

I raise a hand to stop him. "It's fine, Logan. It's none of my business, anyway."

Logan places the bottle on the glass coffee table in front of him before lifting off his cap and running a frustrated hand through his hair. It's distracting how casually hand-some he is. His jaw clenches before he looks at me again. "I don't have a girlfriend. The woman you saw got the wrong idea somewhere during our friendship. In fact, what you didn't see in that picture is that I pushed her off me when I registered what was happening. I made it clear that I wasn't interested in her in that way. "

I huff out an unfair and bitter laugh. "Seems like a common occurrence for you." *What the fuck is wrong with me? Who is this child in the body of a twenty-two-year-old grown ass woman?*

"Anisa."

"No, it's fine, Logan." I look down at my hands in my lap, feeling the prick of embarrassment at my behavior and the ache that I still can't reconcile. "You don't owe me any expla-nations."

"Anisa." This time his voice holds a command, making me look up at him. "Come here."

The heat in his intent stare has me shifting in my seat. It's taking all the strength of my mind and heart to keep my body from complying to his demand. But I lose the battle as soon as he says, "Please."

Moving over to the couch, I sit next to him before he swiftly captures my legs and brings us back to the familiar position from last time where my knees are on his lap and my back rests on the armrest. I force away the thoughts of the position I was sitting in afterward.

I'm still playing with my fingers on my lap when he gently pulls them through his. "I know you have questions, and I can't imagine how you must have felt all week." He lifts my chin and I raise my head to look at him. "I *do* owe you an explanation. I owe you several. If I was in your spot, I'd want some explanations, too. In fact, if I saw someone else touching you ...." He snaps his mouth closed and I see his jaw work as he grinds his teeth.

I nibble my bottom lip, not entirely sure what to say when he starts again. "I met someone when I was nineteen. She was sweet and beautiful." I shift uncomfortably in my spot, my stomach feeling uneasy, when Logan's hand tightens on mine. "She vaguely reminded me of you. But she wasn't you. Nobody is you, *Batgirl*."

Swallowing, my eyes roam over his face. I take in his admission, along with his perfectly chiseled jaw and his Roman nose. My hands beg me to bury themselves in his hair, feel the back of his neck on my fingertips.

"Anisa." Logan's voice comes out a little breathier than before. "If you keep looking at me that way, I'm not going to get very far in my explanation."

I hadn't realized he'd stopped talking. Heat rises to my cheeks at the thought of him catching me shamelessly perusing his face. "Did you . . ." my voice is a whisper, "did you want her to be me?"

"Yes," he states without hesitation. While he gives me a moment to recover, there's nothing that can be done about my spiked heart rate. "I started seeing her, but with my crazy work schedule and some health issues she was dealing with, we decided to separate after a few months. But a month after we broke up, she told me she was pregnant."

"What was her name?"

Logan distractedly rubs circles on the back of my hand with his thumb. "Mandy. She was dealing with some of her own demons, and when Lainey was one, she dropped her off with my mom. I haven't heard from her since."

My heart breaks for Lainey, for Logan. He's had to take on a lot from a young age. Yes, he has the means to do so, but that doesn't account for the responsibility he's had to bear. I squeeze his hand back, showing him the only support I can. "I'm sorry, Lo."

He shakes his head, looking down at our clasped hands. "Honestly, it's Lainey that I feel the worst for. Her mom and I weren't meant to be, but I know how much Lainey misses having her in her life."

I don't quite understand which demons lead to someone leaving their child, never to get back in touch, but I can't imagine that Mandy doesn't think about Lainey. I only met her for five minutes today and her infectious personality and sweet voice are ingrained in my mind.

I run a hand over Logan's forearm. "Thank you for telling me."

"I'm sorry I didn't tell you about her before. I was planning to during our next conversation, but then it was crazy trying to clear up the mess with Tessa and I didn't have a chance to get in touch all week."

I believe him, though it doesn't take away the sting of seeing someone with her hands and lips on him. Nonetheless, I nod in response to his apology. It seems to finally break the tightness surrounding our conversation thus far.

"Lainey wanted me to ask you to come over for a play-date tomorrow." His mouth finally tips up into a small smile.

I can't help the next question out of my mouth. "And what does Lainey's dad want?"

The blue in Logan's eyes ignites like I've seen it do before. "A very different kind of playdate." The innuendo lands perfectly with our hands and eyes still against each other.

I exhale, trying to compose myself, when Logan gets up abruptly. Putting his cap back on, he heads for the front door and opens it. Without turning around, he says, "I'll text you my address."

16

ANISA

"So let me get this straight. Your old BFF is Logan Miller? As in DJ Access?" Nelly gawks at me though my phone screen, her onyx-colored eyes and dark skin glowing under the Boston sun. She's sitting on her balcony in her pajamas.

"Yes."

"And you had no clue he was famous because aside from living inside your games, you pretty much live under a rock."

I'm not sure if that was a question or a statement, but I respond with a "Yes," nonetheless.

"And you're going to his house tonight for a playdate with his daughter?"

"Yes." I stifle a laugh at the way Nelly is repeating everything I've told her during our FaceTime date.

"But this so-called *friendship* between you and him . . . has crossed the line? And goddammit, Nees, if you just say *yes* again, I'm going to find a way to punch you through this camera."

I giggle. "Yes, but we can't do that again. We're both

trying not to complicate our lives and our rekindled friendship. It means a lot to us. He's focused on his work and raising his daughter, and I'm focused on my own shit."

"Uh huh." Nelly looks unconvinced. "And tell me again why you can't be focused on all that while banging each other's brains out?"

I huff, both out of frustration of her not accepting my excuse and of sounding like I'm making up an excuse. I choose the easy path of avoidance. "When are you coming to visit me?"

She smiles, knowing I'm dodging her question. "Actually . . ." she elongates the word, "I found some cheap tickets to come there next weekend, unless you're busy."

My heart leaps. I can't wait to show Nelly my new town. "No! I'm not busy. Book the flight!"

"Great! But, Nees?" She looks at me intently, like she's about to tell me a secret.

"Yeah?"

"We are going to talk about this. And then we are going to go clubbing on Sixth Street or Fourth Street or whatever street the youngins are at these days."

My face twists in part disgust and part annoyance. Ugh, Nelly and her love for clubbing. "Maybe you shouldn't book that flight then," I tease.

"Too bad. I already booked it before I called you, bitch."

GROWING UP IN A WEALTHY FAMILY, I've seen my share of excess and affluence. My parents' home is no small shack, with its ample square footage, big backyard, and large guest house. But taking in the sprawling, perfectly manicured estate in front of me, I'm once again having to redefine my perception of true wealth.

After being cleared at the security gate--similar to one would at the Pentagon--and driving down a long, winding entryway, I park my Audi in the front of Logan's house. The word 'house' doesn't really do this behemoth justice because it looks like it eats houses for lunch.

Holding the plate of brownies I baked for Lainey earlier, my heart races as I walk up the front steps and ring the doorbell. I don't know her well, but the fact that she was standing in the longest cotton candy line at the festival yesterday tells me she's got a sweet tooth.

I assess my cutoff jean shorts and white tank top--this one picturing one of my favorite characters from the *League of Legends*--to make sure nothing looks amiss. With the heat beating down even through my tinted windows, I put my hair into a loose, messy bun in my car.

The door unlocks and my eyes have trouble figuring out who to land on first. The mouthwatering man with freshly tousled hair, wearing ripped jeans and his signature black T-shirt--his gorgeous sleeve of tattoos touting themselves shamelessly--or his adorable daughter with her messy braid and a smudge of something blue on her cheek. Honestly, it's overstimulation for my brain.

Deciding to direct my greeting at the little girl I'm here for a playdate with, I hand her the plate of brownies. "Hi, Lainey."

Her mouth falls to the floor as she takes in the tower of sweets. "Oh my gosh! There's sprinkles on them!"

"I figured you were a sprinkles kind of girl." I smile, looking from her to her delectably handsome dad. God, how am I going to stay on this "friends forever" path with him when all I want to do is climb him like a tree and unabashedly rub myself on him, marking him with my scent like an animal. "Hi."

He leans in, folding me into his arms, his freshly showered, soapy smell wreaking havoc inside my ovaries. "Hi," he murmurs against the shell of my ear, and the vibration of his voice travels all the way down to my panties.

I've been here less than two minutes and I already need a change of underpants.

The duo welcome me into their home, and I pause to take in my surroundings. Two large, circular staircases from the entryway lead to what appears to be different quarters of the house. As I walk with them through the enormous family room, I peruse the sophisticated furniture, modern decor, and plush carpet. And while all the lines are straight and clean, the house doesn't lack homeliness. A smile touches my lips as I take in some of Lainey's toys littering the family room rug, a long fishtail blanket lying messily on the sofa, and a coloring book on the massive marble coffee table. I imagine Logan laying on the sofa, answering messages on his phone while Lainey plays with her tea set on the carpet.

"This is such a beautiful home, Lo," I say, following them into the kitchen.

"Thanks." A flush stirs on Logan's cheeks like it always does when he receives a compliment. Even if he wasn't a world-famous DJ, the guy should get a compliment everyday just for being so damn beautiful. "Can I get you something to drink?"

"No, I'm okay. Thank you." Remembering that Logan said his mom stays on the same property to be near Lainey, I ask, "Hey, so where's your mom? I thought she lived here."

"She's out with her sister and a friend of theirs for a ladies' night, but she said if she finishes up early enough, she'll come say hi. She was excited to see you when I told her you'd be here."

"I'm excited to see her too, after all these years." She was always such a supportive and caring mother to Logan. I remember her coming to all our school events with her husband.

Lainey puts the plate of brownies on the enormous island and climbs atop one of the barstools, quickly working her fingers under the plastic wrap. I slide into the seat next to her.

"Lainey." Logan's tone is firm as he addresses his daughter. She looks from him to me with a sheepish expression on her face that makes me burst out into laughter. Logan shakes his head, laughing. "Those are for after dinner. I'm making pizza."

"Okay." Lainey hops back off the barstool and links her hand with mine, her crystal-blue eyes dancing with excitement. "Daddy said you and him used to skateboard and ride bikes together."

I catch a wink from Logan before he takes out some ingredients from the wall-to-wall stainless-steel fridge behind him. I don't miss the crayon artwork haphazardly affixed to it. "We did! Although, I have to tell you a secret . . .."

Lainey's gapes at me at the thought of me revealing a secret. She whispers, "What?" as I lean down toward her ear.

"I was better than your dad at riding bikes and skateboarding. He was a scaredy cat and never let me do stunts." My whisper is purposefully loud enough for Logan to hear.

Logan coughs and it sounds much like "Bullshit," but Lainey doesn't seem to catch it. He flicks his gaze at me before directing his comment to her. "Don't believe her, Lainey. She acts tough, but she's not."

He's right. I never was tough when it came to him.

Lainey giggles. "I don't know, Daddy. You *are* kind of a scaredy cat. Remember when I was trying to hang upside down from the monkey bars, and you wouldn't even let me go?"

Taking out what looks like fresh pizza dough, Logan unwraps it from the plastic wrap and points the rolling pin in his hand at his daughter. "Monkeys travel with their families. I was doing you a favor by grooming you and eating lice out of your head."

"Eeew!" Lainey squeals in disgust, and we both scrunch our noses. "I don't have lice, Daddy!"

"Well, no. *Now* you don't. Thanks to me."

Laughing with them, I watch Lainey and Logan interact. Their adorable relationship and easy banter warms my chest. A slow, lazy swarm of butterflies whoosh around in my belly.

It can't be easy being a single father, but Logan makes it look that way. He's a natural with Lainey, like being her father is effortless for him. Like this was always what he was meant to do. I don't even know if I want kids, but if it was with someone like him . . . if it was *with* him--

No, can't go there.

"Want me to show you the new skateboard Daddy got me, Anisa?" Lainey pulls me out of my thoughts. Her face lights up, looking from me and then to her dad for permission.

"Sure, I'd love to see it!"

As I follow Lainey, her leading me by the hand, Logan calls after her to remind her to wear her helmet. Yup, he was meant for this.

Lainey takes me to a courtyard where she pulls out her new skateboard to show me how far she can ride on it. She hasn't quite figured out how to get both feet on the board, but she looks adorable lifting her two arms up, airplane-style, trying to balance on one foot.

"Want me to hold your hand so you can get both feet on the board?" I ask.

She nods her approval and I help her get both feet on the board, pulling her around the courtyard and she squeals in delight.

After showing me some of her other ride-on toys and asking me about all my favorite things--Disney movie, ice cream flavor, color, song, and food--Lainey decides to show me her room.

Walking through the halls, I notice framed pictures of her and Logan, and some have Logan's mom in them as well. Along with the photos, there are also frames with artwork done in finger paint, charcoal, and crayons, all signed with Lainey's name. It's endearing to see that with the means to afford the most coveted artwork in the world, the only ones Logan proudly displays throughout his home are the ones made by his four-year-old daughter.

Try as I may, there's no stopping the warmth spreading from my chest to the rest of my body as I reluctantly come to a conclusion. I'm falling for the man who lives here. Truth be told, I fell for him years ago, before I even knew what it felt like. *This* is what it feels like.

"Do you like to draw?" I ask Lainey as I admire the sketches leading to her room.

"Yes! Want me to show you some more?"

"I would love that."

As if it's a replica of something from a fairy tale, her room is a perfectly matched ensemble of sheer, soft pink drapes, faint green glittering lights, and plush white rugs. Her white, four-poster bed is covered with a beautiful pink-and-green quilt and soft, white and pink pillows. It suits her bright and lively personality perfectly.

We're crouched on folded knees on her white rug and Lainey's showing me some drawings she recently made. I'm impressed by how advanced her artwork is for a girl so young.

Remembering something, Lainey suddenly gasps and looks at me. "You like to draw too, don't you?"

"Yeah, I've been drawing since I was a little girl, like you. How did you know?"

"Because my daddy showed me your artwork."

I'm sure my fluster shows on my face. "He did?"

"Uh huh. Want me to show you?"

She doesn't wait for my response before she grabs my hand and leads me once again through another hallway, speckled with more pictures and homemade artwork. At this point, I'm not sure where we are, but I'm positive I won't be able to find my way back to the kitchen alone.

Her little hands pull down two handles on two very heavy doors to what looks like an enormous room. As soon as it opens and I see the slew of shiny studio equipment and turntables, I grab her hand, trying to get her attention. I feel like I'm invading Logan's privacy. "Lainey, maybe we should ask your dad if we can be in here. I don't think he'd want us to be in this room."

"Daddy doesn't mind." Her gaze shifts like she doesn't even believe herself. "We'll be really quick, I promise. I just wanna show you something."

Still feeling uneasy, I follow her to where she's standing in front of a wall directly behind what I assume is the main turntable. Lifting my eyes to what she's examining, I draw a sharp breath, placing my hand over my mouth. My brows furrow as recognition sets in.

He kept it.

I still remember the first time my parents bought me a full sketch set with all the tools and pencils I'd ever need. The first thing I did was think of something I'd be proud to draw for Logan, something he'd find interesting. It had taken me longer than I'd expected to draw the pterodactyl, but once I'd gotten it right, I couldn't wait to show him. I recall telling myself not to act like it was a big deal if he told me he didn't want it, but my heart soared when he said he did.

Now, looking at the same sketch, displayed in a glass shadow box as if it was the most valuable item he owned, my eyes glisten with unshed tears. It's only when I lean in to read the tiny inscription on the wooden frame that my tears break free.

In beautiful, slanted script, it says, *Anisa, my first muse.*

17

LOGAN

"*D*id you show Anisa any cool tricks on your skateboard?" I ask my daughter, who's happily eating a slice of the margherita pizza I just took out of the oven. I set her up with her iPad on the island, next to Anisa--which is where she insisted on sitting--so I could have at least a little time to talk to Anisa privately.

Lainey nods, looking up from her screen. "Yup! I showed her how I do the airplane trick, but then Anisa helped me get both feet on the skateboard, and we went *weeee* around and around the courtyard! It was so much fun, Daddy!"

Laughing, I look over at Anisa from across the kitchen island. She gives me a small smile before dropping her eyes back to her salad. I get the feeling she hasn't even heard what Lainey just said. Focusing more on her expression, I notice the rim of red around her eyes. *What the hell?* Has she been crying? Did something happen? Lainey is really sweet and affectionate, but sometimes she can be unfiltered. Did she say something to upset Anisa?

My feet move toward her on their own accord, and I

reach out and run my thumb along Anisa's cheek. "Are you okay?"

She exhales softly, trying to school the emotion on her face. Her voice comes out gravelly when she speaks. "Yeah, absolutely. Lainey is the most adorable little girl I've ever met."

That's a relief. At least it's not something Lainey said or did to cause this downcast expression. So, what is it?

Sitting down at the bar next to her with my plate, I'm about to probe further when she speaks. "This salad and pizza are really great. Thank you for making it."

I notice she's only taken a bite of the pizza, so I nod toward it with my chin. "I should have asked if you even like pizza. It doesn't seem like you do."

Catching my meaning, she turns to me. "No, I love pizza. And this is delicious. It's just . . .." She casts her head down at her plate with an abashed smile. "I'm trying to watch what I eat a bit. You know, trying to make some of these curves look more like straight lines instead."

Huh? It takes me a moment to understand what she's referring to, and I can't help the way my teeth clench to hold in my immediate response. *Trying to make her curves look like straight lines?* Is she out of her mind? If she had any idea of the lewd things I want to do to her, the thoughts I've had about running my hands and mouth over her incredible curves, she'd probably think I was outright insane.

Working hard to suppress the irritation in my tone and keeping my voice a whisper to avoid Lainey's ears, I speak loud enough so Anisa doesn't miss a single word. "I love every fucking one of your curves. Now, eat the damn pizza."

She turns her head slowly to meet my gaze, and my fingers tingle in an effort to stop themselves from pulling her toward me, devouring her instead of the pizza in front of me. I know she's taken aback by the command in my voice, but she's mistaken if she thinks I'll apologize for it. I won't. She's fucking beautiful exactly the way she is, and I won't let her diminish herself in my presence.

Since she's gotten here, I've done everything to not openly ogle her long, lean legs and round ass under those cutoff shorts. Like a fucking sleaze, I eyed the slightest amount of cleavage showing under her tank top. And don't even get me started on how many times I've had to avert my gaze from licking up the exposed skin on her neck.

She searches my eyes for a few seconds, silently asking me questions I don't have the answers to. The same emotion that I'd seen earlier when she walked back into the kitchen treads on her face momentarily before she schools her features and looks back at her plate. This time, she picks up the pizza, turning toward me before taking a slow bite. Almost mockingly, she makes a show of it--licking the sauce off her lips and humming around the bite. She has no idea how hard I am just watching her mouth move. Something must show on my face because the moment her eyes dart up to meet mine, realization sets it. She's goading a ravenous tiger.

Quickly turning back to her plate, she tries to change the subject. "Do you cook often?"

Clearing my throat, I fist my hands under the counter while trying to even out my breathing. "I try to cook a few meals whenever I'm home. What about you? Do you like to cook?"

Her delicate hands pick up her fork again. Clear-polished nails at the end of her fingers make them appear long and lean. Fingers that I know are soft yet firm. Fingers I want on my body, inside my hair. Fingers I'd love to see wrapped around the hard-on I've had to hide all fucking evening.

Jesus, Logan, get a grip. Your daughter is sitting mere feet from you.

Shifting uncomfortably in my seat, I almost miss the first part of her response. "... not great at it. My mom's been nagging me to learn how to cook Indian food." She laughs before turning to me, but all I can hone in on is her dimple. "Apparently, that's the only cuisine she thinks is worth learning."

"What's your favorite kind of food?"

"Tex-Mex!" Lainey chimes in, startling both me and Anisa. "And her favorite Disney movie is Moana! Just like me!"

I raise an eyebrow. "Oh yeah? And is her favorite color still gray?"

Lainey gasps, and I can't help but relish the astonishment in Anisa's face. She's surprised I remembered. "Yes!" Lainey answers.

"Looks like you both got to know each other well."

Lainey nods. "Can we watch Moana after dinner, Daddy? Please!"

I turn to Anisa. "It's up to our guest. If she can stay past dinner, then we can definitely watch a movie."

"Please, Anisa! Can you stay a little longer?" My daughter's hopeful eyes meet Anisa's.

"My night is reserved just for you." Anisa smiles at Lainey. "So yes, I can stay for a movie."

Lainey squeals, pumping her arm. "Yes!"

Finishing up dinner, Lainey asks if we can finally have the brownies Anisa made. They're both plating the brownies--though, I notice Anisa takes just a quarter of one--when I hear my mom's voice in the foyer.

"Hello?" Her heels click on the marble floor.

"Grams! We're in the kitchen with Anisa!" Lainey responds before anyone else can.

My mom makes her way to the kitchen, wrapping her arms around Lainey in a quick hug before gasping at the sight of Anisa, who lifts off her barstool to come toward her. Pulling Anisa in for an embrace, she says, "Well, heavens! I always thought you'd turn heads when you grew up, Anisa Singh, but goodness me! You are just the most beautiful woman I have ever seen!"

Anisa blushes, her tanned cheeks picking up a rosy hue as her arms unwrap from my mother. "Thank you. It's so great to see you."

"How have you been? Logan tells me you're working here in Austin now. How are your parents and that studious sister of yours?"

Anisa tucks a loose strand of hair from her bun behind her ear, and I force myself not to lick my lips. "I'm good. Yes, I'm working as a game developer for a company nearby. And both my parents and sister are good, too. Jeena works for my dad's company on his legal team."

My mom glows. "Well, your parents must be so proud to have raised such exquisite daughters."

Anisa shrugs, glancing at me as I take a bite of my brownie. "You must be proud of everything Logan has accomplished, too."

Mom sighs. "Oh, I am, but I do wish he would travel less. He's just burning himself out. He won't listen to me though, but maybe you can convince him." She winks at Anisa and the flush on Anisa's cheeks grows brighter. I can tell just from the way my mom notices it that she's really quite proud of herself.

"Mom," I clear my throat, "do you want to have dessert with us? Anisa made brownies."

"Oh, no. I'm stuffed after my dinner with Beth, and I'm ready to call it a night. You kids carry on." My mom regards Anisa warmly. "I just wanted to come see this lovely young lady."

After finishing dessert, Lainey pulls Anisa by the hand into the family room for the movie. It's such a small gesture but something in my chest unfastens seeing it. They've only known each other for a few hours but it's as if their connection has spanned years. The way Anisa listens intently to Lainey when she speaks, the way she folds down to her knees to make eye contact with her, the way they share conspiratorial looks--it's something I hadn't fathomed.

Up until today, I hadn't seen past just Lainey and me. It was always going to be just me and her. Of course, I was lucky to have my mom's help, but even I could see that managing an active four-year-old on a daily basis was a lot for anyone, especially someone my mom's age.

Up until today, I hadn't considered anyone for *both* me and my daughter. Up until today, I hadn't needed anyone else. But until today, I hadn't wanted anyone more.

Turning on the movie, Lainey and Anisa settle into the couch under a blanket as this startling new feeling settles somewhere deep inside of me.

I want Anisa.

All of her.

But would she give me everything, knowing I couldn't give her the same in return?

Because I couldn't give her everything, and definitely not all of me. I'm a father first, I have a stressful job that keeps me away from home. I have a life in the public eye--something I can't see her ever wanting, given how reserved she is.

Would being with someone like me even make her happy? Could I make her happy?

No, I couldn't.

I can't ask her to accept what little I have of myself to give. I can't ask her to accept my two-for-one deal where I came packaged with Lainey. Just because I was young when I became a father, doesn't mean Anisa wants to play that role in any way with my daughter. Nothing about where my own selfish hopes are leading me would be fair to Anisa. And I can't ask her to fulfill them.

Even if I did ask, and by some miracle she said yes, how would I ensure that she'd stay? What if after seeing how complicated my life and schedule are--after seeing how little she got of me--she decided she couldn't handle it? Like Mandy.

I can't bring her into Lainey's life only to have her leave. Lainey already struggles with feeling abandoned by her mom. I won't let her feel that way again when Anisa decides to leave.

No. My hopes, wants, and desires would all have to wait. And if that meant that I'd lose my chance at being with Anisa, then that was a bitter pill I'd need to swallow.

Finding a spot on the other side of Lainey, I watch Lainey rest her head on Anisa's shoulder. Her knees are up on the couch, under the blanket, and she looks content with having found a new friend. Anisa gently tilts her head to rest on top of Lainey's as they whisper about the first scene of the film.

The movie progresses but the only thing I'm acutely aware of is the movement of my girls next to me.

Holy shit. My girls? Did I just think that?

They're singing along to the songs, laughing at Maui-- their eyes glimmering in unison because somehow, they find this movie just as funny even after having seen it multiple times--and generally in a world of their own. I, on the other hand, see nothing but them.

At one point, Anisa lifts her arm so Lainey can snuggle into her side. Anisa's arm lays over my daughter protectively, as if it's the most natural thing. The movement is so small yet so momentous, that without even thinking about it or the resolution I *just* made not even five fucking minutes ago, I pick up Anisa's hand. I have absolutely zero self-restraint when it comes to this woman.

Her breath catches at the contact and her gaze meets mine above Lainey's head. Her eyes are turbulent, questioning me this time, unlike the past few times I've reached for her hand. And even though I know the questions they're asking--What is this? What are we?--I'm unwilling to answer them.

I don't know what this is.

No, that's not true. I know *exactly* what this is. I just don't know how to stop it . . . and I don't know if I can.

Threading my fingers through hers, I turn back to the TV, barely aware of what I'm even watching. The only awareness I have is the soft feeling of her skin against mine. The small contact burns through me, threatening to awaken the parts I've kept dormant all these years.

18

ANISA

*L*ainey is snoring peacefully at my side, her little body cuddled close to me. And while the feeling should be foreign to me--of having a little girl crawl her way into my heart--*that's* not the feeling I'm finding unfamiliar.

It's the rough thumb that's currently brandishing my skin, running against the pulse point on my wrist. It's the heated blue gaze scorching me in its descent over my body. It's realizing that someone--the same someone I've always wanted it to be--has a place in his heart for me. Just for me. Just as he has a place in his recording studio for a silly sketch I once drew for him.

But it's also the realization that, despite the place I take up in his heart and the written declaration on the shadow box, that despite the connection we share, and what I believe is mutual sexual chemistry, he's made it clear that he doesn't want anything more.

He doesn't want me, and I just need to come to terms with that.

Because this rallying back and forth, this tension and this cyclical logic are doing nothing for my mental sanity. I'll be damned if I throw myself at him again after it took me almost a week to get over my previous humiliation.

He's sending me contradictory signals. Holding me, touching me, staring at me one moment, and then telling me how we can't be anything more the next. It's giving me whiplash, honestly, and I just need to extricate myself from this situation. I can't go from a relationship where I was made to feel worthless to one where I don't feel worthy. I'm done being with men who define my worth and take out their resentment for their life situations on me.

Finding my mental fortitude, I shift in my seat and run a hand over Lainey's soft little braid. Her head lands in my lap and my heart clenches at seeing how trusting she is. What I wouldn't do to be able to put that level of trust in someone to take care of me and my muddled heart.

"Um . . ." I whisper, pulling my hand out of Logan's, "I'm going to get going."

"Oh." His shoulders deflate. "Do you want a cup of coffee? I can put Lainey to bed and we can hang out for a bit." I can see the hesitation in his face.

Knowing that I'm the cause of the hesitation, that I've contributed to this awkwardness between us, has the room feeling smaller. I don't want to be anyone's hesitation.

I need to get out of here.

Getting up gingerly, I place a small cushion under Lainey's head and adjust the blanket on her. "Um, actually, I have work tomorrow, and I want to make sure I get a decent night's sleep."

Logan gets up, putting Lainey's legs on the sofa and searching my face. "Okay."

He moves in closer but I scurry to the front door. "Thank you for having me. I had so much fun with Lainey, and I hope I can see her again soon."

"What about next weekend?"

"W-what?" His question throws me off.

"Come over next weekend." His eyes bore into mine as if challenging my sincerity.

"My friend Nelly is visiting from Boston next weekend. I promised to show her around." I cringe at the next thought. "She wants to go clubbing and bar-hopping downtown, so I thought I'd take her out on Saturday."

Logan nods, but I don't miss the disappointment on his face. "Where will you be downtown?"

I slip on my sandals. "Oh, I don't know just yet. I'll probably ask my friend Sydney from work to join us since she knows the area better."

"I'll make sure you have a table at *Club Vex*."

"Oh, no, that's not necessary, Lo. Anyway, Nelly wants to see a few other bars, too."

"Then end the night there." His expression tells me he's not going to take no for an answer.

Good heavens, this man is pushy! Sighing, I concede. "Okay, but no tables. She'll want to dance and mingle, so the table will be a waste."

"Fine." He relents, closing the distance between us. My heart jumps inside its cage at the proximity, but I keep my gaze affixed to his. Raising a palm to my face, he runs a thumb over my cheekbone. "Thank you for today. Thank you for hanging out with Lainey." His soft breath fans my face and I have to hold myself back from tilting forward in a request for him to meet my lips halfway.

"It was my pleasure. She's all the wonderful parts of you,

which is why I fell for her immediately." I snap my mouth shut as soon as the words are out. His thumb stops abruptly on my cheek and his questioning gaze tells me he heard exactly what I said. He understood exactly what I meant.

Damn brain to mouth filter! It's always jacked-up around him.

What in the actual hell is wrong with me? I literally just said I wasn't going to throw myself at anyone, and now I'm insinuating that I'm falling for him? Can I have one meeting with this man where I'm not feeling utterly exposed and humiliated by the end?

He looks like he's about to speak but I don't want to hear it. I can't hear another rejection, another fucking '*it's not you, it's me.*' I won't be told that whatever I feel would just end up being unfair to me, because he's goddamn right. *It would.* "I- I need to go."

And with that, I rush through the door and down the steps like a bat out of hell. How appropriate, given my nick-name. I leave Logan looking like he's lost for words, and I don't blame him.

I'm lost, too.

"GREAT WORK on building out the first version of Eterna last week, Anisa. I had a quick conversation in the hall with Rosa this morning, and she said you surpassed her expecta-tions." Travis leans back in his office chair during our one-to-one Monday morning.

"Thanks. I had fun developing her," I respond, wondering if Rosa told him about Blake's asshole behavior last week as well.

"I'd like to see it when you're ready to show me a demo."
Travis types something on his laptop, likely in regards to our
meeting. He has many people to manage, and I'm sure he
can't remember every conversation so he has to keep it in his
notes. He looks back up. "We've had a decrease in daily
active users on one of our main games as well. This is an
anomaly from past years because kids play more online
games during their summer vacations rather than less. So,
I've assembled a task force to tackle the issue. I'd like you to
join it as well."

"That sounds good. I'm happy to help."

"Great. Anything else you want to talk about?"

I consider telling him about Blake, but I decide to wait
until there's more to say or after I talk to Rosa. "Nope. I'm all
set."

The rest of the week progresses just as fast as the last
one. I work on animating the scene I'm responsible for,
along with taking part in the meetings with the new task
force. I'm even able to go to lunch with Sydney a couple of
times. Of course, we mostly end up talking about Logan
since she's still starstruck after seeing him and finding out
that I know him.

While I tell her about our history, I keep out the part
about me and Logan making out at my apartment. I'm sure
Sydney is trustworthy, but it's always taken me time to open
up with new people. So far, Jeena and Nelly are the only
ones who know anything more--minus the grinding. No one
needs to know about the grinding.

I don't even want to know about the grinding.

I'm on my way to a meeting when I hear what sounds
like a woman's distressed voice in one of the small conference rooms I'm passing by. Not wanting to snoop too obvi-

ously, I decide to look through the mesh glass window to see who it is. Before I can get a glimpse, the door opens and Rosa rushes out, looking flustered and shaky. She doesn't seem to see me as she passes, but just from the look on her face, I can tell she's barely holding it together.

Behind her, Blake exits the room, adjusting his crotch.

Wait, what?

Adjusting crotch?

What. The. Fuck?

He catches me glaring and his expression indicates he's not happy about what I might have seen or heard, but he keeps moving toward his desk.

Even though I know I'll be late for my meeting, I decide to chance a visit to the ladies' room to see if Rosa might have gone in there. With my heart beating fast, I enter the multi-stall bathroom.

"Rosa?"

I hear a quick inhale from one of the stalls like she's trying to stop herself from sobbing. "Go away, Anisa. This is not your problem."

"Are you okay?"

"Yes. Just . . . don't worry about it."

"No. I'm going to be right here when you come out. You don't have to talk about it if you don't want to, but I'll be here just in case." I'm not normally one to pry or insist that someone talk to me when they clearly don't want to, but this doesn't feel like a *normal* situation, either.

After sniffling some more, Rosa comes out of the stall to wash her hands. I can't help but rush to her when I see the red streaks on her cheeks. Pulling her into my arms, I let her sob on my shoulder. "He's such a fucking asshole."

I run a hand down her blue-streaked hair. "What

happened? Do you need to go to HR? I'll go with you, if you want me to."

Rosa stiffens in my arms before pulling away, as if I've burned her. "No. Are you kidding me?"

"Wha--"

"Anisa, I'm a Latina woman in the gaming industry. I'm also one of the first college graduates in my family, and this is the best job and team I could hope for--if you don't count that asshat. I don't have the luxury of going to HR and making this a *thing*!" She puts the base of her palms into her eye sockets and leans her head back. "God, I'm such an idiot."

I bristle against her response. "Rosa, you did nothing wrong." I understand how she feels about not wanting to go to HR. I don't agree with it, but I understand how sometimes it can bring an undercurrent of shame for women, even though they have nothing to be shameful about.

"I did." She releases her hands and looks to the side. "Blake has been known to make stupid comments and jokes about women's bodies. He usually doesn't do it at work though, but I heard him once when some of us were out at a bar. I shouldn't have provoked him today. I told him I didn't think his comments from Friday about Eterna were appropriate, and he just lost it. He cornered me in the office and put his hand--" She shakes her head. "He said I shouldn't have any issues with voluptuous women since I am one."

My teeth grind so hard, I feel like they're going to fall out. "What an asshole. Look, if you change your mind and want to talk to HR--"

"No, Anisa. I'm fine. I'm just going to stay away from him and keep my head down. I don't need drama. If they start an investigation on him, then people will look at me differently."

I scoff, "That's simply not true, Rosa!"

Her eyes become stone as she focuses on me. "It is. I'd appreciate you keeping this whole thing to yourself."

I nod, feeling completely at a loss, as she straightens her shirt and makes her way out of the door.

"*O*h my god. You weren't kidding about the Tex-Mex here!" Nelly makes a humming noise around the bite of her fajita. Her curly black hair is pulled off her face and tied up on her head. The natural glow of her dark skin makes her look airbrushed. She's so ridiculously beautiful, it's inappropriate. "It's so good!"

"I know, and it's not doing anything for my waist." I take another bite from my taco salad, remembering *Asshole Aunty's* comment, "*A moment on the lips, forever on the hips!*"

I'm glad I'm wearing a loose-fitting dress tonight. I'd ordered it online this week to update my generally simplistic wardrobe of tank tops, jeans, and shorts. Looking at it now, I'm quite happy with the way it hits right above my knees and the draped V-neck design. I don't have the largest breasts, but I'm loving how this neckline shows off my cleavage in a tasteful, yet flirtatious way. And of course, I'm wearing Nelly's large earrings and bracelet. In typical Nelly style, she'd looked at the accessories I *was* going to pair the dress with and scrunched her nose.

"Whatever. You look hot. Between those beautiful light

brown eyes, that head of gorgeous wavy hair, and curves for miles, I'd wanna hit that if I was a guy." Nelly giggles while I roll my eyes.

Sydney nods, agreeing with Nelly. "Yeah, you look stunning. I'm so used to seeing you in casual work clothes with your hair up in a knot. Don't get me wrong, Anisa, you look great at work too, but this look really suits you."

I'd asked Sydney to meet Nelly and me at the restaurant, and it was as if the two were estranged peas from the same pod. They immediately launched into complementing each other's clothes and talking about celebrity fashion trends.

Speaking of celebrities and trends . . ..

After running out of Logan's house last weekend, I'd come to a decision sometime this week that I was done waiting for him to make a choice about this so-called friendship. A friendship that felt more like a mutual agreement to avoid the proverbial large elephant in the room. Currently, the proverbial elephant has the words "attraction," "tension," and "sizzling chemistry" written in big block letters all over it.

And while I'm not on the hunt for a relationship or even a date at the moment, I'm also not going to keep myself locked up inside my apartment behind a chastity belt. Part of finding myself and enjoying my newfound independence is going to be putting myself out there a bit more, talking to strangers, and letting myself have a little bit of good, old-fashioned fun. I'd decided I was going to summon my inner Nelly and truly let myself be free tonight, instead of lingering behind my own self-constructed walls.

After paying for our dinner and calling an Uber, the three of us are on our way to a club on Fourth Street when I get a text from Jeena.

I miss you. Wish I was going out with you
guys. Tell Nelly I said hi and have fun
tonight. Send pics and let me know if you
have any 'celebrity sightings' ;-)

I'd had a chance to update her this week on meeting
Lainey and finding the shadow box in Logan's home
recording studio. I'd conveniently skipped over the part
where I told Logan--in not so many words--that I was falling
for him. There was no point in adding that to the litany of
embarrassing things I'd said or done when it came to the
man at this point.

And now, reading her text, I giggle to myself, remembering our phone conversation.

"I don't know, Nees. I feel like neither of you are willing
to put your heart out there and make a move. And until one
of you does, you're just going to dance around each other
like a pair of prairie chickens performing an unsuccessful
mating ritual."

"I've already made a move by basically jumping him on
my couch the first time he came over!" I responded. "I'm not
making a fool of myself again."

She sighed. "Yeah, I suppose he either needs to show
you his special chicken feathers or be okay with another
chicken booming on his booming ground."

"What the hell are you even talking about, weirdo?"

"There's this National Geographic footage on, and well . .
. I just really felt that metaphor."

I send her a quick text back right as our driver pulls up near
the first club we'll be visiting. Should I send you pics
of any Wayland sightings, too?

Her response is a single-word statement that says a lot more than she's ready to admit. No.

We get out of our Uber and follow Sydney into the club she'd recommended. It's a large space, currently sparkling with multi-colored strobe lights. A balcony overlooks the massive dance floor below, where it seems like all of Austin has congregated to gyrate on one another to the rap music blasting from every speaker.

Nelly whoops with her hands up in the air, already walking backward to the dance floor. "This song is my jam!"

Sydney pulls on my hand. "Let's go dance." I'm already having to read her lips with the blaring loud music.

"You guys go ahead. I'm going to go get a drink."

After confirming that I really don't want to dance, Sydney follows Nelly onto the dance floor while I walk straight to the wall-to-wall bar in the back.

Waiting for my drink, I pull out my phone and check my text messages. Specifically the last one I'd sent to Logan.

He'd messaged me in the middle of the week with a video of Lainey on her skateboard with both feet on the board. I smiled and responded with a GIF of Moana yelling, "Woohoo," with her hands up in the air. But that was it. No other communication.

As the bartender hands me my drink, I feel my phone buzz in my hand and see a new message come in. Surprisingly, from the devil himself.

Where are you?

At a club called Talisman on Fourth. I wave to Nelly and Sydney after sending my response to Logan.

`Just give them your name at the front when you get to Club Vex and come find me.`

`Thanks.` Putting my phone back inside my clutch, I think about whether I even want to see Logan tonight. Maybe I can tell him we called it an early night and avoid going to *Club Vex*. I'm in no mood to do the weird prairie chicken dance my sister pointed out.

Taking a sip of my drink, I let the cool liquid wash the haze from my mind. I'm here to have fun with my friends, not let a guy who's been oscillating between hot and cold consume my thoughts. Pulling my phone back out, I type out another response.

`I think we're just going to stay here for the rest of the night. Thank you for the offer, though. I'll see you later sometime.`

I re-read the message I just sent, waiting to see if Logan responds. After about a minute, I put my phone away, feeling good about taking back control of this situation. If being friends is what he wants, then I need to distance myself a bit and not act like a lovesick puppy . . . even if I feel like one.

"Can I buy you a drink?" A voice behind me has me turning to look. It seems to have come from a broad-shouldered, tall man who's looking at me with a smile.

I pick up my drink, showing it to him in response. "I'm all set, but thank you." I'm speaking loudly but with the music thumping against the walls, I'm not sure he heard what I said. Still, I think he gets the gist.

"How about the next one?"

Looking at him once more, I notice he's probably a few years older than me, in his early thirties perhaps. He's dressed impeccably in a light blue button-down with black trousers and his dark hair is slicked back, making him look like a stereotypical banker or hedge fund manager. He's actually quite attractive. I smile back, reminding myself of my decision to put myself out there more. "Sure."

"I'm Evan." He leans into my ear so I can hear him clearly, but my nose is assaulted by the strongest cologne I've ever smelled on a man. *What is that? Beet juice?*

"I'm Anisa," I say, leaning in toward his ear as well and holding my breath momentarily.

"Anita?" He focuses on my lips as he places his hand at the small of my back.

I shake my head. "Anisa." I'm pretty sure he still thinks I'm Anita, but whatever.

"So, what do you do, Anita?"

"I'm a game developer for *Escapade Games.*"

He still hasn't removed his heated focus from my lips or his hand from my back. "Wow. Sexy and smart, the perfect combination."

My cheeks heat up and I'm about to respond when Evan turns to see someone standing at his back. Tilting my head, I follow his gaze and immediately regret it.

Shit.

"She is, isn't she?" Comes the voice of a man I know well, and right now that voice sounds anything but friendly. Logan looks from Evan's face to the hand at the small of my back. His gaze slowly travels to meet mine and holds it. He's wearing dark jeans, fitted perfectly to what I'm sure are long, muscular legs and a black hoodie with the hood pulled up, presumably so people don't recognize him. But *I* recognize him, and there's no mistaking the look on his face or the tick in his jaw.

He's pissed.

20

ANISA

"*D*o you guys know each other?" Evan looks from me to Logan before something registers in his expression. "Hey, wait. Aren't you . . . aren't you DJ Access?"

Logan doesn't respond. Sliding in behind me, he places a possessive hand on my elbow, effectively creating a wall between me and Evan. "We need to talk." His deep growl sinks into my core.

I take a seemingly casual sip of my drink. *When one finds themselves in the presence of a large territorial cat, one should reclaim one's nerves and figure out an exit plan.* "I'm here with my friends, Lo. I'm happy to talk to you another time." No, I'm not, but that's as much as I can get out before my heart dispatches itself from my chest like a speeding bullet.

Logan leans into my ear. "Either you walk upstairs with me now, Anisa, or I throw you over my shoulder and take you. Your choice."

Holy mother of motherboards! This man knows how to elicit so many shivers in my body, you'd think I was catching a cold.

I lean back to look at the caveman's face and astonishment sets in my expression. He's fucking serious. Growling in frustration--though I'm sure no one can hear me--I take two more long sips of my drink and beg for the alcohol fairies to give me the courage to fight off my feelings for this infuriating and confusing man. "Fine! Let's go."

I send a quick text to Nelly and Sydney, telling them I'll be upstairs with Logan and that I'd find them later before following him. Within seconds, he has my hand gripped in his like a vise as we maneuver through the crowd to the stairs.

Upstairs, Logan turns toward a hallway with what looks like private rooms before tilting his chin toward a large man who looks like a Spartan. Seriously, this man has more muscle on his body than I have hair on my head. The Spartan nods at Logan in recognition before opening the door to one of the rooms.

This is stranger than the sign language conversation I saw between Jeena and Wayland.

As soon as the door closes behind us, I notice the absence of the music blasting outside. I only have a moment to take in the large red sofas lining the wall and the huge wooden table laden with every type of glass bottle conceivable. My eyes adjust quickly to the dim lighting before focusing on the man--uh, carnivorous tiger--standing before me with his hands stuffed inside his pockets.

Logan's eyes flash with the anger I saw earlier, and he does a quick survey of my entire body before meeting my gaze again. I wonder if he likes what he sees, but then I quickly remember that he's been with women a hundred times hotter than me. "Is there a reason you didn't come to *Club Vex*?"

I swallow, leaning back against the door, begging my knees not to wobble. "We were . . .. I was having fun here."

Logan takes a step closer, eliminating the space between

us and any chance of me escaping. "Yeah, I got that based on the slime that had his hands on you not five minutes ago." His breath fans my face and my body reacts, arching toward him. *What the heck, stupid body?*

"Why does that bother you, Lo?" I summon any boldness I can find inside of me to meet him head-on. "*Friends* let friends flirt with strangers at bars."

His hands stretch out and capture my hips, his fingers pressing firmly at my sides, creating a warm current inside my core. His heavy bulge rests unabashedly on my belly. "Well, I guess we're not friends then, *Batgirl.*"

My breath snags on an exhale. The way his hands are holding me steady right now, they're both my life raft and the anvil pulling me under. "Then what are we, Logan?"

He doesn't respond. Instead, his stormy eyes bore into mine, mixing with equal parts of the same emotions I have swirling inside me--hesitation, vulnerability, and lust. He licks his lips and watches as I follow the movement. "Are you?"

My eyebrows crease. "Am I what?"

"Falling?"

Before I can even come to terms with what I'm doing, my hands lift, as if possessed by someone else. I push back the hood from his head before digging my fingers into his soft brown hair. With my head tipped up, I hold his gaze. I'm tired of fighting it, tired of denying it. "Yes."

And just like that, his mouth is on mine, seizing the last of my breath. His hands slide down my hips and over my ass before resting on my bare thighs. A pool of heat gathers between my legs and I moan, bending into him. My nipples pebble against my bra as my body asks for more. His tongue finds mine, and I relish the sweetness I've been craving ever since I first tasted it. He squeezes the backs of my thighs and I feel his chest pound against mine.

The sounds of our lips and moans fill the room, spurring my arousal. I feel needy and heavy, and I'm shamelessly writhing under his touch. He pulls back slightly, capturing my bottom lip between his teeth, pulling and biting before deepening our kiss again.

Cupping his cheeks between my hands, I open my eyes, watching as his lips work over mine. It's as if I need to see him devour me to believe it's actually happening. As if he can feel my gaze on him, he opens his, too. And now we're kissing--like freaks--with our eyes open.

It's always been this way, hasn't it, I wonder. *Our eyes have always said everything our words never could.*

His hand travels up, under my dress, lighting a fire over my skin. His eyes search mine for permission, and at the arch of my hips and the thumb I tenderly swipe over his cheek, he seems to have the approval he's looking for. His lips unlock from mine before he finds my neck, licking, sucking, biting. "Baby . . ." he rasps.

It's sensation overload as his scruff slides over my neck and his hand finds the hem of my panties. Pushing aside the thin fabric, his fingers trace up and down my slick opening, and I gasp into his touch.

"This," he whispers, traveling over my wet seam again and again. "*This* is for me." His other hand comes to my face, curving over the back of my neck, as his thumb brushes my lips. I pull his thumb into my mouth, sucking gently, and he hisses. His light blue eyes become pools of obsidian as he watches his thumb disappear into my mouth. When I let his thumb go, he slides it over my lips again. "These lips, this body, you . . ." he inhales as if surprised by his own admission, "all *mine.*"

Before my brain and heart can catch up to my body, Logan pushes a finger into my opening and I groan, my hips seize momentarily before I start to undulate shamelessly against his hand. Squeezing his shoulders, all I can get out is, "More".

Continuing to push and pull his finger out of me, he puts his mouth to my ear. "Do you let other *friends* do this to you, *Batgirl*?" His voice is whispered, but I hear the warning in it clearly.

My eyelids squeeze shut, singularly-focused on fulfilling my own need. My short fingernails dig into his shoulders as my body jolts, teetering on the edge of something but not getting enough to push forward. "Please, Logan."

"Eyes on me, Anisa." *God, I love when he's bossy.* When I comply, his finger plunges into me, rewarding me for my good behavior with more pleasure, making me moan again. "Good girl. Now, answer the question. Do you do this with other friends?"

I shake my head against the door. "No. Just you. Only you."

At my confession, a tenderness pulls on his features and his forehead comes to rest on mine. "It's always been you, baby."

I melt into him, my heart expanding in my chest, as I will my tears to stay at bay.

Finally, showing me the mercy I've been begging for, Logan pushes another finger inside me, making me moan against the sweet pressure.

My dress is brazenly pulled up to my waist and I'm riding his fingers when he pushes his thumb against the ball of nerves in my center, giving me the exact pressure to push me over the edge. Tilting my head back, I cry out my release--thankful of the soundproof room--as he continues to pleasure me, slowing his movements only when he's taken every last bit out of me.

Taking his hand out of my dress, his eyes pierce mine. He keeps me focused on him, even as I pant from what feels like a near-death experience. He's so magnetizing, I couldn't look away even if I wanted to.

Sliding both of his fingers into his mouth, licking them as if they were sweet cherry popsicles, he says, "Next time, I'm going to taste the source of this."

21

LOGAN

*B*lood surges through my veins like hot lava as I take in her bewildered and satiated form. She can barely stay steady on her feet. The taste of her--like holy water and bourbon--lingers on my tongue, and I wish I could keep it there forever. With her hair tousled like she's been rolling around in my bed, her pink bee-stung lips, and her crumpled dress hoisted to her hips, she's a goddamn wet dream. Reaching out, I pull her dress down, listening to her deeply inhale to regulate her breathing.

This wasn't part of the plan. Texting her tonight like an obsessed teenager, walking into this club, and finding her smiling up at a dark, greasy-haired version of Richie Rich wasn't part of the plan. I wanted to break every bone in his hand for having the audacity to touch her. And the way he was leering at her lips made me want to grab him by the back of his neck and slam him down on the bar. I hadn't felt such a wave of anger before.

It was then that I realized I'd lost the battle I'd waged against myself for the past couple of weeks. I'd lost my battle to *her*, and I'd never felt happier accepting defeat.

She's softened my resolve against needing someone--against needing her--like a stream over jagged rock. For the past two weeks, I've tried to hold on to the sharp edges of my resolution, convinced that I'd be happier alone. Convinced that being with someone would complicate my life and that of my daughter's. Convinced that no one would understand that I would need to put Lainey first.

Until Anisa came along. Until she put cracks in that resolve.

And seeing that asshole's hand on her tonight was the last hit to crumbling my resolve into pieces. I knew that if I didn't accept my fate right then--as the loser in this battle of wills--then I'd have to accept seeing her with someone else. And *that* wasn't going to happen.

From the moment I laid eyes on her--with her raven hair, dimpled smile, and psychedelic tights pretending to be the next Tony Hawk--I knew she'd be imprinted on my brain until the day I died. She may have won this battle, but she never had a fighting chance against me. She was always mine.

Moving back in close to her--because I can't even stand the half foot distance--I capture her face in my hands and place a kiss on her forehead. I'm hard as rock--a usual occurrence around this woman--but I'll worry about myself later. Right now, I see the questions rising like tides in her eyes. Eyes I've been able to read since I was a kid.

Her hands tremble as she clasps them around my wrists. "Logan." The whisper of my name travels down my spine, and I beg the heavens that she doesn't say it again. Because one more breathy whisper and the weak hold on my fortitude will shatter and I'll do anything to bury myself inside her.

Brushing my lips against hers, my voice is gravely. "I know, baby."

"What--" she tries again. "Did that really happen?"

I search for a sign of remorse in her expression. "Do you want it to happen again?"

"Yes."

I kiss her. My tongue travels along the seam of her mouth and she opens it, giving me another taste. I don't think I'll ever get my fill of her. "Then I'll make it happen again."

She places her hands on my chest, pushing away slightly to search my hooded gaze. "But you said you didn't want this."

I chuckle. "There's not a single thing about you I don't want, *Batgirl*." I continue, knowing she wants more of an explanation for my sudden onslaught of *caveman* earlier. Pulling her by the hand toward the sofas in the back, I grab her hips and sit her on my lap. "I haven't been in a relationship since I was with Mandy. And even that was short-lived because my work schedule kept me on the road so much. And then when Lainey came along, I knew she'd be my number one priority. My life sort of orbits around her, and I'm scared to pull anyone else into it." I wrap my arms around her waist. "Do you know what I mean?"

She nods. "Of course, I do. That little girl deserves all of you, Lo."

God, she makes it so easy. It's like falling into a pool of pillows. "I don't want to be unfair to you. I want to give more to you--more of me, more of my time--but I don't know if the little I have will be enough."

She turns around, straddling me, her fingers in my hair again. My hands immediately run up the side of her thighs.

"Do you know how long I've lived with just memories of you, Lo? Do you know how many memories I've made since we were kids? All without you." My face falls, hating how much I've missed. "But all my sweetest memories, all the best parts of me . . . have you in them." She leans in, trailing kisses along my scruff and down the side of my neck. "I don't want to make any more memories without you, Logan. I wasn't even looking to get into a relationship right now, but you changed everything." Her thumbs caress my cheeks. "I'll take whatever you give me. If that means that all you have time for is a quick phone call to say good night, then so be it."

I lean up to kiss her. How is this girl real? Our tongues tangle again and before long, we're ravenous once more. I know she can feel me hard in my jeans and she's pressing down on it, trying to find the friction. My mouth travels to her neck, my teeth scraping her skin. I already see the slight bruise I left earlier, and I won't apologize if I leave another one. Palming her breasts over her dress, I groan into her neck, "I want you."

She moans and I am just about to flip her onto the couch when there's a knock on the door. "Sorry to interrupt, Access, but there are a couple of girls here saying they need to speak to their friend. Apparently, the young woman who's inside with you."

Anisa immediately jumps off of me, fixing her dress and trying to catch her breath. "It must be Nelly and Sydney."

I tell Jason to hang on a moment as I adjust myself. When I left *Club Vex* this evening, I'd given him instructions to find a private room for me upstairs. Grabbing Anisa's fingers, I tug so she looks at me. "When does your friend leave?"

"Tomorrow morning."

"I'm fishing with Lainey tomorrow afternoon, but I'd like to take you to dinner in the evening."

She giggles. "This is for real? As in, are we . . .. Is this happening?"

I stand and caress her cheek, already thinking about a few phone calls I need to make so tomorrow will be perfect. "It's never been anything but real, baby. Can I pick you up at six?"

"Okay," she whispers.

My eyes stay on Anisa as I call out to Jason, "Let them in."

As soon as the door opens, two women, about the same age as me and Anisa, walk in. One is a petite black woman who reminds me of my friend Zoe Saldana, with her high cheekbones and spectacular smile. The other is a blonde I remember from the food festival last weekend. I give her a smile and notice her bangs are only barely concealing the state of surprise in her eyes. Her mouth is agape and her gaze is firmly set on me. Frankly, I'm concerned she's not breathing.

"Nelly, Sydney, this is Logan," Anisa introduces as they tentatively move toward us. I shake Nelly's hand first. While she looks a little stunned as well, she's masked it with a smile. "Logan, these are my friends Nelly and Sydney."

I reach out to shake Sydney's hand but she doesn't move. It's only when Anisa starts giggling that Sydney notices my stretched out hand. "Oh, my gosh. Hi! I'm sorry." She shakes my hand with a flush rising in her cheeks. "I'm a huge fan."

I smile. "Thank you and no worries. It's great meeting you both." I turn to Anisa. "I should head back. I'll see you tomorrow?"

She pulls in her bottom lip, a smile forming at the

corner of her mouth and I hide the rumble forming inside my chest. "Yes, tomorrow."

Leaning in, I give her a quick kiss on her cheek before moving to her ear so only she can hear me. "Dinner's on me, but dessert is always on you. You feel me, *Batgirl*?"

Her breath stalls momentarily, and I know heat is rushing to her face but she just gives me a quick nod.

22

ANISA

"How's work going?" Dad takes a sip of coffee and I watch as Mom walks to the breakfast table with her own cup on my computer screen.

I stroke the back of Lynx's ears. His head is currently on my lap and he's taking up most of the couch. We've gotten into a really good rhythm in our new relationship, and the more I get to know him, the more I fall in love with him. Aside from needing some help getting on and off the couch or getting up in the mornings, he really doesn't require a whole lot more. He's quiet and observant and possibly one of the easiest older dogs I've owned. "Work is good. It's been really busy actually, but I'm really happy with the projects Travis has put me on."

Talking about only the positive things about work will be the best course of action with my dad. Even alluding to the situation that I witnessed last week with Rosa and Blake could have him breathing down my neck about coming back to work for him. He can't make me, of course, but it would be just another *thing* for me to deal with. Anyway, it's not like Blake's behavior had been directed toward me, though I'm still very concerned about Rosa.

"So, how are you settling in?"

"Really well, actually. I've even made a friend at work, so I haven't been a complete loner sitting at home." I smile thinking about Sydney's reaction to Logan last night. She was so starstruck, a feather could have knocked her over.

It was fun going out with Nelly and Sydney last night. God knows how Nelly got up to catch her flight this morning, especially after we talked until two in the morning. They both asked me about Logan, giggling and squealing when I told them about my run-in with him last night. I made Sydney promise to keep things between him and me to herself.

My dad nods his approval as my mom leans in. "Have you seen Logan again? How is he?"

Thick, hard, and long from what I remember.

I take a physical and mental breath. As progressive as they are for being Indian parents, neither my mom nor my dad will be thrilled that Logan has a kid. My dad already judged Logan for his career choice, and I can only assume he'll be harsher about him being an unwed father. My parents aren't naive enough to assume that "kids" my age are virtuous virgins, but they also aren't lax when it comes to conversations about sex. "He's doing good. I um . . . I need to tell you guys something."

My dad straightens in his chair while my mom says, "Okay," ominously.

Pull the band-aid off in one go. Let's get this over with. "So, me and Logan have been hanging out a little bit again. Except, I think we're also attracted to each other. So, we're going to give dating a try."

My mom processes what I've said. I suppose I get that trait from her; it always takes me a bit to decompose information and come to terms with what's been said. My dad glances at her before turning back to me. "I see. So, it's over between you and Naveen?"

If I never hear that name, it would be too soon. "Yes. It's been over with Naveen for a while now, Dad." It's been interesting to watch Naveen charm my dad over the past several months, pretending to be the most humble and amicable human being on the planet. My dad still has no idea what a contemptuous asshole Naveen really is, or at least, that's how he was to me. But as long as he does good work for my dad and stays away from me, I'm also not merciless enough to show my dad Naveen's true colors.

My mom asks the next question, seeming to have digested the news. "But Jeena told us that he travels a lot and his life is very public. You, on the other hand, are a private person. How will you manage a public relationship with him?"

I can understand her concern. She knows me as well as a mother can know her child. She knows I prefer the company of my pets and my work to the company of strangers. Though, there are a handful of people I love being with, and currently, that includes Logan. I take that back. I've *always* included Logan in that handful. "I think we'll have to take it one step at a time. I'm going out with him tonight, so I'm sure we'll discuss how to move forward."

Dad continues to sip from his cup, obviously trying to hide his disappointment about things really being over between me and Naveen. My mom is about to ask something else, but I decide to face the music with the next part. I've always been able to talk to my parents about everything so there's no point in keeping this hidden. "Also . . . Logan has a four-year-old daughter."

My dad goes still for a moment, his cup covering his mouth, and my mom opens her mouth to speak but all that comes out is a tentative, "Oh." If the previous information about me and Logan dating was something she had to process, this is going to take her a bit.

Putting down his cup on the table, Dad folds his arms and looks into the camera. "Anisa, it appears to me that in the matter of weeks, you've gone from a fairly uncomplicated life to one that is layered with unexpected responsibilities and obstacles. It was one thing to move to another city on your own, leaving the comforts of what I could provide you here, but it's another to now be tied up with a man who seems not only to have little time for you, but a rather complex life situation."

This is typical of how my dad generally shows his objection with my choices. He'll state the situation he's observing in a rather unadorned and factual way and wait for me to raise my defenses. Well, I'm not taking the bait this time. "Yes. I don't disagree with you."

We all sit there staring at each other in a silent stalemate before my mom finally speaks. "*Beta*, we're just worried, that's all. We really like Logan. We haven't seen him in years, but I know that if you like him, then we will, too. But just the other day you were saying you didn't even want kids, and now you're dating a man who has one. If it becomes serious, you'll end up being responsible for his daughter as well."

I rub a hand over my eyebrow. "Yeah, I know, Mom. I'm happy to accept taking care of her one day." I think about the sweet little kid. "I can understand why you're concerned but right now, I'd just like for you guys to support me instead of giving me reasons to rethink or overthink this. If you know me, you know that I've probably overanalyzed and over-processed this decision."

"And if we know you, which we do . . ." Dad adds, though I see a smile forming on his lips like he can't decide if he should be upset or proud, "then we also know that once you've made a decision, there's little that can be done to change your mind."

Staring at them for a moment in silence, I give a quick nod. "Can you still find it in your hearts to love me?"

Mom sighs exasperatedly. "I suppose we can. Now . . . did you ever end up making that *rajma*?"

AFTER TAKING a shower and rubbing lotion on my freshly shaved skin, I take down the towel my wet hair is wrapped in. I have an hour to get ready before Logan comes to pick me up, and I'm going to wear one of my new outfits.

Before going into my closet, I check my phone, noticing a text from my new dog sitter, Tamara. She's made my life so much easier over the workdays by coming to take Lynx out for a walk and letting him relieve himself.

Still good for me to come check on my guy, Lynx, tonight at eight?

I type her back an emphatic, Yes!

Taking in a few deep breaths, I try to calm the bubbles in my stomach. Last night was the most unexpected, yet welcomed surprise. There was something raw and unbidden about Logan. From the moment he found me at the bar and the way he glared at Evan to the moment his hands ravaged me--taking and giving--in the room upstairs, I knew I was seeing a side of him that he kept leashed. It was also the side of him that I wouldn't tire of seeing again and again. A side I felt like only I got to see--a perfect balance of vulnerable yet bossy, sweet yet surly--and I absolutely loved it.

The way he moved against my mouth, claiming it and leaving promises for a lot more. The way his fingers felt on my most sensitive skin. And the way he let my wanton need culminate, leaving me breathless and riding his hand. It was all too much and so not enough.

I missed his touch the moment he left the room, and I had to ask myself if I'd just signed up for the impossible. How was I going to get through weeks of him being on the road? I told him I'd be satisfied with even a goodnight phone call if that's all he could afford me, but it didn't mean I wasn't going to miss him every day.

Deciding to unravel the convoluted emotions when I had more time to process, I lay the ankle-length, blush-colored, spaghetti-strapped dress on my bed and step back to examine it. It's a new addition to my generally gray graphic tank top-filled closet, but a part of me venturing out and exploring myself is also about working past my comfort zone.

"You're growing up, Anisa," I mutter to myself.

After blow-drying my hair, I put it into a loose, messy braid. I don't own a lot of makeup, so after smoking up my eyeshadow the best I can, I swipe on some mascara and lipgloss.

Logan texted earlier, telling me to wear comfortable shoes. Apparently, we'd be climbing a good number of steps. I'd squinted at the text, wondering if maybe he had plans to take me to a gym, but I didn't ask.

After putting on some ear crawler earrings, I'm just sliding into a pair of casual white sneakers when I hear a knock on my door.

Right on time.

Opening the door, I feast on tousled brown hair, sky-colored blue eyes, and the most delectable scruff on any man. My gaze snags on the creamy skin peeking out of his collared, light gray button-down shirt, moving down his solid chest, and soaking in his exposed arms under folded sleeves. In typical Logan fashion, his hands are casually tucked into his jean pockets.

When my regard travels back up to his face, he smirks, definitely cockier than I've seen him before. "Like what you see, gorgeous?"

I roll my eyes, though it's too late to suppress my grin. "Maybe . . . though the jury's still out."

Throwing his head back, he laughs, giving me a chance to admire his beautiful white teeth and that voice that has a way of traveling to all the untouched places of my soul. "Maybe I can convince the jury to come back with a verdict tonight."

Grabbing my crossbody purse, I give Lynx a little rub behind his ears, telling him to be a good boy. As I'm locking my door, I feel Logan's chest push against my back and his arms wrap around my front. Leaning into my ear, his voice sounds gruff. "Well, I see all of you, and I like everything I see. You look beautiful, baby."

I turn in his arms and lock my fingers behind his neck. Tugging his face toward me, I stand on my tiptoes to meet his mouth. Within moments, we're moaning and breathless. Logan's hands leave a trail of fire wherever they roam--my waist, my ass, my breasts. Pulling back from me, he pants, trying to catch his breath. "You're killing me, woman. Either you open that door back up and let me have my dessert before dinner, or you get into my car. The choice is yours. Either way though, I'm feasting on you tonight."

Warmth takes over my whole body as I smile up at him coyly. Grabbing his hand, I lead him to the car.

23

LOGAN

"This isn't the car you drove over in the past couple of times." Anisa tucks her body into the passenger seat before I close the door and round to my side.

Getting in, I look over at the beauty sitting next to me. She's wearing some sort of flowery perfume. It's barely there but it's enough to linger and make my mouth water. "I have a couple of cars."

Having her back in my life is a surreal feeling. I've thought about her countless times over the years, wondered if she remembered me, hoped I'd see her again. I guess if you make the same wish enough times, the universe has no choice but to grant it. It's a battle of wills, really.

She smiles, giving me a side-glance. "Somehow I doubt we have the same definition of 'a couple.'"

I reverse out of her parking lot and get on the road leading to the freeway. I'm a little nervous about tonight. I'm leaving tomorrow night for a two-week tour, so I had to call in a few favors to get everything booked quickly for our date. I wanted to show Anisa a special time, something her daredevil side would appreciate.

Reaching over, I grab her hand and bring it to my lips. "I'm leaving tomorrow night." I kiss her soft skin. I'm not trying to dampen the excitement building for the evening, but I want to make sure I don't spring it on her at the last minute, either.

She squeezes my hand in return. "For how long?"

"Two weeks." I brush my mouth against the spot I just kissed, looking ahead at the road, not wanting to meet her gaze.

I hate that I have to leave the day after our first date, but this is how it's going to be for us for the foreseeable future. I also don't want to sugarcoat any of it. Being in a relationship with me isn't going to be easy. Truth be told, she could find someone a lot better, without the baggage, who could give her more time and more of himself. A constriction builds in my chest at the thought of someone else's hands and mouth on her.

"Lo." She squeezes my hand again, urging my gaze toward her and bringing me out of my unpleasant thoughts. A look of understanding and support graces her expression. "I know what I signed up for. It's not going to be easy, but if your four-year-old can do it, then I can, too. Plus, I'm looking forward to hearing your sexy voice through my phone."

Her wink has a smile spreading over my face. "So you *do* think I'm sexy."

She pretends to be appalled, but I don't miss the way her mouth tips up. "I said your *voice* is sexy. The rest of you is just okay."

"I have my work cut out for me, then."

She laughs. "Clearly."

Anisa looks out her window as I drive down the long

stretch of highway. "I don't think I've ever seen this part of town before."

"Well, I'm glad I get to be the one to show you first."

Twenty minutes later, we turn onto a gravel path and I park on the rough terrain in front of the large warehouse-looking building. Getting out of the car, I go to the other side to open the passenger door for Anisa. "Let's go, beautiful." She takes my hand with a confused expression but doesn't ask for clarification of our whereabouts.

Gravel crunches under our feet as we walk to the other side of the warehouse where I find Tim leaning against the building. Before I look in the direction of where the helicopter stands, rotor blades in motion, I give him a wave and he makes his way toward me.

"Wha--" Anisa exhales sharply, clearly having noticed the helicopter as well, but her voice is overpowered by the noise from the rotor.

It's my turn to wink at her. Pulling her into my arms, I kiss her forehead. "It won't be like us riding our skateboards, baby, but I think you'll have fun."

Her response is to pull my mouth down to hers. I'll never fucking get tired of this.

Tim walks up next to me and Anisa as we pull away from our embrace. He shakes my hand before introducing himself to her. I've flown with him before and he's become a good friend. Even though he had the day off today, he generously offered to take me up on my last-minute request to show us around the city. I made sure to add a generous tip to his hourly rate.

After walking us through some safety information and policies for the aircraft, Tim leads us toward the helicopter. Anisa is already so excited about the trip, she's bouncing on her toes like a little kid while I'm barely able to control the swelling in my chest. Seeing this energy and excitement on her face reminds me of the little girl from so many years ago.

After buckling ourselves in and putting on our headsets, I reach over to kiss her again. Tim says something in our headsets about the path we'll follow and some areas we'll see, but Anisa and I are already somewhere else. Our slow kiss travels down my throat, burning in my chest as we leave the ground.

Pulling away from me, her face is a mixture of emotions--gratitude, elation, and something else I've seen often over the past two weeks. Something I feel inside every bone in my body. Something I never want to lose. "Thank you," she says into my headset, her smile brighter than the sky outside.

We hold hands as Tim flies us over the Pennybacker Bridge above Lake Austin toward downtown. The sun is still bright this time of day since it sets a lot later in the summer, so it gives us a chance to capture the views below the river bordered by dark green hills and large homes, the beautiful Austin skyline, and large, glass-faced commercial buildings. Even as the chopper turns and rolls onto its side, Anisa's smile doesn't falter. She points out sights like the Texas capitol building and the football stadium, and I secretly send up a prayer that we get back on land safely after this.

An hour later, we make our way back down to the helipad and Tim helps Anisa get out, with me following behind her. After giving our thanks once more to him, we make our way back to my car, our ears still ringing from the noise of the helicopter.

She stops us halfway to the car and wraps her arms around my neck, still winded from the experience. "Thank you so much. That was incredible, and I'll never forget it."

"You're welcome, beautiful." I give her a kiss and she deepens it.

After sending a text to Jason to confirm our ETA to the next location, we get back onto the paved road. Reaching over, I lay her hand on my thigh and cover it with my own. She lays her head back on the headrest. "Do you think Lainey would enjoy that? I can't wait to do that again with her."

And *that*, ladies and gentlemen, is the reason I'm head over heels for this woman. Even though she knows this evening is all about her and this is our first official date together, she still thinks about my daughter. "There isn't an age requirement per se, so she could ride in one, but knowing her grandma, I'm pretty sure Lainey won't be getting on a helicopter until she's in her fifties."

Anisa giggles. "She's lucky to have such a fiercely protective grandma taking care of her."

Exiting the expressway, I follow the road going toward the river. "That she is." I look over at Anisa, thinking about her own fiercely protective family. "I know it's only been a short time but knowing how much you talk to your family, have you mentioned anything about us?"

She exhales a long breath and glances out the window, and I get the feeling I'm not going to like what she's about to say. "Well, Jeena knows, of course, and she's ecstatic about us. I mean, the entire reason I ran into you at *Club Vex* that first night here was because she set it up."

"And your parents . . .?"

Circling her finger over the back of my hand, she turns to face me. "My mom is happy; she absolutely adores you. But my dad is . . .." She pauses, thinking about it a bit more. "Well, he's going to take some time. Lately, I've pushed a lot of his buttons, and telling him about you this morning was probably another item to add to his already growing list of grievances." She turns her hand so our fingers tangle. "The thing is, my dad really wanted me to work in his company. He also really wanted me to keep dating my ex."

My caveman blood starts to run a bit hotter at the reference to her ex. "The guy who called when I was at your apartment that one night? The one you said can't get it through his head that you're no longer together?"

She nods, looking forlorn. "He works for my dad. In fact, I got him the job there."

I'm sure she can see my confusion even through my profile. I push down on the accelerator slightly in an effort to release some of the irritation building inside me. I get the feeling she's holding something back. "What are you not telling me, Anisa?"

She's quiet for a moment, likely thinking about her next words. "My ex is an asshole, Lo. He treated me like shit while we were together--"

"Treated you like shit, how?" I practically growl, cutting her off.

She puffs out a breath. "I mean, he wasn't physically abusive, but he threw plenty of verbal punches, calling me names, making me feel like I had no redeemable qualities." She stares at our entangled fingers and when I glance over to look at her face, I know firmly in my heart that I will rip this guy to pieces if he's unlucky enough to cross my path. "I think getting him a job at my dad's company actually made things worse because he started to resent me for it."

My molars are grinding so hard, I'm on the verge of cracking them. "So, why is he still working at your dad's company?"

From what I remember and know of Anisa's dad, he's always been protective of her. So, if this douchebag ex of hers is still working for his company, then I'd bet he has no idea how she was treated.

She sighs. "It's not that simple. Naveen got into some trouble with the law while we were in college. He's a really smart guy, but because of his record, he was getting passed up for jobs. So, I asked my dad to help him." She looks out the window again, though I don't think she's aware of her surroundings. "In hindsight, I shouldn't have done that, but I also didn't know how bad it would become with him."

Finding the parking lot, I line up my car in one of the spaces. I've always known Anisa to have a big heart, but her ungrateful ex didn't deserve her kindness. Looking through my window, I try to control the edge in my voice but my possessiveness for this woman makes it hard for me to accept some of her choices. "You haven't answered my question, Anisa. Why is he still there?"

She pulls her hand away from mine, taking her warmth with it, and crosses her arms over her chest. Her tone comes out firm, and I get a glimpse of the dichotomy that lives inside her. She may be gracious but she's no pushover. Her principles may not be ones I understand, but I have to accept them if I want to be with her. "I'm not going to be spiteful just because he hurt my feelings and made me feel bad about myself. He needs this job and I don't have it in me to tell my dad. If my dad actually knew . . .."

She trails off but I finish for her, "He'd punch the asshole. Similar to what I'd do if I ever see him." I'm staring straight ahead at nothing in particular. My eyes are in danger of burning anything in their path, like Cyclops from the *X-Men*.

Dammit, this has me so pissed off, I'm using Marvel references!

Reaching for me, she puts my face between her palms.

Her expression softens as it skirts over the irritation on my face. "Listen, I already told him when he called me last time that if he did it again, I'd have him fired. Will you trust me to do that if he tries to contact me again?"

"Will you tell me if he gets in touch with you again?" I feel like I'm begging. I get that her heart is in the right place--even though she doesn't owe this guy a goddamn beat of it--but it doesn't mean I have to like it. "Or give me his information and I'll get in touch with him myself. It won't be over the phone, though." *It'll likely be over my fist.*

She giggles, lifting both of our moods. "Okay, tough guy. I'll tell you if that happens. Now, where have you brought me?" She looks around, taking in the lush trees and the path toward the hill we'll be climbing soon.

"To dinner."

24

ANISA

*F*ollowing Logan, hand-in-hand, on a well-paved path, I survey my surroundings. Aside from one other car, Logan's is the only one in the parking lot. I wonder if that's normal for an early Sunday evening.

Both sides of the wide path are surrounded by sprawling oak trees and short, lush bushes. The air is cooler up here, too--likely because we're pretty high up on a hill--with a smell of fresh flowers and strangely enough, something that reminds me of grape *Kool-Aid*.

I realize that I may have a slight obsession with grapes.

Logan stays relatively quiet, letting me take it all in, as we hike up the short path to a large staircase going up the hill. A large sign sitting atop a stone base says we're at *Mount Bonnell*.

Turning around to look at me in front of what appears to be stairs leading to outer space, Logan's eyes glimmer in the evening sun. "Ready to work up an appetite, *Batgirl*?" The mischief in his eyes tells me he's not referring to just the stone steps.

"I am," I whisper, smiling. "You hungry?"

His eyes go from glimmering to dark, knowing I'm flirting with him. "So fucking hungry." He pulls me in for a kiss, and I giggle into it before pulling away. If I don't stop it right here, we'll never make it to the top.

My thighs cramp and I almost decide to call it a day after the fifth step, but I keep following the gorgeous man in front of me, grateful for any chance to be with him.

He has this way of reading me. He could have easily taken me to a busy restaurant or a loud concert, but instead, he chose something private, just for us. And even though he'd rather have both his feet--and mine--planted firmly on the ground, he recognized my love for adventure and took me on the most breathtaking helicopter ride.

My legs feel like jelly when we finally reach the top of the stairs, but the thought of it falls to the wayside as I take in the breathtaking views of the Austin skyline. "Oh, wow," I breathe out the last word into the light breeze. "This is absolutely beautiful."

"Stunning," Logan responds, perusing me from head to toe.

Taking my hand, he leads me down a limestone path and I draw in another breath. A picture-perfect view of Lake Austin stretches as far as the eye can see on both sides. In the distance, I can even see the Pennybacker Bridge we flew over just a few hours ago. "Logan . . .."

I'm speechless, taking in the beauty and the sights. My gaze travels along the rooftops of what look to be very large waterfront mansions and lush foliage.

Pulling me toward a flat stoney area, Logan sits on a large, heavy looking blanket that I hadn't noticed until now. The blanket is secured at each corner by a large picnic basket, an ice bucket with a bottle of champagne, and some large boulders.

He must see the bewilderment on my face. Pulling me in between his legs and wrapping his arms around my stomach, he kisses me behind my ear. "I have a couple of guys guarding the entrances but I, uh . . ." he almost sounds sheepish, "I booked the entire area for us for the evening."

My surprise registers in my expression as I turn to look at him. "You booked this whole place . . . just for us?"

Logan smiles, making me feel lightheaded. "I thought you'd like watching the sunset from here."

I press my lips to his, not able to express with words what the past few hours with him have meant to me.

As if he was waiting for me to make the move, his hands work themselves over my breasts and I can feel his heartbeat pound against my spine. His long, thick length pulses on my lower back and aside from the sweet chirping of birds amongst the trees, all I can hear is the sound of our lips working against each other.

"I want you, Logan." My voice quivers as goosebumps light up on my skin and I feel a strange tightness in my chest, as if my heart feels like it's too big to be contained. This beautiful man was already burrowed deep in my heart, but now he's threatening to possess my soul.

Wasting no time at all, Logan lays me down on the blanket and I breathe out a trembling sigh into the breeze. Putting his forearms on both sides of my head, he hovers over me, panting gently against my skin. Leaning in to seize my mouth again, his tongue battles with mine as my hands find their favorite place inside his hair.

Breaking our kiss, he slides down my body, kissing my neck and shoulders, his hands kneading my breasts, feeling my erect nipples. I arch into him, my body demanding more. *So much more.*

His mouth travels over my covered breasts, leaving a wet

spot on my dress, before moving down my stomach. Getting up on his knees before pushing my dress up to my waist, his eyes lock with mine. Gone is the gentle and sweet Logan I know--this is the same man who fingered me against the door last night. This man is the single-focused tiger, ready to ravage anything in his path to get to his goal.

I tuck my bottom lip into my teeth, trying to silence a moan as I feel his hands sear my skin on their ascent to my hips. His fingers latch onto my panties and he pulls, his eyes desperate to feast on my skin. I lift my hips and he gently takes my panties off, growling his appreciation. And even though I should feel exposed and indecent, uncovered under the expanse of blue, all I think about is my need. My need to be devoured like the meal he's making me feel like I am.

"Jesus." Logan licks his lips, taking in my bare, delicate skin. Scooting down the blanket so he's lying on his stomach, he places both of my legs on his shoulders while one of his hands rests on my bare stomach. The anticipation is both long-awaited and short-lived as he plunges his face deeply into my heat. My hips rocket up as his hand pushes down on my stomach to keep me from moving. He moans his pleasure against my skin, lapping at my heavy mound. His tongue trails up and down my folds, driving me crazy, before he bites down gently. "Fucking delicious."

My fingers trail into his hair, pulling and pushing him farther in, as I writhe under his face. "More," I pant out.

The vibration of his laugh inflames the blazing inferno inside me as he continues to lick me with abandon. Pressing a finger into my opening, Logan continues to suck and I groan, indifferent to anyone hearing us. Sliding his finger back out, he lifts his face. "More?"

I want to scream, "You better not fucking stop!" but I

keep things as lady-like as possible under the circumstances. "Yes. Please."

I can tell he's smiling as he goes back to work, lashing at my wetness and moaning in pleasure. Driving another finger inside me, he makes me yell outright this time. "Say please again, baby."

"Please."

My insides feel like they're about to explode as I feel another finger enter me. "Oh, god." He continues thrusting into me, keeping me steady under his other hand as I shamelessly ride his face.

Within seconds, minutes, hours perhaps, I scream into the wind as every other sensation ceases to exist except for the one inside my core. An explosion of sweet ecstasy detonates through me as my body trembles from the eruption. Logan continues to lap at me, easing off slowly as I come down from my high.

As soon as the thought of what we just did registers, my hands come up to my face and I laugh, the heat captured inside my palms. *God, this man makes me crazy.*

I feel him lay out above me, secured on his forearms before he pulls at one of my hands. When I meet his eyes, I see the swirl of something that makes my breath catch in an exhale. "I'm crazy about you, *Batgirl*. Fucking head-over-heels, can't-even-stop-myself kind of crazy." His mouth crashes down on mine and I taste myself on his lips. He breaks away from our kiss and looks at me again. "It's always been you, baby."

My eyes prick with tears as I absorb his words. In a strange dichotomy of responses, a tear slides down the corner of my eye and into my hair as my hands work urgently, tugging on his zipper.

Knowing exactly what I'm asking for, Logan helps me

with my task. Before pulling down his jeans, he reaches into his back pocket and takes out a foil. His gaze is almost unsteady, becoming unfocused with lust as I watch him roll on the condom, his need coming to a head along with mine. We're ravenous, and he rasps out his command gruffly, "Take off your dress." How does this man's growled demands make my insides melt?

Maneuvering, he helps me out of my dress before lining us up, need and desperation flowing through us like a live wire. His gaze questions me once more, silently asking for permission.

"Yes." I nod. "Plea--"

I don't even get a chance to finish my pleading before he plunders deep inside me in one movement, piercing my soul.

25

ANISA

I feel like I'm floating. Like a cherry blossom falling gracefully to the ground, having exhausted all its power to stay secured to the branch it fell from. Satiated and content.

That's what this feeling is, to give in to the man I'm in love with. The man who I think feels for me at the same deep level I do for him. The man who is currently inside me in every way possible--heart, body, mind, and soul. I'm done for him. Lost to him.

Cupping his face in my palms, I stare into pools of blue, inhaling as he exhales. Moving with him rhythmically like a ballad. My body is alight, tingles running through my arms and legs as he pushes into me, stretching me impossibly to accommodate him. It's never felt this good. I've never been filled like this. "Logan . . ." I whisper, arching into him as he pushes deeper inside me.

"Do you feel that?" he pants. "You feel us?"

I manage a nod and answer definitively with a moan, "Oh, god."

Logan pulls one of my knees up to my chest and pushes his thick length into me even deeper, deeper than I've ever thought possible. We both exhale the most pleasurable groan as I feel him savagely move inside of me, my body covered in a thin veil of sweat and my heart running a marathon it's ill-prepared for.

His mouth finds mine urgently and our tongues collide. He tastes like confection and need, like an answered prayer, one I'd been waiting for all this time. His mouth pulls back before he takes my bottom lip between his teeth, biting and sucking. "I always knew it would be this good." I don't know if he's said it or I've thought it, but it's the truth, nevertheless.

He lets go of my knee and his mouth moves to my breast, shoving my bra down to expose my nipple and doing to it as he did to my lip. Sucking and humming around my pebbled peak, he continues to pound into me. Biting as he builds another pyre of need inside of my core, a need that demands release. I thrash underneath his delicious weight, my fingernails digging into his shoulders. "Logan! Oh, god. I'm about to . . .."

"Yes. Come for me, Anisa."

God, that growly voice inside my ears and my bones, the smell of cloves surrounding me in a lust-filled bubble, his taste, his touch . . . it's all too much. *It's not enough.* Bowing under him, my hips meet his thrust for thrust, and my heels dig into the blanket below. I feel the clap of thunder roar inside of me, pulling me into a haze as everything behind my eyelids turn white, just like the sky before a lightning storm. Unconcerned with who can hear me, I scream out his name as I fragment from the inside.

I'm still gasping for air, coming down from my release, when Logan pummels me faster, desperately chasing his release. Grasping his face between my hands again, I kiss him gently--a complete contrast to the way he's pillaging my body.

Within an instant, he combusts, burying his release deep inside me and groaning with every last thrust. "So good."

"Can I ask you something?" I lay my head back on Logan's shoulders, my body tucked between his legs as he wraps his arms around me from behind. My clothes are back on, though in a more rumpled state than before. Our Caprese sandwiches and an array of various cheeses and crackers lay half-eaten next to our champagne flutes, bubbles dancing happily to the top.

The sun is on the horizon, diffusing the most dramatic arrangement of oranges and yellows that create an invisible boundary with the blue sky. The air is slightly cooler--but not enough to cause a chill--sweetly caressing my damp skin.

If he rewrote the basic qualifications for a kiss when he first kissed me, then he's obliterated the requirements of love making. I feel like I've been awakened from a lifeless slumber. As if I'd just been a shell for my soul up until now. Until he breathed life into me.

Logan's lips skirt over my neck. "Always."

"Why me?"

His mouth comes to a halt on my neck. "What do you mean?"

Shrugging, I mindlessly trace a tribal-looking design on his arm. "I never looked at your pictures online, but Jeena and Sydney have shown me a few and well . . . every woman I saw you with was so different from me. So model-esque, beautiful and stick-thin. I guess I just wonder . . .."

Turning my face toward him with his hand, Logan's face is stern. "Listen to me, Anisa, and get this through that hard head of yours. You're the most beautiful woman I've seen. Your body, your curves, your fucking lips that have driven me mad since the day I met you wearing your multicolored tights, and even your preposterous claims that you're a better skateboarder than me. I want it all." He smiles, his face softening. "Those other women were a temporary salve when I was really looking for the cure."

He shifts, turning his arm around for me to see. My eyes skim over the various designs in dull blue--even a hidden one in cursive that says Lainey--to find one that beckons my touch. *A bat.* I trace over the design with my finger as a slight tremor wobbles my chin.

He clears his throat. "I've always known what the cure was."

I kiss him like if this night ends, there would be no tomorrow. Turning around, my hands roam along his shoulders and down his chest. He never took off his shirt, but next time around, I'm going to demand that be a requirement because if the weight of him on me and my roaming hands are any indication, his body is to be revered.

Pulling back, his hands unravel my braid. "Come be with me in L.A. next weekend."

It's not a question, but damn if I don't love his demands. Still, I smile, trying to rile him up. "I'll have to check my calendar . . .. I might be busy."

His mouth quirks up around the edges as his hand winds around my untangled hair. He pulls my head back slightly. "You're damn right you're busy." His breath ghosts across my face before he kisses the corner of my mouth. "With *me*. You feel me, *Batgirl*?"

I lean in for another kiss but he evades it, his eyebrow cocking up in demand of an answer. *So bossy.*

"Yes," I answer, giving in. "I feel you."

26

ANISA

*T*he following week inches along at a turtle's pace. Even though I'm consumed with work every day, getting to the weekend seems about as long and arduous as a journey to Mars. The only thing I'm thankful for is that Blake is off this week, and it's made a world of difference in everyone's mood. Even Rosa seems to have a bounce in her step.

I've started a new after-work routine--to the behest of my mom--by trying out new recipes on myself. While I'm not a natural in the kitchen like her, I can't deny the satisfaction I get from making a good meal. And surprisingly, it's pretty darn decent! Maybe even delicious, if I do say so myself.

"I thought you said you didn't want to learn to cook," Mom taunts me on the phone Tuesday night after I tell her I'm cooking the *rajma* she's been so persistent--ahem, annoying-- about. Thankfully, she's in my earpods so I have both hands free to chop the vegetables--and I can roll my eyes to my heart's content without her seeing them.

"I never said I didn't *want* to learn. I just didn't want to be *pushed* into it."

"So, what's changed now?"

Thinking about that as I add the vegetables to the pan for frying, I open up a cupboard and get out the can of kidney beans. What *has* changed now? Could it be that I like the idea of being somewhat domestic now that I have other reasons to learn to cook, aside from just for myself? Reasons named Logan and Lainey? "I don't know . . . I suppose it feels like the right time. Plus," I open the can of beans using a metal can opener, "I was getting tired of eating the same stuff from the food delivery service."

Mom laughs. "Of course, you'd come to that conclusion on your own. You couldn't just listen to your mother."

"Of course," I retort, grinning.

"And have you also changed your mind about wanting kids?"

Pouring the beans into the pan after washing them under cold water, I stir the entire mixture. Even though my initial inclination is to tell my mom that I'm too young to answer that question seriously, I can't seem to convince myself that that's truly the case. "I don't know. Maybe." I add some Indian spices to the mixture. "Yes."

I don't have to see her face to know that there's a smug smile on it. "I figured as much."

"Oh, really? You *figured*, did you?" My smile matches hers as I come to some new conclusions about what I want.

"Mm-hmm. After you told me Logan has a daughter, I had a feeling you'd change your mind about having kids." She waits for me to respond but while I'm quietly processing her words, she continues, "Tell me more about her."

For the next few minutes, I recount my visit with Lainey.

I'd already given my sister and Nelly the same synopsis, but I hadn't realized how much I wanted my mom to ask me as well, to show me that she truly approved of this new development with Logan. I suppose regardless of my age, I'd still seek my parents' approval and support.

For as long as I've known it, my parents--though overbearing and protective--have been my biggest champions, my loudest cheerleaders. They'll express their concern or disappointment; they'll even nag me about it until I snap at them. But, in the end, they'll do their best to understand my choices. Though, as experienced by my move here to Austin, they don't always agree with them.

"She sounds like a special kid. Similar to how Logan was--sweet, polite, and caring. I still remember how he would light up when he'd see you walk down our hallway to get to the door."

"Yeah . . .." Nostalgia hits me as I think about our sweet, carefree summer days, playing and talking with him under the Texas sun.

"Neesu, listen. I know you're going to visit him this weekend. Jeena mentioned it to me." Mom clears her throat and I grimace, knowing that she's about to launch into overprotective-mom mode again. "*Beta*, I know you and your sister are adults--very capable young women with very capable heads on your shoulders--so I don't want to lecture you too much. But be careful with this new relationship. I have no doubt that Logan is a wonderful man, but he's also been a single parent for a while. His first priority will always be his daughter--"

"I know, Mom. We've discussed this, and I'm completely in support of that." I add salt to the *rajma* and then put a lid on it to let it all simmer.

"I would expect nothing less from you. But sometimes

even being understanding or supportive isn't enough. From what you've just told me about Lainey, that little girl is yearning for her mother. She may have her grandma there, but she knows the difference between grandma and mom."

A wrinkle forms between my eyebrows. "Okay," I stretch the word, indicating I'm unclear. "What are you saying, Mom?"

I hear a sigh on the line before Mom responds, "All I'm saying is that this relationship with Logan may be more complicated than you've considered, and it's my job as your parent to make sure you think a bit more before you really jump into something. I don't want you getting hurt."

"Well, it's too late to stop me from jumping, but as far as getting hurt," I open my rice cooker to check if the rice looks like it's cooked, "I think that's a risk in any relationship. I just hope that with how much Logan and I talk, we can work through any situation. He wouldn't hurt me."

"Okay," Mom says defeatedly. "Your dad just came in. Let me give the phone to him so you can catch up."

After updating Dad on my new job, life in Austin, and even Logan for the next ten minutes, I finally sit down for dinner. The *rajma* isn't quite as good as Mom's, but it still reminds me of her home-cooking and I realize that in my search for being on my own, I truly miss being home as well.

After putting my dishes into the dishwasher, I'm just confirming plans on text with Tamara for her to take care of Lynx this weekend when a message from Logan pops up, making my face light up.

I miss you.

Smiling broadly at my phone, I wipe my hands on a towel

and type back, `I miss you, too. Why can't this week go by faster? I can't wait to see you.`

`Same. I'm on my way to the concert arena. You'll probably be asleep by the time I'm done tonight, but I wanted to text you because I can't stop thinking about you, Batgirl.`

My heart soars and clenches at the same time. `Call me no matter what time it is tonight.`

His response comes a few seconds later. `Are you sure? I don't want you to be tired at work tomorrow.`

`Positive. I want to hear your voice.`

`Okay. Talk to you soon.`

I send a final message to say bye to Logan before getting into the shower. Afterward, I work on my sketches, laughing out loud with an episode of *Friends* playing in the background, before heading to bed.

A buzzing sound on my nightstand wakes me up and for a few seconds, I feel disoriented, trying to figure out if I'm dreaming or awake. Picking up my phone, I notice it's around two in the morning.

Turning on my lamp and sliding the button to answer the FaceTime call, I say, "Hey."

Logan's face comes into focus and I'm assured that I'm not dreaming because he looks even better in real life than he's ever looked in my dreams. He's laying against his headboard with his tattooed arm folded above him. His sharp features and his smile make my heart rate spike. "Hey yourself, beautiful."

"Hardly. I probably look like I've been electrocuted." Wincing internally at seeing my messy, pillow-squashed hair in the little frame at the bottom, I immediately try brushing out the knots with my fingers.

"You look like the girl I dream about," he states seriously.

I smile into my pillow before looking back at him. He's such a charmer. "How was the show?"

"It was good. I think the audience really liked the new artists I've been working with."

Always modest. "They loved *you*, Lo." Color rises to his cheeks but he shrugs. "I listened to some of your new music at work today. You're so talented."

"Thanks," he says softly. It's always surprising to me that a man who has such a public life, who wins accolades and praise wherever he goes, could be so shy about taking compliments.

"I also watched a music video of you from a few years ago. It's crazy because I'd heard the song on the radio before, but had no idea *you* were DJ Access."

"What would you have done if you knew it was me?"

I nuzzle the side of my face into my pillow, considering my answer. "I don't know. I suppose I would have been happy and sad knowing it was you."

He doesn't respond for a beat, just stares at me. "I always wished you were out there listening. So much of it was for you . . . because of you."

I press a hand against the ache in my ribs. "I'm listening now."

He grins. "How was your day?"

"Busy, but tiring." I tuck a strand of hair behind my ear to get it off my face. "I'm glad Blake wasn't at work; I feel like everyone was a bit more relaxed."

Logan squints. "Who's Blake? I thought your boss's name was Travis?"

For the next couple of minutes, I tell Logan about Blake and the strange encounter I witnessed between him and Rosa. By the time I'm done, Logan't face has turned so grave that I wish I hadn't told him anything.

"Anisa, you need to report this asshole."

I imagine going to HR to report Blake and the subsequent events that would follow. Travis would definitely find out and there would likely be a bigger investigation where Rosa would be questioned. I'd promised her I wouldn't say anything and it would be unfair to break that promise when Blake hadn't explicitly *done* anything to me besides making me feel uncomfortable. At this point, just based on my account, it would feel like I was making a mountain out of a molehill. "I can handle it at the moment, but if I can't, I'll go to HR."

Logan runs a hand over his face, as if exasperated. "Of all the women to be crazy about, I had to pick the one who was also the most stubborn."

I wink at him. "You wouldn't have me any other way."

His face gets serious again. "I'm going to have you in so many ways."

"Mmm," I hum in response. "I'll be there soon."

The heat swirling in his eyes has my skin on fire. "I need to touch you, taste you." His arm lowers so it's no longer on the screen. "Show me what you're wearing, Anisa." This time his eyes flare, leaving no room to guess where this conversation is headed.

My core clenches at his command and I comply, turning

to remove my blanket. Dragging the phone camera down my body, I watch his face as he takes me in. I'm only wearing a simple white camisole and some plaid blue shorts, but with the way my body is warming under his gaze, my clothes feel like heavy parkas. My nipples are as hard as rocks, and I know he can see them through the thin material of my top.

Bringing the phone back so he's now looking at my face again, I smile abashedly. "Gotten enough?"

"Never," he responds without hesitation but his face looks pained. "I want you so bad."

"You have me," I whisper.

The side of his mouth tilts up but his eyes haven't lost the glint. "You taste so fucking good when you come into my mouth."

Wetness gathers in my panties as his words incite recent memories. My hand travels down my shorts, pushing past the elastic as my breathing accelerates. I run my fingers through my folds and the smug smile on Logan's face tells me he knows exactly what I'm doing.

"Did you like it, baby? When I feasted on you?" I watch as Logan's bicep flexes under his white shirt sleeve and a tint of pink travels up his throat.

"Yes," I hiss softly.

"Push your fingers in, Anisa."

I immediately comply like a diligent student. Even through the phone, he has my body begging to be dominated. Pressing my fingertips past the barrier and into my hot tunnel, I gasp at the slight burn. "Oh, god." I bite down on my lip, holding in another moan as my head presses back into my pillow and my eyes close.

Logan's voice comes out unsteady, and I imagine him

doing exactly what I know he's doing. "What does it feel like, baby?"

"Wet . . . warm," I breathe. My fingers push in and out as I imagine his mouth, his fingers, *him* in their place. "God, Logan, I need you."

Panting, we both watch each other as our heads rear back against our pillows. I can hear a rhythmic sound through the line and images of Logan holding himself threaten to make me lose my mind and composure. It takes only a few more thrusts into myself before I feel the rough and sensitive bundle inside of me and I erupt on a loud groan, breathing hard into the empty space above me as Logan watches.

"You're so beautiful, baby." Logan's jaw tightens as the flush on his neck deepens. I know he's close. "And you're all *mine*." He groans louder and I recognize it from the last time we were together. Even as my heart tries to steady its wild beating, it sails knowing that I'm the reason for his pleasure.

Once we've both caught our breaths, I look at him shyly. "God, what are you doing to me, Lo?"

"Giving you a taste of your own medicine." His chuckles, sending an extra jolt of tingles to my frayed nerves. "I hope you sleep even better tonight. I know I will."

I smile into the camera. "Good night, Logan."

"Good night, *Batgirl*."

Exhausted, I sleep better than I've slept in days.

27

LOGAN

*H*anging up my morning call with Lainey, I put on my hat and step out of the hotel. It's been a week of the same routine--traveling, rehearsing, and performing. The only reprieve has been knowing that I'll wake up to the chirpy sound of my little girl, giving me a rundown of every poop-head at her preschool, and I'll fall asleep to the sexy voice of the seductress I now call my girl.

My girl.

The girl who turned into a goddess. The woman whose moans and sighs sing in my ears long after I've coerced them out, keeping me hard for hours. The vixen whose blessed body makes me want to sin. *That* woman is all mine.

And this weekend, that same woman will be in my arms and in my bed, where I plan to do a lot more than just sleep with her.

Getting out of the limo on a private tarmac near LAX, I put my anxious hands in my pockets and lean against the car, waiting for her to deboard the plane. My hands itch to feel her smooth skin.

My phone buzzes inside my pocket, and I pull it out to see a text from Wayland. I'd sent him a message earlier letting him know that I'd invited Anisa to spend the weekend with me and that I was going to be picking her up at the airport. As my manager, he gets really pissy if I don't keep him up to date on my whereabouts. And a pissy Wayland was the last thing I wanted ruining my weekend.

How private are you wanting to keep things with you and Anisa? You know that shit's going to go viral the second a picture gets taken.

Reading his text, I sigh. I don't give a shit about who sees what. I'm not putting things on display, but I'm not going to hide them, either. The only person I worry about finding out is Lainey, but I'll talk to her after this weekend.

His response comes in a few seconds later while I watch the airstairs descend from my private jet. You sure Anisa wants that kind of attention? Do you want to make a formal statement to stay ahead of it?

Putting the phone back in my pocket, I don't reply to his text. I don't know if Anisa is ready for the type of attention she's sure to receive if we get photographed. I don't even know if she really knows what it all means or how relentless the media can be.

I shove the thoughts to the side as I watch Anisa emerge from the plane. She's wearing torn, white jeans and an olive-green, spaghetti-strap blouse that exposes miles of luscious tan skin. Her hair lifts in the wind slightly as she pulls her roller bag behind her. One of the attendants says something to her as he grabs hold of her bag handle. She nods, smiling at him before her head inclines to look for something. Someone. Her searching eyes finally land on mine, making me grin. Her lips turn upward as beautiful teeth come on display. Her dimpled smile is worthy of poems.

Before I even know it, I'm rushing toward her, impatient to get her in my arms, desperate for the smell of her hair in my nose, and hungry for a taste of her lips.

She steps off the last stair and her feet pick up speed before she starts running to close the distance between us. My arms open up on their own as she launches herself at me, wrapping her arms around my neck and her legs around my waist, burying her face into my neck.

Holding her in a vise grip, I speak into her hair. "Fuck, I missed you, baby."

She doesn't answer but I feel her nod against my neck before I feel her lips brush against my skin. Kissing. Licking. I was already hard at the sight of her, but her mouth has me pulsating inside my pants. I don't stop her, though. I let her carve her path with her wet lips from one side of my neck to my ear before she moves to my jaw, leaving a trail of warm kisses. I don't give a shit that the flight crew is watching. That one of them is walking around us to hand my driver Anisa's bags. That I probably have unwanted paparazzi taking pictures of this entire display of our love.

Our love. Because I'm as sure of it as I am of the sky being blue. I love this girl with all my fucking heart, and I'm pretty damn positive that the way she's ravaging me is more than just lust on her part.

She lifts her head slightly and I catch sight of the wild

look in her eyes before she urgently presses her lips to my smiling ones. Sliding my hands into her hair, I take over, fusing our mouths together. A groan escapes from my chest as I taste the sweet flavor of lemon and sugar on her tongue. *All mine.* For a few minutes it's just us in the world. Our mouths moving as one, our tongues colliding softly in battle, our breaths fanning each other's skin. For a few minutes all I feel is the press of her fingers at the nape of my neck, the heat of her body around my stomach, and the sweet vibration of her moans inside my throat. For a few minutes I just want to disappear with her.

Having finally had a taste of me to her satisfaction, she breaks the kiss. "Let's get out of here."

Walking her back to the car with her wrapped around me, I tell her again how much I missed her as she nuzzles into me, saying the same thing without words. At the limo, she tucks her body into the backseat as I come around and do the same. I immediately put the privacy window up and within seconds, we're ravenous for each other again.

Moving off my lap, she pushes my chest so my back rests against the corner between the seat and the window. Just from the glint in her almond-colored eyes, I know that this is a side of Anisa I haven't seen before. A side where she's decided to take control. A side I'm more than willing for her to show me.

Her hands work to unbuckle my belt and the heels of her palms press against my solid and unyielding shaft. A groan breaks free from my lips at the anticipation of what she's about to do. Leaning over my hips, she unzips my jeans and I help her by lifting so she can lower them to my knees. "Anisa." I'm fucking dying to have her warm, wet mouth on me.

My swollen erection falls heavy against my stomach as I

watch her lick her lips, looking at it like she's trying to solve a physics problem. Her gaze draws up to mine and my lips tip up at the look of concern on her face, but I stay silent, letting her take charge.

Her chest rises and falls as she seems to come to a resolution and leans over my hips once more, wrapping her long fingers around my hard-on. I hiss in response at the feel of her grip around me as she licks her lips again. I lift into her touch and she puts her mouth over my enlarged head. "Jesus," I whisper as my eyes roll back into my head. I feel her tongue slide around the crown, knowing that she's tasting the droplets that trickled out in forethought.

She hums as she strokes me from root to the middle where her mouth is pulling me in farther. Aside from the whir of the car on the freeway, the only sound I hear is the roar of blood rushing past my ears and the sounds of her mouth drawing me in, consuming me fully.

As she pulls me in even farther, I moan again at the feel of my tip hitting the back of her throat and the sight of her head bobbing over me. I take in her bent form--her gorgeous ass barely on the seat--in complete control of my fate. She's an enchantress, a fucking siren in disguise.

"Fuck." My hand tangles in her hair as I try my hardest to not take charge. To not use her mouth for my own selfish needs. To just let her take this at her own pace. "So good, baby," I pant, not wanting to blink and miss even a single second.

She continues her ministrations on my heavy length and my stomach clenches. A thrill gathers at the bottom of my spine. "Anisa," I warn her, knowing I'm close. This is not how I want to finish. "I don't want to come down your throat, baby."

Either I haven't said it loud enough or she doesn't care,

because she continues like she's on a mission. And she's well on her way to accomplishing said mission because within seconds, a charge of thunder builds inside me and all I can do is roll with it. The pounding in my chest comes to a crescendo before finally ebbing as I pour into her mouth with a roar.

My head falls to the headrest as my gaze becomes hooded. I feel like I've just survived a bomb blast. Anisa eases off me slowly, and I keep my eyes locked on hers as I pull my jeans back on. I couldn't look away even if I wanted to; she has me in a trance. She helps me with my belt before straddling my hips.

A lazy grin precedes my next thought. "I don't know if I should thank you or be annoyed."

Her face twists slightly with confusion. "What do you mean?"

I place my hands above her ass, looking at her swollen lips. I now have a new image ingrained in my mind of her beautiful mouth. An image that will keep me company for the rest of the lonely nights here after she leaves. "You being so good at what you just did means you've had practice, and just the thought of you doing that to someone else has me itching to strangle the guy."

Smiling at me teasingly, she leans into my ear to whisper, "Maybe if you had kept in touch with me for the past ten years, you would have been my practice subject."

I squeeze her ass and she jumps. "I don't give a shit about your practice subjects as long as I'm your only one from here on out."

She giggles before looking at me and I see a swirl of vulnerability that wasn't there before. "As long as you promise the same thing."

I steady my gaze on her. "Only you, Anisa. I promise. Only ever you."

Her hands curl into my collar and she looks at it instead of my eyes. "So, that Tessa girl and all those other women you've been photographed with before . . .. Are they completely out of the picture now?"

I lift her head, needing her to see the truth written on my face. "They were never in the picture. Not long-term, anyway. Tessa was a misunderstanding. She came onto me when I was in Paris and I cleared it up afterward, letting her know I don't have feelings for her. In fact," I lean in to kiss the side of her mouth, "I told her I had feelings for *you*."

Anisa gives me another one of her shy smiles. "I have feelings for you, too."

"I'd surely hope so."

"Pretty strong feelings, in fact," she whispers.

And all of a sudden this moment feels even more important than it already was. "Yeah? Want to tell me more about those strong feelings?"

She stares at me, her thumbs brushing lightly over my jaw before leaning over so the moment feels even more private. "I love you, Logan Miller. I've always loved you."

I lean my head back so I can see her face and take in the sincerity of her words. Words I've heard her say with every look and every action, but words I didn't know I was dying to hear aloud. My chest feels like it's too small to carry my heart, like it's begging to be released into the wild. Crushing my lips to hers, kissing her more deeply than I've kissed anyone, I let my tongue and lips speak silently before actually voicing what I've always known. "I love you, *Batgirl*. I've loved you since the moment I saw you in your psychedelic tights."

A tear slips down her face. "You just couldn't resist the jelly sandwiches I made for you."

I'll never have the heart to tell her the truth about how much I hated those grape jelly sandwiches. Circling my hand around the back of her neck lightly, I run my thumb over her wet cheek. "You're right. It was probably just that."

Giggling, she punches me gently in my chest and kisses me all the way back to my hotel.

28

ANISA

*A*fter taking a shower together, where Logan washed me from head to toe, we moved back to his bed so he could dirty me up again. Tenderly kissing and loving every inch of skin, we explored each other's bodies and memorized each curve and indentation as if they were land-marks. *Landmarks to find home.*

I relished the weight of him over me, the feel of his hard muscles against my soft belly. I ran my hand through the smattering of hair on his chest. I kissed every mole, every freckle, and every imperfection on his skin, bestowing it with love and attention. His hands did the same, though his mouth did more--sucking on my nipples, leaving trails of heat over my stomach before turning me around to do the same to my back.

When it all became too much, I begged him to take me, to fill me, and he promptly obliged. Bringing my bottom to his hips, he lined us up and took me from behind. I moaned into the pillow under my face, savoring the feel of being full of him. And when I brought my fingers to the apex of my thighs to release my bundle of nerves, he moved them away, telling me it was his turn to satisfy me.

Covering my back with his chest and pummeling into me over and over, he reached around to run his fingers through my wet and needy arousal, and I screamed into the pillow as he loosened an orgasm out of me, whispering how much he loved me into my ear before spilling into me.

To say that Logan was an attentive lover would be akin to calling a world-class chef a good cook. He was so much more. Determined to give more than he took. Tuned-in to the way my body reacted to each touch. Completely committed to my pleasure. All while making me feel like I was the one doing all the work, telling me how beautiful I was or how crazy I made him.

And now as I lay here, facing him, satiated, with my limbs entangled with his and my heart coming back to its normal rhythm, I think about the words we said to each other in the limo ride here. I'd known it for so long that it felt only natural to share them with him.

Some people win your heart piece by piece, but Logan had all of mine the minute I met him. And once it was his, it was never going to be anyone else's.

Logan absently draws circles with his index finger on my back. He's been pondering something for the past few minutes, looking at me but somewhere beyond. "How do you feel about not keeping all this hidden?"

Snuggling into his chest, with the smell of cloves and soap surrounding me, I consider the question. "I don't know if it really matters as long as I get to lay claim on you." I smile into the crook of his neck.

He runs a hand through my hair. "You're the only one who gets to lay me."

I grin, looking up at him, getting lost in the gray

perimeter around the blue tides in his eyes. There's a map of my future in them--beautifully paved paths and long winding trails, all meant for my private perusal and wandering. "What about Lainey and your mom? Have you told them anything?"

"Not yet. I'm thinking I will after this weekend. I want to talk to Lainey one-to-one and not rush through the conversation."

I nod, though a speck of concern floats up, sullying my sex-induced haze. "Do you think she'll be okay with it?"

Logan tightens his hold on me before leaning back to look at me. "I think she'll be thrilled. She already loves you."

I give him an uncertain smile. "Okay."

We're still curled around each other when Logan breaks the silence a few minutes later. "Do you like to travel?"

I shake my head and he laughs at my unexpected response. "No, I hate the actual traveling part. I hate the rush to pack, the anxiety that I've forgotten something, and the scramble to get to the airport."

Logan chuckles again, letting me admire his beautiful teeth. "Okay, fair enough. Do you enjoy yourself once you get to the destination, at least?"

I purse my lips to the side, thinking. "Yeah, depending on the destination. I love places that promise adventure. Somewhere I can go zip lining, bungee jumping, skydiving--"

"So basically anywhere with the possibility of breaking bones or risking your life," he interrupts, deadpan.

I laugh, kissing his lips. "Yeah, basically."

"I have a feeling I'm going to die from an early heart attack because of you."

I roll my eyes. "Such a scaredy cat. Some things never change." He tickles me around my stomach and I yelp before grabbing his hands to stop them. "What about you? What's your favorite kind of vacation."

"Hmm . . .." His palms make a warm trail down my torso and over my thigh before his fingers glide up to my center and into my folds, making me moan. "I like warm and wet places," he whispers, making me shiver from head to toe. "Somewhere I can explore and also relax. You feel me, *Batgirl*?"

My lids flutter closed as my body responds to his touch. "Somehow I don't think you're talking about vacations anymore."

~

"Hey, Anisa! Good to see you again." Wayland greets me and Logan downstairs that evening. He leans in to give me a warm hug before fist bumping Logan. "You ready for day seven?"

Logan shakes his head and I see the exhaustion in his appearance. "Let's get this over with. One more week to go."

"You guys coming to the party after the show?" Wayland looks from Logan to me, but I turn to Logan for direction. I'm not keen on being in a crowded room with a bunch of strangers, even if they are mostly all famous celebrities. I've never been the fangirl type, but I'm here to support Logan in any way he needs. *I fangirl for only one.*

Searching my gaze, he answers, "Yeah, I think we'll join for a bit."

Wayland raises both eyebrows, seeming surprised by Logan's response. "Well, alright then." He motions to a couple of very large men in suits standing near the hotel entrance to come over. Looking back at us, he says, "You guys head to the venue and I'll find you there. Anisa, one of these guys will escort you to the private viewing box we have set up."

I nod, taking Logan's outstretched hand as the body-guards escort us from the hotel to the black Escalade waiting outside. A large group of people--many holding microphones and cameras--line both sides of the hotel exit, shouting questions at Logan as we come out, but Logan keeps his hands secure over mine, leading us.

"*Access, how is your tour going? Looks like your new record is killing it on the charts!*"

"*Who is the woman with you? Are you dating her?*"

"*How is Lainey doing? Is your mother still taking care of her?*"

"*Logan, any information you can share about your daugh-ter's mother? Is she still in the picture? Does your daughter miss her?*"

We quickly walk to our SUV and I hear a jumble of various questions, along with clicks and flashes from cameras. Keeping my gaze focused on getting to the car, my heart picks up speed. Logan's bodyguards push a few overly excited fans aside, and I notice the tension in Logan's jaw.

Grabbing his hand in the car as we finally make our way to the concert venue, I look at him, studying his demeanor. Even in all his beauty and perfection, tension rolls off of him in waves. Turning my body toward him, I place a hand on his cheek and he visibly jolts; his eyes meet mine as if he'd forgotten I was there. "Do they ask about Lainey a lot?"

His posture relaxes a bit at the sound of my voice and he shakes his head almost imperceptibly. "Sometimes. I just . . .." He huffs and I let him gather his thoughts. "I just hate that everything about my life is so public, you know? As if Lainey's well-being is any of their concern. It fucking pisses me off that she doesn't have a normal life as it is without both her parents being together, but what's worse is that it's also scrutinized and judged by complete strangers."

A constriction surrounds my airway as I fully process Logan's words. I'd known he was always concerned by Lainey's lack of privacy, but that she didn't have a normal life because her parents weren't together stirred something uncomfortably in my gut. "Lo." I muster up the strength in my voice to cover up my own hurt. Because why should his words hurt me? They weren't about me. They were about his life situation and the fact that he wasn't with Lainey's mom. So why am I still feeling like I'm a stand-in for the real thing? "Just because Lainey's parents aren't together, doesn't mean she doesn't have a normal and happy--"

"Don't you see, Anisa?" Logan's voice cuts me off and an irritation I've never heard before comes through loud and clear. "It's just one of many things that isn't *normal* in my daughter's life. It's not normal for a four-year-old to be raised primarily by her grandma. It's not normal for her to see her dad's pictures in gossip magazines, ranting out bull-shit. It's not normal for her to spend weeks without me. No part of my life is *normal.*"

I am. We are.

Aren't we?

I regard our entangled hands before slipping mine out of his, giving him the space he seems to want. He's looking out of the window and I don't have to be a genius to know that he's not actually seeing anything.

At the concert arena, Logan's bodyguards come around us as we walk through a secured entrance through the back. As soon as we enter, Logan looks over at me and I can see his shoulders collapse. His fingers brush my cheek and remorse lines his features. "I'm sorry. I usually have my reactions to the media under control. I'm not sure why I let it get under my skin today."

Nodding, I let him press me into the wall and kiss me, trying to mask my own emotions with a smile. "Sure."

"Tell me how much, *Batgirl*."

My heart constricts as I look into his tired blue eyes--conflicted with the worry of keeping his world from spinning out of control--and I finally grasp the severity of his struggle to insulate and protect the most important people in his life. His eyes beg me for acceptance and reassurance, giving me a glimpse of the same protective boy who rushed to my side when I fell off my bike. Giving me a glimpse into a man looking for land when he's surrounded by an ocean. Nothing could stop me from being that firm ground for him right now. "I love you, Logan Miller. So much more than you'll ever know."

29

ANISA

*W*atching Logan perform is like watching a thunderstorm sweep through a dry creek, replenishing everything in its path. He's magnetic on stage, his hands moving a million different buttons, his body swaying to the rhythm as he creates the perfect remix. In his standard black T-shirt with a muscular tattooed arm raised to his headphone, he bounces in sync with the beat. I recall what he told me about being in a trance when he's on stage, and that's exactly what it looks like. Every movement of his hand and every reaction of his body is attuned to the music. What appears to be a million bodies move to the hypnotic sound in unison as they let the notes flood their bloodstream. And though there are other artists on stage, my eyes are glued to the only one that matters to me.

I'm entranced in the melody when I hear shuffling next to me. Looking to my side, Wayland comes to stand next to me. "Hey. You liking the show?"

I smile up at him, noticing his gray eyes and relaxed posture. The cut on his eyebrow where the hair no longer grows, along with his broad shoulders tucked snugly in his suit, make him look imposing and somewhat threatening. But his smile gives away the huge bear of a heart he holds protectively inside that massive chest. "I'm loving it." I look back to the stage. "He's really something."

"He is."

After a few moments of silence where we're both entranced in the music, I glance at Wayland again. "So, do you travel with Logan every time he goes on tour?"

He shrugs. "Sometimes. This tour has a lot of moving parts, so I came along with him. I can usually get most of my work done for him from home, though."

"And where is home now? Austin?"

He runs a hand through his dark hair, a few of his curls landing over his collar. "For now. I've been thinking about moving here, to California."

My eyebrows arch. "Oh? You mean L.A.?"

"Nah. I'm not really into the L.A. lifestyle or scene. I'm looking at some places in the Bay Area, maybe Sausalito."

Well, isn't that interesting? "That's not too far from where my parents and Jeena live." I watch Wayland's reaction carefully at the mention of my sister's name, noticing the way his eyes shift to mine momentarily before he moves them away. *Gotcha!*

"My brother and his family moved there a few years ago, actually. They've been wanting me to move closer to them."

I smile, knowing we've just had a silent exchange in between our banter, one that neither of us is willing to ask about openly. "Well, my parents would love for you to visit them too, if you do end up moving."

"I'd like that."

After the concert finishes, Wayland escorts me to the SUV where I wait for Logan. He finds me inside a few minutes later, after he's taken pictures with fans backstage.

His eyes light up when he sees me and the fog that surrounded them before the concert seems to have cleared. "Hi."

"Hi," I whisper. "You did amazing. I couldn't take my eyes off you."

He scoots in next to me, entangling our fingers. "I never want you to take your eyes off me." Lifting my knuckles to his mouth, he kisses them before asking, "Are you okay with going to this afterparty? I promise not to stay too long."

"Of course. I'm happy wherever you are."

As the car comes to a stop near the club, I notice the huge crowd gathered around the entrance. Logan's body-guards work to move people away as we exit the car, shielding us from the mob. Logan wraps his arm around me possessively as we enter the club, and being under the gaze of so many people, my heart speeds up uncomfortably.

We're guided to a large private space inside the club, decorated with massive chandeliers, red walls, and framed black-and-white photographs of various celebrities in the same venue. Famous personalities--some I recognize and others I don't--are gathered, both around the bar and in groups, mingling and laughing. Some are taking selfies with drinks in their hands as waiters walk around with trays of food and beverages. It's exactly what I would have expected from a star-studded gathering, yet completely surreal.

As soon as we're spotted by a group of men--one I recognize as a performer from a famous boy-band--they call Logan over, patting him on the back and giving him a friendly "guy hug" where they clasp hands and bump shoulders. "That was sick, Access! You're a fucking musical genius," one of them says to Logan.

"Thanks," Logan responds before looking over at me. I

know how uncomfortable he must be right now with the attention. "This is my girlfriend Anisa."

I swoon in the title as seven pairs of eyes turn to me, a few reaching out their hands to shake mine, introducing themselves. A couple of them exchange covert smiles and winks with Logan, making my cheeks heat. "I'm going to find the restrooms," I say, leaning into Logan's ear, needing a little break from the attention myself.

He kisses the side of my neck. "I'll be right here."

I walk past groups of people standing near the back wall. A few beautiful, Amazonian-like women with voluminous blonde hair, in short sequin dresses eye me warily, as if they can't decide if I'm part of the waitstaff or a lost fan.

While I'm happy to be wearing the expensive black strapless dress and diamond earrings Logan surprised me with and carrying the overpriced clutch Dad gave me for my birthday last year, I have never felt as self-conscious as I do today. Every one of my insecurities scream inside of my head in *Asshole Aunty's* voice. *I should have worked out more this past month. I shouldn't have eaten the pasta and bread this afternoon. If I could just lose the extra ten pounds, I'd be so much happier. Maybe I should wash my hair with dead seahorse shampoo, too.*

Finally finding the restroom, I do my business and am washing my hands when the door opens and a stunning, tall blonde walks in. She looks familiar, so I assume I've seen her on TV. Smiling at me tightly through the mirror, I notice she lingers near the door. I give her a smile and turn to find the hand towels.

"So, you're Anisa?" The cold blue stones in place of her eyes scroll up my body, judging, assessing, and offending.

I suck in my stomach and imagine myself with a six-pack similar to the one I'm sure she has under her tiny dress. *Yup, definitely should have had a salad for lunch today.* "I am. And you are . . .?" Maybe she heard Logan introduce me to his friends.

"Tessa. Tessa London." She introduces herself like James Bond would. Her lips lift slightly, doing nothing to warm her features. "My family owns *London-Bridge Organic Foods.*"

Realization hits me as I recall her from the picture I saw a few weeks ago, where she was plastered to Logan. "Nice to meet you."

"I'm sure it is." Her lips purse as if she's decided to mimic a fish.

My eyebrows furrow. "I'm sorry?"

"Are you here with Logan, then?" She doesn't answer my question.

"Yes. In fact, I should be heading back. He's probably looking for me." I move toward the door but Tessa shifts, holding my attention.

"Do you enjoy breaking up relationships, or is it just that you don't mind being another groupie he fucks?"

I gulp in a breath, trying to ignore the dull pain that's started somewhere in the hollow of my chest. Mustering up all of my courage, I straighten my spine. "Maybe you're speaking from experience, but I don't partake in either. Now, if you'll please excuse me."

Tessa puts a hand on the door, looking down at me from her full gargantuan height. "Take a look at yourself, honey. You're basic fish eggs when he deserves nothing less than caviar. You're neither in his class nor his world. He might be giving you the few minutes of attention he can spare as charity, but most of us around here change our causes and charities as often as we change our designer purses."

I forcibly school my features, not giving her a second of gratification, even though my insides feel like they're on fire.

"Well, I'm terribly sorry that I've been the cause for your insecurities, Tessa. I can't imagine how you must feel being passed up for basic fish eggs, especially after you threw yourself at him so desperately, but thank you for your cautionary words. I'll let him know you said hello." I pull the door handle and step out of the bathroom, looking back at her briefly to see her gawking at me.

My legs feel like unstable stilts walking back toward Logan. Tears threaten my eyes as I process Tessa's words. Am I really a charity for Logan? Is he with me just because he feels obligated to our childhood connection? Would he want me if we didn't have the history between us?

He's speaking to a couple of women--both of whom look like they are pin-up models--with his back toward me. Their eyes roam all over him, licking him up from head to toe. In fact, I'm pretty sure they'd swallow him whole and not gain an ounce.

Deciding not to interrupt their conversation, I walk the other way to find a corner seat at the bar, hidden from the crowd and order myself a vodka and soda. After swallowing the first cold sip, I take a long inhale and release the built-up tension through my lips.

Maybe Tessa is right. Maybe I *am* just too ordinary to be a part of this world. Maybe he's not looking to find someone *normal* so much as someone extraordinary. Someone who can thrive in the public eye. Someone who can live up to the expectations of his world, instead of almost collapsing in the face of scrutiny.

He doesn't deserve to have to take care of another person when his life is already laden with worries. He deserves someone self-assured and confident, who can free him of more responsibilities; someone who can be his partner, not his burden.

And wouldn't I be a burden if I can't handle coming to these things without getting rattled by women like Tessa London or women who look like they want to make him their next meal?

As much as I want to be the land he finds in the middle of his vast ocean, I also don't know if the ground he'll stand on can withstand his weight.

The only *extraordinary* thing I have to offer Logan is my love, cultivated and coddled over the years and across the miles, just for him.

But will it be enough to shield us from his world?

30

LOGAN

*E*xcusing myself while talking to Hannah and Kennedy, the twin sisters who are the face of Victoria's Secret at the moment, I walk toward the restrooms in search of my girlfriend. She's been missing from my side for the past fifteen minutes, and I mentally kick myself for not checking in on her already.

This is her first time at an event like this, and I know how overwhelming it can be. It takes someone with a spine of steel to walk through the room and not be intimidated by the excess of pretension and plastic surgery. And while Anisa looks better than any woman in this room today, I wouldn't be surprised if she's hiding somewhere, feeling like she's not good enough. Just the thought of her feeling that way boils my insides.

I'm just about to knock on the ladies' restroom door when a familiar voice catches me off guard. "Hey, stranger. Looking for me?"

Turning my head toward Tessa, I regard her with a tilt of my chin. "Actually, no. I'm looking for my girlfriend." I annunciate the last word so she doesn't miss it. "Have you seen her?"

"No." She pouts. "What does she look like? The only people I've seen today are the ones everyone sort of knows."

I try to ignore her underhanded remark, but one thing I've learned about Tessa is that somehow she misses anything that's not explicitly explained to her. "About five-seven, gorgeous Indian girl with light brown eyes and long wavy hair. I don't think you'd miss her if you did see her. She's a knockout."

Tessa's blue eyes pale but her jaw sharpens. "Oh! Now, I remember! I did talk to someone who might have been her. We had a good chat, her and I. What's her name again? Anita?"

My fist clenches at my side. "Anisa."

"Right." She waves a hand in the air. "Anyway, she asked me about what it's like to date someone so famous. She seemed kind of clueless, to be honest. I'm sure this is all just a lot for her. It's never fun to be a small fish in a big pond." She giggles. "So funny, I actually used a fish reference with her earlier, too."

My temper soars through my head and past the fucking roof, and I make a move to get past her before I say something I'm going to regret when she grabs my arm. "Logan, listen. Please talk to me. I'm sorry about what happened in the lounge at your hotel that day. I just . . . I told you, I misunderstood and thought you felt the same way about me. I want us to be friends again."

"Tessa, let me make it crystal-clear so you don't *misunderstand* again. We're *not* going to be friends again. Please stay away from Anisa and stay the fuck away from me. Next time, you'll be hearing from my lawyer."

Leaving Tessa looking like she'd just been slapped, I

glance into the bathroom before walking past her to find Anisa. After asking around for a couple of minutes, I spot her with a drink at the bar. She's twisting her cup like she's fastening it to the counter.

Coming up behind her, I put my arms around her waist and lean into her ear. "You hiding from me, beautiful?"

She shakes her head. "Not you. This guy who looked a lot like a Hemsworth. He was all over me earlier and just doesn't care to get the message."

Knowing none of the Hemsworths were even at this party, I play along. "I guess he's asking for an ass kicking then, because I'd never allow an Avenger anywhere near my girl."

She giggles. "I saw you in a deep conversation with a couple of women and I didn't want to interrupt."

Coming up next to her so I can see her face, I turn her chin to me. Tucking her hair behind her ear, I regard her beautiful face with the reverence I've always known for her. "*You* are the most important woman in my life. Everyone else is an interruption. Do you hear me, *Batgirl*? I love *you*. I want *you*."

She nods, but I see doubt whirling in her eyes. I don't know exactly what Tessa said to her, but I'll be damned if Anisa feels anything less than the queen she is. "I ran into Tessa just now."

Anisa bristles at the mention of Tessa's name. "Yes. I did, too. She has quite the charming personality."

"Listen to me, Anisa." I slide my hand to her shoulder, peering into her eyes. "There's not a woman on Earth who holds a candle to you. You're the only one I think about and the only one I want. In fact, ever since you've said yes to giving us a chance, I've wondered how the fuck I got so lucky. So, before you let assholes like Tessa or your ex or whoever else take any space inside your head, remember that I love you, I cherish you, exactly as you are." I lean into her ear, licking it gently, feeling a shiver run down her body. "And I'm happy to show you how much once again. Just say the word."

A smile pulls up her lips before her mischievous eyes dart to the exit on her other side. I follow her movement and smile back, knowing exactly what my girl is implying without so much as a word. Lowering my mouth to hers, I bite her bottom lip before sucking it gently. "You lead and I'll follow, baby."

She looks around conspiratorially before grasping my hand and taking us through the exit and into a small stairwell. Pulling me up the stairs, she ushers us to the top of the club to a door leading to the roof. Luckily the door is open, and I follow her as she takes in the sight of the L.A. night sky, twirling in place as if she's finally free. She smiles into the wind. "Wow, it's beautiful up here."

I breathe in the slightly cool breeze mixed with the scent of magnolias and pineapples--the smell I love more than any other. I casually tuck my hands into my pockets, watching her shoulders relax and her beautiful figure sway under the black strapless dress. I'm solid as stone inside my pants but I'm too mesmerized by her beauty to do anything about it just yet.

After a minute or two of taking in the sight of flashing lights from the high-rises around us and the sounds of the L.A. traffic humming in the background, Anisa finally makes her way back over to me. Putting her arms around my neck, she leans up to kiss my nose. "So, what was it that you were saying about showing me how much you love me?"

I take my hands out of my pockets and find her ass,

pulling her into me before kissing her lips again. "Take your dress off."

A shudder moves through her at my words. "Here?" She looks over her shoulder to the buildings near us. "What if someone sees us?"

"Then, let them."

A final look of hesitation crosses her face before she smiles--the same mischievous smile I saw inside the limo before she leaned over my waist to take me into her mouth. Wiggling out of her dress, she lets it pool on the ground unceremoniously before stepping out of it. My eyes rake over her black strapless bra, the beautiful bronzed skin of her torso, and her tiny lace underwear before combing over her long, bare legs.

She lifts a foot to take off her high heel when I stop her. "Keep the heels on."

Palming her ass, I press my erection against her, walking us to the glass wall at the edge of the building. She looks down and around her at the large windows from neighboring buildings shining into our space, creating the perfect glow around our bodies. Unbuttoning my pants and lowering my boxers, I lift her up to my waist. She moans at the touch of our bare skin--hers wet and warm while mine is dry and smooth--wrapping her legs around me. With her back firmly on the glass, I use a hand to slide her underwear to the side to look at her wet mound. She follows my movement with her eyes and squirms around me, asking for more.

Using my first two fingers, I slide up and down through her wetness, making her huff and pant. "Please, Logan."

God, I love hearing those words.

Grabbing her mouth with mine, I continue to press into her with my fingers, feeling her warmth around them and telling myself to be patient. It'll only be a matter of minutes before I'm inside her. Continuing my exploration, I add another finger inside her and she groans, her head hitting the glass behind her. To anyone looking in, it'll look like she's suspended in air. "Please."

Taking my fingers out of her, I line us up and find her eyes. I have a condom in my wallet but fuck, I want to take her bare.

She hears my silent question. "I'm on the pill."

"I'm clean, baby. I would never hurt you."

"I know." Her thumbs tenderly brush my cheek like she always does. "Please. Don't make me wait anymore, Lo."

Pushing into her slowly, I force my eyes not to roll to the back of my head at the feel of her warmth around me. We both groan at the same time as I bury myself to the root and I honestly think I might pass out if I don't start moving. With both of our eyes locked to where we're merged, I start plunging inside of her, trying to get deeper than before.

Holding her ass in my palm, I continue to pummel into her, feeling her core clench around me. Her nails bite into my back through my shirt and I love the feeling of pain mixed with pure pleasure in the most perfect disunion. Groaning into each push, I pant into her neck, "How's this for showing you how much I love you?"

"It's pretty good."

"Pretty good, huh?" I drive into her harder, making her yell out and giggle at the same time.

"Really good," she pants. "The best."

With a few more thrusts, I find the pressure point at the back of her core, focusing on teasing it, taking from it exactly what I'm here for. "Let go, Anisa."

I shove a cup of her bra down and grab her nipple in my mouth, sucking hard and causing her to catapult into my waist. "Logan!" Her fingers tighten over my shoulders as I finally feel her insides uncoil and release. She lets out a long groan and I devour it inside my mouth, driving into her to find my own release before the completion of hers.

Within seconds, I'm flooding her insides with my release, moaning into her ear. "Fuck, I love you, baby."

"I love you, Lo," she breathes. "I love you."

31

LOGAN

*B*y Saturday morning, my phone is blowing up with texts from both Wayland and my publicist. Apparently, Anisa and I were caught going upstairs hand in hand through the stairwell last night, and prior to that, a picture was taken of us kissing at the bar. As much as I want to care, I honestly don't. Instead, I turn to face my gorgeous girlfriend sleeping with her hair in her face and her arm haphazardly thrown over my bare chest.

Brushing her hair from her face and tucking it behind her ear, I lean in to kiss her shoulder. Even begging didn't convince her to sleep naked with me last night. After taking her once more after we got back from the party, she said she was going to put on a chastity belt if I didn't let her keep her pajamas on for the rest of the night.

Sliding my hand over her back, I palm her ass inside her boy shorts and wonder if the no-more-sex restriction has been lifted this morning. God, this ass is the best thing I've ever held. I may dedicate my next single to it.

She wiggles sleepily but I see the smile on her pouty lips and the outline of her dimple on her cheek. Turning around to give me access to her front, she murmurs, "You're relentless."

"Making up for lost time." I skate my hand up her stomach to her breasts, pulling her camisole up with me so I can pull a nipple into my mouth. She lets out a gentle hum as her body heats up under me when her phone starts buzzing on her nightstand. "Ignore it," I murmur against her nipple.

She giggles then gasps as I slide my hand back down into her shorts, finding her wet and ready for me. I kiss her neck and put my mouth on her lips when she shakes her head. "I have morning breath."

"I don't give a shit. Now, kiss me, woman." I continue my ministrations with my fingers inside her and she lets me find her tongue with my own, kissing me lazily when her phone buzzes again. "I'm going to break your phone," I growl in frustration.

Giggling again, she reaches over to the nightstand to retrieve it. "It might be important." She brings the phone to her face and reads the message she's received. "Oh god. I have all these texts and links from Sydney and Jeena."

"Let me guess, pictures of us that are about to be printed in gossip magazines everywhere this morning."

A look of shock passes over her face. "These are pictures of us from last night, but they're all over the internet already. Are you saying they'll print these, too?"

"Yes, most likely." I watch her expression carefully. It's a mixture of ambivalence and worry. "Tell me what you're thinking, Anisa."

She scrolls through something on her phone, her mouth forming a frown. "Showdown over Logan Miller," she reads out loud, and I lean in to view the side-by-side picture of her and Tessa that's been cropped over a picture of me in some online article. "*Access* granted to Logan's mouth and his money!" Anisa continues to read in outrage, and I notice she's looking at a paparazzi-taken picture of her getting off my jet and one of us kissing near the tarmac. "What the hell?"

I take the phone from her hands and place it back on the nightstand. Pulling her into me, I kiss the top of her head. "I know it's not easy, but please don't let this bother you, baby. The media will spin up anything that will sell. I can understand how hard it is to see your face plastered everywhere, but I promise they'll cool down. We just have to show them a united front and that none of this affects us."

"They don't even know me!"

She lays her head on my chest and I run a hand over her hair. "They don't know me, either." She lifts her head to look at me and I continue, "But we know each other, *Batgirl*, and that's all that matters."

SATURDAY PASSES in a love-drunk haze with me showing Anisa my star on the Hollywood Walk of Fame, spending time on Venice Beach, and making love to her every chance she gives me. I've never been so insatiable, but she makes me ravenous.

Often, I find myself staring at her, compelled by the need to commit everything about her to memory. Like the way she throws her head back when she laughs or the way she doodles on any piece of paper--be it a receipt or a napkin. She's the song I want to memorize, even if learning the words takes me an entire lifetime.

On Sunday afternoon, I'm in the back of the limo with her as we drive back to the airport. My mood is shot at the prospect of being away from her for yet another week, but Anisa's hands in my hair and her body pressed up to mine, with her legs straddling my hips, is a good deterrent. I run my hands over the sides of her thighs when my phone vibrates on the beverage tray next to me. It's a call from my mom.

Anisa removes herself from my lap while I reach out to pick up the phone. I hadn't had a chance to tell my mom that I was spending the weekend with Anisa, but I had sent her a message saying I'd chat with her and Lainey tonight, which is why I'm surprised she's calling now. Maybe Lainey is giving her a hard time and Mom needs me to talk her down about something. "Hey, Mom," I answer the phone.

"Logan." The concern in her voice immediately has me straightening up. "There's an issue. Mandy dropped by a few minutes ago."

Mandy?

"What?" I'm trying to process what she just said and notice concern line Anisa's face. She can't hear my mom, but she knows something is up based on my reaction.

"She got through security somehow and rang the doorbell. I was in the kitchen and Lainey opened the door. She's seen enough pictures of Mandy that she immediately recognized her mother. Logan, they were both crying in each other's arms when I came out to the foyer to see the commotion."

My voice strains to hold in the anxiety building through my body. "Where are they now?"

The limo driver takes the exit for the airport and I look out of the window, keeping my face impassive. With everything new that Anisa has had to deal with this weekend, this is the last thing I want her to worry about. "Honey, I tried to stop them but Mandy insisted she's recovered and has had a chance to really think about things. She told Lainey how much she's missed her--apologized profusely for leaving her and even said she moved to Austin to be with her. You know how soft-hearted that little girl is. She forgave her immediately."

"Mom." I clench my jaw, hoping to tamp down the anger swirling in my voice. "Where are they now?"

"Mandy took her to get ice cream. I sent Roger from security with them."

"Fuck!" I curse, hearing my mom take in a sharp breath. She knows there's no point in scolding me about my foul language right now. "I'll take the next flight home."

"Okay, honey. I'm sorry. I don't think there was anything malicious or worrisome in the way Mandy was behaving, and Lainey refused to let go of her mom."

"Did you get her phone number?"

"Yes, I have it. I'm also getting updates from Roger every few minutes. I told him not to call you because I wanted to tell you myself."

I run a frustrated hand through my hair as the limo comes to a stop on the tarmac. "I need to go. I'll be home tonight."

Hanging up with my mom, I press the heels of my palms into my eyes. How the fuck did this happen? After years of breaking her heart, Mandy finally decides that her daughter is worth a visit? What does she want now? God, this must all be so confusing for Lainey. My mind is racing with incongruent thoughts when I feel soft fingers wrap around my wrists.

I lift my head out of my hands, seeing Anisa's face come into focus. "What's going on, Lo?"

Plastering a milder look on my face to camouflage my internal turmoil, I decide not to divulge more until I know what Mandy really wants. My relationship with Anisa is still new, though my love for her has spanned years. And while I know she'll do everything in her power to understand and accept this new complication, I don't feel it's fair to ask that of her so soon. She's already been so accepting of my work situation and so loving with Lainey. Shaking up the foundation I'm building with her so soon after we've just gotten together seems undue. "Just something going on with Lainey that I need to get home for."

Anisa scans my face but doesn't ask for more of an explanation. A twinge of guilt hits me in the chest at the thought of keeping this new development from her, but I tell myself I need to sort it out before I involve her. In all honesty, it doesn't impact her anyway, so there's no point in worrying her. "Do you want me to take another flight home or wait for you? I can do either so you can go on your jet."

I shake my head. The limo driver comes to Anisa's side to open her door before rounding the back and coming to my door. I get out of the limo and meet her on her side. "You go ahead, I don't need the jet. I'll make other arrangements after I get my things together in the hotel room and meet with Wayland to let him know I have to cut the tour short."

Anisa's face falls. "Logan, whatever it is, I wish you'd tell me. You'd never shorten a tour if it wasn't serious."

Wrapping my hands over her shoulders, I look into her disconcerted eyes. "I'll tell you everything once I figure out what's going on. I promise." She moves her face to the side defeatedly and I bring it back so she can see the sincerity in my eyes. "I love you, *Batgirl*. Nothing will change that. You feel me?"

She nods, giving me a watery smile before I reach down to her mouth and leave a tender kiss. The flight staff has already loaded Anisa's bags onto the plane and she looks over at the aircraft absently. Her hair flutters in the wind, bringing some to her face before she pushes it back behind her ear. She looks so beautiful, it momentarily takes my breath away. "Okay, just . . . call me whenever you want to talk." Her voice sounds hesitant and I tell her not to worry once more before she gets on her tiptoes, encircling her arms around my neck.

We hold each other for another few moments, my head buried in her hair, before she turns and heads to the jet.

32

ANISA

"*H*oly shit, your face is all over the internet right now! I had no idea you even went to Los Angeles! How was it? Are you even able to walk after what I imagine was a very satisfying weekend?" Sydney throws her purse into her desk drawer before pulling out her chair to face me on Monday morning.

I groan, both from the conversation and from the massive headache I'm sporting this morning after sleeping a maximum of two hours last night. I waited for Logan's call and even texted him to see how things were going, but I didn't hear back--not even his usual good night message. After tossing and turning until almost four in the morning, I finally dozed off before my alarm woke me up again for work. And like a nervous, overzealous schoolgirl, I've been checking my phone nonstop for any missed messages from him. "It was a good weekend, but it sucks that so many people have already weighed in on it."

"Girl, that's what you get for dating a celebrity." Sydney backhands my bicep gently. "Tell me everything. What did you do? Did you meet any other famous people?"

"I did but--" I giggle when Sydney squeals, almost falling off her chair. "But I have to get to a meeting right now. I'll tell you all about it over lunch."

"Oh my god! I hate that I have to wait so long! I'm going to die!"

I shake my head at her dramatics before painting on a smile that doesn't reach my eyes, even if I tried. "I think you'll make it until noon."

Walking into the conference room, I see Rosa and Blake already waiting for me. Rosa seems to have a distressed look about her already, but I suppose I don't blame her after what happened the week before last when Blake was here. Why couldn't he have taken another week off? Or better yet, why can't he just move to another side of the business? *Or another planet.*

Today is the demo for Eterna and the scene I worked on last week. Once Blake approves it, the demo will be shown to the extended development team and Travis before being incorporated into production code and launched to our users. "Good morning," I address both of them as I connect my laptop to the projector above.

"So, I'm assuming you were able to include the changes I specifically asked for before I went on vacation?" Blake's pompous voice and his raised eyebrows dismiss any pleasantries.

I start the demo and look over at Blake. "Rosa and I came to an agreement on how many of those changes we would incorporate into the design. I think you'll be happy with the ones we've included."

"Firstly . . .." Blake looks at Rosa, who cowers in her chair, before looking back at me. My spine stiffens at his tone. "There isn't an agreement to be made by you because neither of you are the lead on this project. I am."

I continue to stare at him before raising an eyebrow in question. "And secondly?"

"And secondly, what?"

Huffing before turning back to the screen where my work on Eterna is being displayed, I start to walk Blake and Rosa through the changes. Before I can even progress to the next sequence of the scene, Blake interrupts, "Those are not the proportions I asked for. Her ass needs to be bigger."

Both Rosa and I flinch at his unprofessional terminology. "With all due respect, these are the changes we felt comfortable with. In fact, Travis has put me on a separate task force to see why the number of players on our platform are decreasing, and I'm finding substantial data that supports a correlation with our games being too sexy."

Blake slams a hand on the table, making Rosa jump. "There is no such correlation! I have said it time and time again, but you are clearly hard of hearing. Eighty percent of our base is made of teenagers between the ages of twelve and nineteen. Guess what they want to see, Ms. Singh? Hot women with big boobs and bigger asses! Now, either make the damn changes or get off my project!" He turns to Rosa, who looks like she's about to cry. "Both of you!"

My heart races as the room turns icy. No longer able to subject myself to his assholery, I shut my laptop. "I think this conversation is best had in front of Travis--"

"You're damn right it is. I'm going to let him know about the insubordination and incompetence from our newest and most junior developer."

I get up, my hands shaking, betraying the confidence in my tone. "I think we're done here, Blake." I look over at Rosa to see if she will follow, but she's sitting in the room stoically. I honestly can't tell what's running through her brain right now.

Before I can get to the door, Blake's soft laughter invades my ears. "Why do you think we hire curvy women like you both to work here, sweetheart?" *Holy shit, did he actually just say that?* "It makes for good prototyping."

Yes. Yes, he did, in fact, just say that.

And today, he's strengthened my resolve.

AFTER CALLING my sister and getting her advice on how best to handle the situation, I head upstairs to HR. I want to text Logan and tell him about my morning. I want him to tell me that he's in my corner and that he's proud of me for taking charge of this situation. But after not hearing from him all night and receiving no response to my past texts, a little part of my dignity strengthens my spine. I won't be the type of girl who calls and texts her man, needing more than he can give.

When I saw the shutters visibly come down on his emotions yesterday, I knew I wasn't getting through to him. Whatever happened with Lainey couldn't have warranted him canceling the rest of his tour unless she was sick or hurt. And from what I got from the one-sided conversation I could hear between Logan and his mom, I don't think Lainey is in any type of physical pain.

It crushed me internally to know that whatever he was dealing with, he couldn't trust me to open up about it. Maybe years of knowing someone has nothing to do with the years it takes to *actually* know them. Still, I would have thought that our love would have been strong enough to conquer some of our fears. I know I was trying--*am* trying--to move past the doubts that had built-up over this weekend between talking to Tessa and finding my face on every online gossip site. I won't let my own insecurities dampen my love for him, and I trust him wholeheartedly when he tells me he loves me. But Logan's hesitation yesterday makes me feel like he doesn't share the same level of trust with me.

I'm just about to open the doors to the HR suite when I get a call from my dad. I don't even get a chance to say hello before he starts. "Anisa. What's this I'm hearing from Jeena?"

I sigh. I should have known Jeena wouldn't be able to keep this from our father. A part of me had held off telling her about Blake up until now, knowing it would only bring out her overprotective side. And now, my dad's. "Dad, I've got it under control. I'm just going to report the guy to HR and let them start the investigation."

"Have you talked to your manager?"

"No. I just came straight here after talking to Jeena. Travis has meetings all day, anyway, so it would be a while before I get a chance to speak to him. I'll inform him as soon as I see him."

"*Beta*, I know you're not going to like me saying this, but this is exactly why I didn't want you to work in a different city. I have no connections there, and I can't even do anything about this guy."

I groan, my fingers coming up to my temple. "Dad, you can't put me in a bubble for the rest of my life. These things happen, and I am sure they've happened at *Techsess*--"

"Yes, and I've fired people over sexual harassment. We have a no-tolerance policy."

"And I'm sure *Escapade Games* does, too. I just need to speak to HR and start the formal complaint."

"Come home, *beta*. Just come work for me, and I will give you whatever it is that you want--freedom, an apartment in the city, whatever."

"Dad." I count to three in my head to keep from losing it on my dad. I know he's just worried and wants to watch over me for the rest of his life, but this is the last thing I need right now. Between being the topic of a thousand news articles online to having this turbulence at work, I've got my hands completely full.

"Okay, fine," my dad relents. "I also wanted to tell you that some magazine was here looking to talk to me about you. I refused to comment and they left. Anisa, are you sure you are okay? Can you and Logan handle all of this on your own?"

I don't tell my dad that at present, I'm kind of handling things on my own and that I haven't heard from Logan in the past twenty-four hours. It would just give him more ammunition to support his argument for moving back. "Yes, Dad, we've got it. Now I have to go, but I'll tell you how it all goes."

After spending a half hour with HR, I come out feeling even more drained. Even though they said they'll start the investigation, I'm worried about their conversation with Rosa and whether she will actually admit to what she saw and heard today. I hope she'll look at this as a way to get rid of Blake without having to be the instigator, even though she has dealt with his male chauvinism and misogyny for much longer than I have.

I'm just about to leave for the day when Travis comes by to ask if he can have a word with me in his office. Walking by Rosa's desk, I see her eyeing me questioningly, and I have the strongest desire to ask her if she's heard from HR but I continue to follow Travis.

"Have a seat, Anisa." He waves to the chair in front of his desk. I can already tell he's been filled in on the situation. "Now, tell me how I can help you. I am here to support you and ensure that you feel safe at work. I've already talked to HR about the case that you filed this morning, but I want you to know that if something is bothering you, I take it very seriously and will support you in any way I can."

My eyes pool, triggered by the sincerity of his words, and I launch into what I witnessed this morning and a few weeks ago. I leave out the conversation I had with Rosa in the bathroom, giving him only the information that I heard myself.

After listening to me and handing me a tissue, Travis leans back in his chair, weaving his fingers over his lean stomach. "I want to thank you for trusting me with this information, Anisa. I am truly sorry that you experienced that kind of behavior here at *Escapade,* and I appreciate you bringing this up to the right people." He takes a moment to observe me. "I think you should work from home for the rest of the week. HR will be conducting a number of interviews with various people on our team and even some of the extended teams, and I want you to be able to focus on work. Get your mind off of what's happening over here."

I nod, feeling like a boulder has lifted off my chest. For the first time all day, I feel like someone has cared about my needs more than their own. "Thank you. I think I'd like that."

Walking back to my car with the same feeling of foreboding that I've felt ever since I left Logan yesterday, I look at the zero missed calls and texts from him. I wish I could talk to him, be wrapped inside his warm arms with him whispering that everything will be alright and that he loves me.

But maybe love doesn't conquer all.

33

ANISA

*H*ave you seen the latest pictures of Logan? My fingers stop mid-code, creating new weapons for Eterna on Wednesday night, when I see my sister's text light up my phone.

I stare at the screen for a few moments, though I don't respond. I'm not the type to go hunting for mindless babble or reported rumors, and a part of me refuses to acknowledge even wanting to know what Logan has been up to the past few days.

My chest feels constricted at the thought of finding whatever it is that Jeena is referring to online. I've waited every day this week to hear from him, staring at my phone like a mindless zombie. I even called him yesterday--foregoing all my talk about upholding my dignity--but only got his voicemail. I didn't leave him a message, though. What would I have even said that my texts hadn't already?

Feeling my nose tingle at the sign of impending tears--tears I've shed every day this week--I pull up my web browser and search for Logan. I don't know what I'm expecting to see, but it definitely isn't what I'm looking at now.

Image after image of Logan walking hand-in-hand with Lainey, who's between him and another woman. A tall, thin woman with dark hair--close to the same color as my own-- and Persian-looking skin and features. She's absolutely stunning. The three of them are walking like a family, down a street in a few pictures, and turning into a restaurant in others. Pressing a hand against the pain in my ribs, I swallow the lump in my throat as I click on an article.

"DJ Access Cancels Tour to Rekindle His Relationship With The Mother of His Daughter"

Can you hear the wedding bells ringing? We can!
An exclusive source reveals that Mandy Monroe, estranged girl-friend of DJ Access, AKA Logan Miller, says the two have "talked marriage" and are ready to fully commit to raising their four-year-old daughter.
The insider tells T&T News that Logan has always had a place in his heart for Mandy, but was committed to ensuring she dealt with her health issues before becoming a caretaker for their daughter. Mandy contacted Logan this weekend while he was with rumored girlfriend, Anisa Singh, to speak with him privately about rekindling their romance.
The source also claims that the two are committed to "starting a relationship" and giving their daughter the sense of family that she deserves.
This week Logan and Mandy were spotted holding hands with their daughter, laughing, and talking as if there wasn't a three year separation between their love. The source goes on to say that Mandy has kept a close watch on how dedicated Logan is as a father and hopes that they can have a bigger family in the future.

With the distance between them removed and all other romantic relationships dissolved, can Mandy and Logan be on their way down the aisle? We think so!

Hot, almost-solid tears roll down my cheeks as I inhale sharply, trying to replenish my oxygen-deprived lungs. I didn't realize I was holding my breath along with my broken heart for the past minute. My chest hurts so much, it feels like my heart is revolting inside its cage. Lynx walks over to examine my tear-stained face before curling up near my feet.

With the distance between them removed and all other romantic relationships dissolved . . ..

And all other romantic relationships dissolved . . ..

Dissolved.

I read the line over and over again, but each time it feels like the sentence is written in Greek. The small rational part of my brain tells me to wait until I get a call from Logan. That this is just a gossip column, not *real* news. I know Logan well enough to know that if he wanted to dissolve things between us, he would have the guts to do it in person. Wouldn't he? I wouldn't be hearing about it from some online chronicle. I have to believe that.

But the acid churning in my stomach and the streams of tears that refuse to stop flowing no matter how many times I've wiped them, tell me that I don't quite know what to hold on to--my belief in our love or my gut telling me something is amiss.

The man I love, who told me he loves me, has reconnected with the mother of his child. He not only kept the truth from me on Sunday when his mother called--undoubtedly with regards to this information--but he hasn't respected me enough to call and tell me about it. As if the love we expressed to each other, the words we said and meant, were nothing more than a bout of lust and insanity. I expected more from him. I expected to be his partner in whatever it is he was facing, but right now, I feel like a mere acquaintance.

Dragging myself off my chair and shutting down my laptop, I find a fresh set of pajamas to wear. It's nearly ten PM, and I've finished braiding my hair and washing my face when I hear a sharp knock at my door. The knock makes Lynx's head snap up and he follows me to the door where I look through the peephole.

Turning my back immediately to the door, I lean against it, holding in a sob so the man on the other side can't hear it. Wearing his white hat, he was looking down so I couldn't see his face, but I'd know his beautiful profile, his presence, even if it was halfway across the world from me.

"Anisa." Logan's voice, dulled through the heavy door between us, still has the power to vibrate down my spine.

Pulling both my lips between my teeth before taking in a big breath, I resolve to open the door. I remind myself that this is what I wanted--to hear the truth from his mouth. There must be a good explanation for all of this and after hearing it, I can decide how to proceed.

I refuse to meet his eyes as I open the door halfway. My hurt and my heart won't let me, knowing I'll crumble if I do. Plus, I don't want him to see the tears that have permanently etched themselves over my cheeks. He stands there waiting for me to look up and when I don't, he starts again. "Baby, can we talk?"

I flinch at the use of the endearment, but my heart leaps in hope that maybe everything isn't as it feels; that maybe I've misinterpreted, misunderstood Logan's silence. I open the door farther in invitation for him to come in. He enters and I quickly wipe the traitorous tear about to make its way down before he turns around. I'm still glued to the door, looking down at the floor when he advances toward me, gently lifting my hand. "Anisa, look at me."

Lifting my head, I meet Logan's weary eyes. Similar to mine, they're rimmed red and bloodshot, like he hasn't slept in days. The look on his face crushes whatever is left of my heart and I instinctively know that whatever he's struggling with, whatever he's come here to tell me, will unravel everything we've worked for.

Like watching a bullet pierce its target in slow motion.

Pulling me against his hard chest, he wraps a hand around my head, burying his face into my hair. Neither one of us speaks for a few moments, relishing the pressure of our bodies against each other, supporting the weight that's floating between us. For a few moments we just listen to the sounds of our tired breaths and cherish the security within each other's arms.

But intuition tells me not to let myself get lost in this moment because something is still off. I pull away, looking up into his face, ready to face my fate like a helpless pin awaiting the crash from a speeding bowling ball.

His thumbs wipe my cheekbones as his fingers wrap around my neck. A resolution passes through his eyes as he decides whatever it is he's about to say. "I love you, Anisa. I will always love you for as long as I live." He pauses, clenching his jaw shut, seeming to get control of his emotions as a tremble catches my chin. Why aren't his words filling me with the same sense of solace and elation as they usually do? Why does it feel like there's a "but" coming? Why does this feel like the end? "But everything . . ." he inhales, "everything in my life feels like too much right now. Work, life . . .."

"Me," I finish for him.

He shakes his head. "I just don't want you tangled up in everything. I need to undo a few knots before I can decide which way to go. Do you know what I'm saying?"

Decide which way to go? Yes, it seems perfectly clear; in fact, the decision on which way we go lies solely in Logan's hands. Apparently, the direction we take has nothing to do with what I want. I nod, lowering my lids so the only thing I see is the way his throat moves when he speaks.

"I don't know how much you've read online, but I know you're wondering where I've been the past couple of days or why I haven't responded to your texts. I don't blame you for being confused or angry with me. You didn't deserve my silence." He huffs out a breath. "Baby, please look at me."

I lift my gaze to meet his again and see the swirl of emotion. "I've just been trying to process it all without losing my shit in front of Lainey, and I needed to find some clarity without mixing you up in all of this." He pauses, searching my eyes--for what, I'm not sure. "Mandy came back and visited Lainey on Sunday. That's the reason I cut the tour short and hurried back home. Lainey is completely smitten with her, refusing to spend a moment without her. It's like they're trying to make up for lost time." He shakes his head as if he's lost in front of a fork in the road. "I'm trying to be as understanding and supportive as possible to both of them because I know how much this reunion means to Lainey. It's just . . . .." He runs a hand through his hair. "It's just a lot, Anisa."

I break away from him, my legs finally cooperating with my brain, forcing some distance between us where the heady smell of cloves isn't invading my senses. He's trying to be understanding and supportive to both of them, as he should be. But who will understand what I'm going through? What about how all this has affected *me*? Does it make me selfish to want to shelter what's left of my battered heart? He watches me, his shoulders sagging. "What are you saying, Logan?"

He swallows, shifting his eyes to somewhere beside me-- past me--so he doesn't have to look at my face. His fists clench at his sides. "I . . . I need to take a break from us." He looks at me briefly before finding the spot next to me, like looking at my crumbling face is too much for him. "I need to figure out how to manage it all between my work schedule, raising Lainey, and now having Mandy back in our lives. I already felt like I didn't have enough time for anything else before, and now I feel even more constrained . . . like I'm drowning."

Anything else. Constrained. Drowning. These are the words that hit my chest like missiles, burrowing deep into my heart. Here I was with my wild dreams of being more than just "anything else." Here I was thinking about integrating my life with Logan's and becoming a bigger part of Lainey's life. Here I was thinking our childhood friendship made us stronger as a couple, where we would face the world head-on, together.

But here I am, proven wrong, disintegrating in my entryway.

Rising above the tide of blood rushing through my ears, I straighten myself as best as I can and keep my face blank. "Okay."

Logan's eyes flit to mine but I see something break inside of them, like my response caught him completely off guard. He nods after a few moments as if he's just heard me. "I'm sorry, Anisa."

"Thank you for coming over to let me know." I bite the

inside of my cheek to keep myself from trembling. "I'll see you around, Logan. Good luck with everything."

He reaches out but drops his hand when he sees me recoil. I refuse to let his touch melt me into a pool of tears at his feet. This was *his* decision, *his* doing. Not mine. I was ready to work through the thick and thin. And I refuse to give him anything less than my most sincere emotions. I refuse to show him that I understand, because I don't.

His frown deepens as he nods again, turning toward the door. Holding the handle, he turns his head to the side, speaking to me over his shoulder before he walks out of my life again. "I love you, Anisa."

34

ANISA

"Hey, Anisa. Can you chat for a few minutes?" Rosa stands next to my desk the following Tuesday morning, twisting her hands in front of her.

Sydney gives me a knowing look before focusing back on her screen. Closing the screen of my laptop, I roll my chair out and get up. "Sure. It looks like the small conference room over there is open," I say, pointing toward said room.

We walk side by side into the room and I pull out a chair to sit down, facing Rosa. It's been quite an interesting week here at the office from what I've heard. Thankfully, I was able to work most of last week from home so I didn't have to be a part of the chaos that ensued here, but from what Sydney told me, it was nothing short of a dramatic TV show.

Travis, along with HR, fired Blake for sexual harassment. Apparently, aside from Rosa, several other women came out against him and validated my claims during the HR investigation last week. Even a few of our male colleagues attested to hearing Blake make misogynistic and inappropriate remarks. And while I'm happy about the outcome, I've felt awkward and antisocial at work. *Not that I wasn't that way before*. But it feels like people have categorized me as a troublemaker. Sydney told me she's heard several women commend my courage for vocalizing what many have felt, but I still feel like I could have done without the dramatic unfolding of events only weeks into my new job.

I give Rosa a few seconds to collect her thoughts with an encouraging smile. "I just wanted to thank you, Anisa." She looks at me from where she's still standing. "That day when Blake was verbally inappropriate and demeaning to you, I didn't stand up for you. I didn't even walk out with you when I knew I should have. It truly made me feel like a coward." She gingerly pulls out a chair and sits next to me, hands folded in her lap. "That one day a few weeks ago, you followed me into the bathroom to check on me, to make sure I was okay. You even told me you'd come with me to report him if that's what I wanted to do. And even then I was a coward. I just thought about the ramifications of the situation for *me*, not for anyone else."

Sliding forward, I place a hand on her hands. "It's okay, Rosa. I don't blame you for what happened."

She nods, looking down at our hands. "I know. You seem like the type of person who has a really good sense of right and wrong, and you stand up for your convictions. I wish I was more like that. I just let my fears get in the way and I shouldn't."

"But you didn't when it counted. You told HR the truth when they asked you about it." I smile at her. "How are you feeling now? He's gone. Do you feel a sense of relief?"

She closes her eyes momentarily. "You have no idea. He's been a menace since I started working here. I want to thank you for what you did. It really opened my eyes to what I was accepting from others. It made me see that I have to stand up for my self-worth and not put up with disrespect."

I give her a watery smile, not wanting to admit that sometimes standing up for my own self-worth and self-respect meant that I had to nurse a broken heart as well. A heart that felt less broken and more butchered.

After leaving the conference room, I walk straight to the bathroom for the second time today to release the fabricated poise with which I've been holding myself up the past few days. Grabbing a handful of tissues from the roll, I sob silently into it, praying for the day when I don't have to fake it any more. Praying for the day that I won't feel like breaking down or just staying in bed all day.

That day doesn't appear to be anywhere on the horizon.

I'M JUST COMING BACK from a walk with Lynx on Friday evening after work when I see another white news van and some people who look like reporters standing in the parking lot near my apartment. I've had someone or another show up uninvited about three times over the past week, and this time it looks like yet another unwelcome newscaster.

"Ms. Singh! I'm Nick Olson from *T&T News*. We wanted to talk to you about your recent breakup with Logan Miller."

"Sorry. No comment," I say curtly, walking past them and through the downstairs alley of my building to get to my apartment.

"Don't you want to state publicly what happened? You can clear the air so people know your side. It looks like Logan and Mandy are still trying to work things out. They apparently took their daughter on a trip to Disney World this week. How does that make you feel?"

It makes me feel really goddamn great! Thanks for asking, Nick!

Every question, every fucking word out of his mouth impales me with the force of a hundred swords. Even when I don't want to know what Logan is up to, even when I've refused my sister or my friends from giving me updates about his whereabouts, someone finds a way to bring him back up. It's like the universe is set on seeing both my heart and soul battered.

Sealing my lips, I quickly unlock my apartment, bringing Lynx in with me and close the door behind us. Sliding down the door, I sit in my entryway with my knees up, weeping into my hands. A new sob emerges from my throat when I feel my sweet dog's tongue sweep across my ear. Even *he* thinks I'm pitiful. "I miss him so much, Lynx. Why did I have to see him again after all these years? Why couldn't we have just forgotten each other? Why didn't I stay true to my promise of being single?"

Foregoing a response to all my questions, Lynx sinks down next to me, laying his head on his paws as the only sign of his support.

After crying for another ten minutes, I get up to wash Lynx's bowls and give him his dinner. I suppose the one good thing that's come out of the past two weeks is that I've eaten the equivalent of what a small rabbit might. And thus, I've lost a good pant size. The bad thing--aside from the shattered soul I'm housing--is that along with the pant size, I've also lost the glow that might have previously been on my face. My limbs feel weak, like they'd float away if they weren't attached to my body. Even sketching doesn't interest me. In fact, I often find myself looking indifferently at the incomplete sketches, wondering if someone else had drawn them. I suppose someone else *had* drawn them.

After scrounging up a few crackers from my pantry and some grape jelly from the fridge, I find a seat on the couch, mindlessly watching an episode for *Friends*. I'm just licking a little jelly off my finger when my phone vibrates with a FacetTme call from Jeena. She must just be getting back from work. For the past week, she's been relentless about Facetiming me instead of doing an audio call. I know she's worried, but sometimes I wish I could just hide from the world.

I click the button to answer, leaning back into the couch. "Hey."

"God, you look terrible," she says, eyeing me--or whoever she sees in the camera.

"You should consider becoming a motivational speaker," I deadpan.

"Nees, I'm really worried about you, okay? I haven't told Mom or Dad anything because I'm respecting your wishes, but seriously, you're starting to look like the Scarecrow from the *Batman* movie."

So glad she's not a motivational speaker.

Putting on a brighter face, I smile into the camera. "It's just the breakup blues, okay? I'll get over it."

Her face turns wary. "Stop trying to mask yourself from me. I've known you since you were born. You're my red-headed, drunken Irish twin."

I squint at her but can't help smiling a little. "Why are you so weird?"

She laughs before we both fall silent. "Any word from Logan?"

I purse my lips. "No, I think he's said all the words he needed to."

"I truly think he loves you, Nees. He just needs time to figure his life out. All of this is a lot for him."

"Yeah, well . . . he's been abundantly clear about that."

I see her grab a large bowl of cereal--of course--and pour some milk into it. It looks like *Fruit Loops* from what I can see. She turns back to the screen when she's done. "So, I have some news."

"Oh?"

"Guess who turned in his resignation at *Techsess* today?"

My brows furrow. "Who?"

"Naveen." My sister waits for my reaction--raised eyebrows with a *whoa* out of my mouth. "Yeah, that's what I said. Apparently, he wants to take some time off to travel. He's been really . . . different lately."

"Different, how?"

Jeena takes a bite of her cereal, crunching away before speaking again. "Well, apparently, he's been going to therapy and does a lot of volunteer work at a youth center. He's been overall just easier to communicate with at work. Which is why it was actually a little surprising when he quit. He says he wants to take some time off to focus on becoming a better person."

Yeah, I bet assholery takes a while to scrub off.

"Well, that's good, I suppose." I put my dishes in the sink and remember my conversation with Wayland. "Oh, I have some news for you, too."

"Sis, I don't think I can handle more of your news. From the shit you've dealt with at work to the stuff with Logan to everyone around the world knowing your business, I'm kind of stocked up on Anisa-news for at least a year."

I roll my eyes. *I'm kind of stocked up on Anisa-news for a lifetime.* "Not about me. It's about Wayland." My sister stops mid-crunch before pretending not to have heard me, but I continue, unperturbed, "He's thinking about moving to the Bay Area. Sausalito, to be exact."

Jeena looks bored. "Riveting. I'll ensure a welcome parade takes place in his honor."

I laugh, finally after what seems like forever. "What is it with you and him? Why aren't you telling me?"

"There's nothing to say. Listen, I have to get going. I have a pretty exciting date tonight."

"Oh?" I reply, surprised. It's not like my sister hasn't been on dates since her last serious relationship, but it's rare for her to sound excited about anyone. "Who is he?"

"His name is Arjun. Mom and his mom met at their reading club and exchanged our numbers." She rolls her eyes but doesn't appear to be truly bothered by it. "Anyway, he called me a few nights ago and we had a good chat. He works for a private equity company."

I eye her cautiously. "And you're okay with Mom introducing you to someone else again?"

She shrugs, knowing what I'm asking. "Yeah."

"Have you seen what he looks like? Is he cute?"

"Nees." My sister puts her spoon down so I know what she's about to say will be attention-worthy. The girl never puts her spoon down unless it's important. "He's fucking gorgeous! Like, scorching hot."

My eyebrows rise, happiness for my sister blooming in what's currently an arid desert in my chest cavity. She's been through a lot over the past couple of years and deserves to have someone she's once again excited about. I still wonder what the deal is with her and Wayland, but maybe I'm overthinking it. "Well, go get ready. Are you going out to eat first?" I ask, regarding her now-empty bowl.

She furrows her brows at me like she's embarrassed we share the same gene pool. "Of course. That was just a snack."

35

ANISA

*I*t took six weeks for my broken wrist to heal, and eight weeks when I broke my ankle. I've never had a broken heart, but I'm guessing that a lifetime will be insufficient, let alone three weeks.

However, I'm eating better and I've only cried in the bathroom twice this week so that's progress, but I still think about Logan every damn day. I miss him in my marrow. And even though news of him is floating around all the time, I can't bring myself to look at it. It's similar to how I felt after I moved to San Francisco as a little girl. I never looked for him because finding him, knowing he was out there living his life without me, would hurt worse. I've even told Jeena, Sydney, and Nelly to stop sending me any information about him. It's the only way I can cope.

Parking my car in my apartment lot, I take out the groceries from my trunk when I see a man's shoes walking toward me in my periphery. Gasping out loud, I almost drop the heavy paper bag.

Naveen lifts both arms in a sign of surrender. "I just want

to talk. I'll turn around and catch my flight back if you tell me to, but I came here with only good intentions."

I rapidly search for sincerity in his face. "What . . . .. How did you find my apartment?" *Is my address plastered on every gossip site, too?*

He cringes, knowing he's going to sound like a stalker no matter what he says. "I did a little bit of sleuthing." His whole face collapses into a frown. "Anisa, I owe you a huge apology. I'm not here for anything but to tell you in-person that I'm sorry for the way I was with you. I was a complete asshole, and you deserved better."

I'm not the most snarky person in the world, but if I was I'd say something like, "Yeah, you're goddamn right, I deserved better!" Instead, I give him a quick nod. "Okay."

His face lights up marginally. "There's a bakery near here from what I saw. Want to grab a cup of coffee?" He must see the hesitation on my face as I look around the parking lot. "Anisa, please give me a half hour, that's all I'm asking for. Just give me a chance to explain."

I bite the inside of my cheek for a few seconds longer and then tell Naveen I need to put my groceries down and let Lynx out, but that I'll meet him back out in the parking lot in a few minutes. I'm not comfortable inviting him into my apartment and fortunately, he doesn't seem to expect that, either.

Once we're both in my car, we chat a bit about his recent resignation with my dad's company while I drive us to *Beth's Bakery*. After waiting in a decently long line for six in the evening on a Wednesday, I get a grape jelly donut--no other bakery around carries them--and a cup of decaf coffee. We find a seat near a window while Naveen looks around, assessing our surroundings. "This is a nice place. Have you been here before?"

"Once, when Nelly visited." The portly woman at the front register--who I believe the bakery is named after--has the kindest demeanor, and I recall chatting with her for a few seconds when I visited the first time.

Naveen turns his coffee cup in its place mindlessly, seeming to be lost in thought. After a few seconds, he looks back up at me. "Thank you for even taking the time to talk to me today, Nees. I know I don't deserve it, but I guess I'm also not surprised. You've always been one to give second chances, whether it was to save an old homeless dog or save a friend's career." His face falls. "I really fucking screwed it up with you."

I circle my finger around the rim of my cup. "Why did you?"

Naveen surveys me before he runs a hand through his thick, black strands. "I resented you. I resented how easy you seemed to have it--your nurturing parents, your supportive sister, your talent, your brains. All of it." He sees the hurt on my face but continues, "My dad can barely keep his own job, let alone care if I had one. Not once did he come to my school events. Fuck that, he didn't even come to my graduation! And then when I got my DUI, I couldn't even call him for help. And that felony on my record from hitting the biker? I had no one to talk to but you." Taking my hand in his, Naveen squeezes gently. "You were the only one who cared, but I resented you. I never felt good enough for you."

I lick my lips, processing his words. "But I never meant to make you feel that way. I was just trying to help."

"That's the thing, Nees. It wasn't *you* that made me feel that way, it was *me*. I saw how you had it all and still worked your ass off to carve your own path while I made bad deci-sion after bad decision and basically took a hand-out from you. I couldn't even get a job on my own after getting two fucking degrees from one of the best universities in the world! I still needed your help!" His face distorts before he regains his composure. "I hated myself for never measuring up to you. And honestly, I never will. I know that now. I've been in therapy for the past few weeks and have come to a lot of realizations. I still have a long way to go, but I wanted to start by apologizing to you. I hope you'll find it in your heart to forgive me."

My heart sinks thinking about how much he's struggled, but I also know there's no excuse to treat me the way he did. I'm not stupid enough to ever want to try to reconcile our relationship--I know a zebra can't change its stripes overnight--but I am compassionate enough to forgive him. Squeezing his hand back, I smile at him. "I forgive you."

As if a weight has lifted off of him, Naveen's demeanor relaxes. We sit there in the same position for a few more seconds before he looks like he remembers something. "Hey! I saw that you were dating DJ Access, but you guys recently broke up. What happened?"

I'm just about to respond when the door to the bakery opens, the bell chiming sweetly above the frame, and a little girl I recognize with blonde pigtails and bright blue eyes enters, skipping in front of a man who looks like he just walked out of a magazine. *He probably did.* The girl goes chirping toward the lady at the counter as my heart falls, meeting Logan's eyes.

Logan's nose flares slightly as he watches me slip my hand out of Naveen's, but I don't miss his pained expression. What the hell? Why should *he* be hurt? He's the one who moved on, made his decision. Why do I need to feel guilty for holding someone's hand?

Naveen notices the exchange and realization dawns across his face. "Should we get going?"

I get up, picking up my cup and half-eaten donut. "Yeah-_"

"Anisa!" Small arms wrap around my legs as I look down at the adorable four-year-old's smiling face. "I haven't seen you in ages! You have to come back and show me tricksies on my skateboard again. Daddy won't let me do anything because he thinks I'll get hurt." She looks over at her dad, making a face at him.

Putting my cup and plate back on the table, I get down on my knees so I'm at eye-level with Lainey. "It's so good to see you again, Lainey!" I put on my most realistic sounding excited voice, hoping it doesn't crack. "Have you been practicing putting both feet on the skateboard?"

She nods animatedly before her eyes move to Naveen. "Who's he?"

Logan shifts in my periphery, his hands finding his pockets. "Um, this is my friend Naveen."

Naveen is just about to extend his arm out to shake Lainey's hand when Logan speaks. "Lainey, let's get your jelly donut and be on our way."

Lainey looks over at me and then her eyes find the half-eaten pastry on my plate. "You like grape jelly donuts, too?"

I smile what feels like the first real smile in weeks. "I do. They're kind of the best."

"They *are* the best! Did you know my dad hates jelly? But most of all, he hates grape jelly. Can you believe that?"

Say what now?

Just as my world turns upside down, so does my smile. I stare at Lainey before my eyes glide to Logan's panicked ones, remembering every single time we'd sat in the sun eating jelly sandwiches, remembering the time he brought one to my apartment. Was it all a lie? My eyes prick with unshed tears as a quake moves my lips. "No. I suppose I didn't know him as well as I thought," I respond, looking at Logan's disconcerted expression.

"Anisa," Logan says with a shaky voice as I give Lainey a quick hug before picking my things off the table and heading for the door with Naveen following behind me.

The last thing that registers throughout the drive back to my apartment is the bell above the door on my way out.

.

36

LOGAN

*G*odammit!

Throwing my cap on the floor, I run both hands through my hair, pulling the ends as if maybe the pain will bring me relief. I need to go after her. She has no fucking idea how much I've missed her these past three weeks, making every fucking effort to get back to her, hoping she'd one day forgive me for being the jackass I was when I walked out of her apartment.

And there she was today, with her hands wrapped inside her asshole ex's. Didn't she tell me she would have him fired if he ever contacted her again? And now she has him visiting her? Had I messed this up so badly that she was running back to the man who made her feel like shit for so long?

"Daddy? Are you okay?" Lainey looks at my cap on the floor before looking at me with a jelly donut in her hand.

Squeezing my eyes closed for a moment, I put on a confident face for my daughter. "Yeah, baby girl. I'm okay. I just--"

"Daddy?" she interrupts my thought. "Are you and Anisa not friends anymore?"

I swallow, a piercing pain shooting through the organ that's no longer in my chest. I'd heard of amputees saying that they felt pain where their limbs used to be, and I could attest to a similar feeling over the past three weeks. "I don't know, Lainey-pants," I say honestly.

Lainey's intelligent eyes assess me, moving to my mussed hair back down to my downturned lips. "Just say sorry, Daddy. Grams says it doesn't make anyone shorter if they apollo-gize."

I smile at her use of *shorter* in place of *smaller*. "I'd even accept being a few inches shorter if she would forgive me."

"She will, Daddy. You have to try."

AFTER DROPPING Lainey off at home, I'm on my way to Anisa's place when I get a text from my attorney. We're all set.

Sighing out a breath of relief, I park in an open spot and race out of my car. I don't fucking care if that douchebag ex-boyfriend of hers is there or not, he'll wish he never put his hands on what's mine when I see him. I need to talk to her, see her, hold her, tell her how much I love her.

All the clarity I was looking for punched me right in the gut as soon as I left her place that night a few weeks ago. I let go of a part of my world and it tilted the axis in the wrong direction. And nothing but Anisa can right it again.

Knocking on her door, I hear a quick bark from Lynx. I send up a silent prayer to let her be home, but if I have to wait all night at her doorstep, it would be a small price to pay. "Anisa." I knock again. "Please, baby, open up."

Fuck! My heart flip-flops inside my chest like a fish out of water, begging for relief. *Please. Please, open up.*

A few minutes--maybe a few centuries--later, I hear the lock click and my beautiful girl comes into view. She has on her sleep camisole and plaid shorts with an open thin robe draped casually over it. Her dark hair is up in a messy bun, her silky tan skin unblemished on her neck. God, how I want to put a fucking blemish on it with my mouth, letting everyone know she's mine. Because she's *mine*.

A mixture of anguish and apprehension outline the contours of her face but she meets my eyes, shuttering her emotions and her heart. "Let me guess. You're going to tell me you don't even like superhero films."

I blow out a breath of air as the true meaning--her look of betrayal--hits me square between my shoulders. *The damn jelly sandwiches.* "Can we talk?"

"No. I'm pretty sure we've already done that a few weeks ago." Her lips turn downward and another part of me breaks inside.

"Please, baby. I just need a few minutes. Please, give me a chance to explain." If she wants me to kneel at her feet, I'm ready.

She huffs out a laugh, incredulously. "What is it with you guys today? Have the stars determined this to be the auspicious day of atonement?"

I look at her, perplexed, but realization sets in when I remember her holding hands with her ex. "Fuck." A sharp pain shoots through my chest at the thought. "Please tell me you're not back together with him."

She looks at me incredulously. "Not that it's any of your concern, but no."

Thank you, Jesus!

"Please, Anisa, just give me ten minutes."

She scrutinizes me, starting at my disheveled hair, steadying her gaze on my exhausted eyes, and then moving to my crumpled shirt. And even though she doesn't look a whole lot better than me in her current state, she's still the most beautiful woman I've ever seen. Pinching her bottom lip between her teeth--making me groan internally--she opens the door wider, allowing me entry.

I hunch over to pet Lynx behind the ears but notice that even his bi-colored gaze on me looks leery. "Hey, buddy."

Anisa moves past me, leaving the smell of her shampoo behind and my mouth waters. God, how I wish I could rewind time and go back to the last weekend we spent together. Bringing her knees up to her chest, she places herself on one corner of her sofa, as far away from me as possible. She waves in the direction of the couch for me to sit.

"Um." I place my elbows on my knees, sitting across from her, deciding to start from the top. "As you know, Mandy randomly showed up in our lives a few weeks ago. When she came over to the house, Lainey immediately recognized her from the pictures she's seen of her and the two spent the rest of the evening together. When I got there later that night, I found out that Mandy had been living in Arizona for the past several years and just moved back to Austin. She's been in and out of therapy and maintaining her medication. In fact, she'd been managing another club in Arizona and working hard to live a normal life--"

"A normal life a thousand miles away from her four-year-old daughter?"

The animosity is plain as day in Anisa's tone, and I can't blame her. I felt the same way after I found out what Mandy has been up to. Here I've been, raising my daughter with my mom and she's been back to work, living a seemingly ordinary life. "Yes."

"Go on."

"Once Lainey fell asleep that night, Mandy launched into these grand plans that she had in her head about us becoming a family. Apparently, in the time that I wasn't there, she managed to tell Lainey about them as well, getting her excited. Even when my mom tried to intervene, both Mandy and Lainey shut her down." I pinch the bridge of my nose. "Basically, I had to do a lot of damage control for the next few days and I needed time to . . . process it all. I spoke to Lainey and clarified that I had no intention of marrying her mother, but that we'd find a way to co-parent together. I cleared that up with Mandy as well. In fact, my lawyer just texted me to tell me that Mandy has signed the paperwork, agreeing to my terms."

Anisa watches me with the same doubtful gaze Lynx gave me earlier. "I thought you wanted Lainey to be raised by both parents in the same house?"

"Maybe at one time, I did," I answer truthfully. "But not at the cost of my own happiness. Not at the cost of you."

"And how does Lainey feel about that?"

"She wanted to have her mom back in her life, and she does. That's what mattered most to her." I give her a hopeful smile. "She knows how I feel about you."

Anisa gives me a curt nod. "Why didn't you call me, Logan? Why was I not your partner, your confidant, in this? You told me you loved me--"

"I do love you. I've always loved you."

"Yeah, well, then maybe we have different definitions of love. For God's sake, we were friends first, Lo!" Her face twists painfully, making me feel like scum. "Forget being your girlfriend, you didn't even let me be your friend during this time."

"I know." My throat feels like it's closing up. "I know, and I see how it all must have seemed to you. But I wasn't trying to hurt you, baby. I just didn't want you to feel overwhelmed with everything else you were dealing with."

"Oh, you mean being called fish eggs when you deserve caviar? You mean having every person within a ten-foot radius of me compare me to the other women in your life? You mean seeing paparazzi hiding in random bushes around my apartment, taking pictures of me? Yeah, Logan, it *was* overwhelming, but I'd willingly, *happily*, signed up for it. I'd willingly signed up to receive any amount of you that you could give me. You know why? Because I loved you and you were worth it!"

Loved.

Were.

Her eyes pool with emotion and I see color seeping into her cheeks. Fighting every atom in my body begging me to grab her and plaster her to my chest, I clear my throat. "Do you love me now . . . still?" My lungs refuse to inflate, burning inside my ribs.

"I found out from an online gossip column that you'd decided to end our relationship, before you even came over here that night." Her lips quiver and I move toward her before she holds her hand up, stopping me. She still hasn't answered my question.

"Anisa, please believe me. I didn't even know what I was going to say until I got to your doorstep that night. I actually had no clue how it was going to go. In fact, when I told you I needed a break and you accepted it, it broke me."

"Clearly. You seemed really *broken* up, Logan. So much so that you took a vacation with her and Lainey," she says sarcastically, and I notice that she omits Mandy's name.

I run my hands frustratedly through my hair again. "I'd

booked that trip to Disney World with Lainey a while ago, and she insisted that we bring Mandy along. Am I guilty of giving into my daughter's whims? Yes. Am I guilty of thinking about anyone else, being with anyone else but you? No. I don't want anyone else."

As if she remembers another betrayal, her face becomes all hard lines and ridges. "You hate jelly? This whole time, you haven't said a word about it."

A little laugh escapes me because as much as the question would sound ridiculous to a third person, for me and her, it created the foundation of our friendship. I refuse to let her see it as cracked because it's not. "Baby, I would fucking eat concrete if you made it with as much love. Yes, I hate grape jelly, but I've always loved you more."

A sob escapes her lips as she puts the palms of her hands on her eyes, rocking herself in the position. "You hurt me, Logan. You can tell me you didn't mean to, but you did."

"Please, baby. Tell me what I can do. Tell me how to fix this and I will." *Fuck! I don't know how to make her see me right now. I'm right here! I just need her to see me.*

She shakes her head before lifting it to face me resolutely, tears streaming down her cheeks. "No. You needed time before and I'd like the same now. I don't know what this means for us but . . . I need to step back from us and put *myself* first. Because in all of this, no one else has."

I nod, though I fucking hate agreeing to what she's asking from me. I guess a dose of my own medicine tastes more like poison. "Okay. Take all the time you need. But, Anisa," my voice trembles, "I can't be away from you for another fucking decade. I just can't."

Sniffling, she wipes her tears with the back of her hands but doesn't respond.

Getting up, I walk over to her and put her head between

my hands. Kissing her on the forehead, I voice the only thing I believe in the depth of my soul. "I love you, my beautiful *Batgirl*."

37

ANISA

"Come on, boy. Let's take you out." I yawn into the back of my hand, stretching, as I get out of bed the next day. Helping Lynx get off my bed, I waddle to my kitchen to turn on the coffee maker before shuffling to the front door.

Opening it, I let Lynx out and both our gazes--and his nose--land on the paper bags and coffee cup sitting in the front of my apartment. Lynx's tail wags a little harder at the smell of whatever is in one of the bags.

"Okay, okay. We'll open it. Give me a second." I peek around my apartment, looking for the deliverer of my breakfast to no avail.

My lips tip up slightly as I examine the contents of one of the bags--a grape jelly donut and a croissant. There's a dog treat in the other one, which now has Lynx's drool all over it. He sits back on his paws like he's the most well-behaved dog in the world and I giggle, throwing the treat in his direction. "Why do *you* get treats? It's not like you're the one with a broken heart."

Taking a sip from my coffee, I notice it's exactly what I

ordered when I went to the bakery yesterday--a caramel macchiato with soy milk. A note clipped to the bag catches my gaze and my eyes well with looming tears.

You. Only you. Always you, Batgirl. - Lo

EVERY DAY for the past two weeks, Logan has left breakfast at my door with a new note. And even though I haven't given it permission, my traitorous heart bounces with happiness and hurts with a dulled pain when I read them. This morning the note says, *Even if I don't see you, this is my most favorite part of the day. I miss you, baby, more than I can say with a bagel and cream cheese. -Lo*

He's respected my wishes to give me time and space, but he hasn't made it easy to have either. As much as I want to tell him not to come by every morning, I also can't deny that I love knowing that he's thinking about me just as much as I am about him. I haven't seen him once throughout the two weeks, but thoughts of him have consumed me nonstop. From the time I wake up to the time I swipe through our pictures on my phone in bed. I miss him with a desperation I can barely contain.

So far I've refrained from texting him, even with a note of thanks. I know that if I start the thread of communication, I won't be able to stop and that will just take me further down the rabbit hole, eliminating the little self-control I've garnered to stay away from him. But something in his words today makes me want to acknowledge his effort.

After thinking about what to type for a few minutes, I settle on a simple, Thank you.

His response vibrates my phone moments later as I'm

getting into my car. You're welcome. I wish we
could be out having breakfast together.
Better yet, I wish I was devouring you.

A surge of electricity zings to my core and I clench down
in my seat. My entire body feels the agony of my self-
imposed distance, and I almost abandon my stupid need for
space by calling him. Thankfully, a call from my dad jolts
me out of the lure known as Logan Miller.

My Bluetooth connects as I put my car into reverse. "Hi,
Dad."

"Good morning, *beta*. You're probably on your way to
work, but I wanted to see if you would be open to an idea I
had." It's always easy for me to tell when my dad is excited
about something, even when it's on the phone. His voice
sounds slightly breathless.

"Okay. What's up?"

"Well, I'd need you to come back home for a couple of
days so I can talk through exactly what I was thinking and
you can get a chance to speak to a few key people."

I squint at the road in response to my dad's vague
request. "What are you talking about, Dad?"

Still working through the entire conversation with my
dad, I get off the elevator at work, ready to book my tickets
to San Francisco to see my family this upcoming weekend,
when I notice an oversized bouquet--more like an entire
tree--of beautiful flowers sitting on my desk. Admiring it
with both my eyes and my fingers, I lean in to smell one of
the many roses before pulling out the note attached.

*These pale in comparison to the smell of magnolias and
pineapples. -Lo*

"Holy shit! These are beautiful!" Sydney slides up next
to me a few moments later, gawking at the ginormous

bouquet that looks like it could provide oxygen to a small country.

A smile touches my lips. "Yeah, they really are."

"So, I'm guessing you're on your way to forgiving him, huh? I mean breakfast, flowers, a public announcement of his love for you . . .. What more could a girl want?

My head swivels to her. "A public announcement?"

She blinks at me a few times like she's wondering if maybe I'm Martian. "Yes. It's all over celebrity news. Anisa, are you kidding me? You haven't been following what he said about you?"

I shake my head numbly as the guilt of agreeing to my dad's proposal this morning curdles inside my stomach. Sydney sends me a link to an article dated from yesterday on my phone and I click it open.

"Only Anisa Singh has 'Access' to Logan Miller!"

Today, in a rare and exclusive interview with T&T News, Logan Miller sets the record straight, saying he's officially off the market and "deeply and desperately in love" with his best friend and girl-friend, Anisa Singh.

This news comes at the heels of his out-of-court custody settle-ment with Mandy Monroe, the absentee mother to his four-year-old daughter. Logan states that while he won't go into the details of the settlement, all previous claims by news sources stating that he and Mandy were rekindling their relationship are false. He has his eyes, heart, and fate entangled with only one other person, the talented game developer working for a large gaming conglomer-ate, Anisa Singh.

Logan tells us that while he and Anisa haven't talked about future plans to settle down specifically, he's waiting for her to give him the green light. Over the past month, the two have been pictured cozying up in various locations in Austin, where Logan currently resides, but sources close to both state that they've been friends since they were in middle school.

Logan's new single, My Perfect Remix--dedicated solely to his sweetheart--drops worldwide tonight!
Move over Nick and Priyanka! There's a new power couple in town, and they'll be making beautiful music together for years to come!

AFTER TAKING the next couple of days off from work and securing Tamara's time to take care of Lynx, I head to the airport early Saturday morning to catch my flight back home.

Music from my radio fills my car as I drive to the Austin airport, and a DJ comes over the airways. "Once again, already topping every list this morning, is the new single by DJ Access, AKA Logan Miller."

A beat of silence follows, during which my heart comes to a complete stop. I'm not even sure I'm going the right way anymore. Logan's deep voice mixed with the most incredible beat flows through my system and my hands tremble along the steering wheel.

Your love, your love is walks in the sunshine
Talks of reaching the moon
Your love, your love is magnolias and pineapples
The scent of finding you

So, I take my time
To learn your lines
Called my perfect remix

Your love, your love was the missing beat
Notes written just for me
Your love, your love is skin and curves
Molded to my heart and soul

So, I take my time
To learn your lines
Called my perfect remix

Days of jelly
Scraped knees and muddy shoes
My first love and my only
Baby, sign your heart to me

Oh, your love, your love is tattooed on me
Carved in stone and dyed in wool
Wrap your arms around me, baby
And bring me home

So, I can take my time
To learn your lines
Called my perfect remix

Oooh, my perfect remix
Yeah, my perfect remix

Tears stream down my face and I wipe one side of my cheek haphazardly, thinking about his words, thinking about how I want to proceed. The timbre of his voice and the intensity of his words cascade through me during the flight back home, giving me a chance to mull over my decision.

Turning my phone back on after landing in Oakland International Airport, I see a message from Logan. I'd felt slightly guilty about not telling him where I was going, but I also didn't feel like giving him a full explanation--which is what he would have expected if I told him the real reason for my visit. No breakfast this morning?

I type back a quick response as the other passengers near me shuffle into the aisle in preparation for deboarding. Do you sit somewhere nearby with binoculars to see if I've taken the bags in?

His next response starts with a smiley-face emoji. Something like that. I've actually been in L.A. the past couple of days.

And here I was thinking you were slaving away every morning . . .. I smile, sending him my response. One of his people must have left the breakfast at my door the past week.

Clearly, it takes a village to take care of you ;) But I'm happy to do it for the rest of my life if you'll let me. Just give me the word.

His response sends a tinge of guilt through me and I'm not

sure how to reply. I finally decide on, `I heard your new single this morning.`

`Yeah? What did you think?`

My throat tightens as I think about the words to the song again, meant for me, written for us. `It was beautiful, Lo. I don't know what to say.`

`Say you're mine, baby.`

I get up from my seat and pull out my carry-on from the overhead bin, making my way down the aisle. I'm planning to respond to him as soon as I get out of the aircraft when I get another text from him. `Will you be home tomorrow?`

`Actually, I came to SF for the next few days.` The dull pain that's been there for the past several weeks throbs mercilessly inside my chest.

I'm on my way toward the airport exit where my dad has a car waiting for me when I see Logan's response. `Oh? To see your family?`

Getting into the designated black car, I pinch the bridge of my nose before responding, `Yes, but also because I'm evaluating a job offer from my dad.`

"Have you had a chance to think about the conversation we had this week?" Dad leans forward on the kitchen table where all our important family meetings have been conducted for the past ten years. His lifted brows tell me he's searching my face for my answer.

I bite the inside of my cheek, thinking about the opportunity he'd proposed--to lead the redesign of the *Techsess* customer portal based on feedback and market research that it was outdated. It would take me away from the gaming industry, but it would still give me a chance to design. It wasn't ideal but maybe moving to Austin wasn't, either. Maybe I wasn't ready to fly out of the nest on my own quite yet.

In just the matter of months, I'd broken up with an ex whose damage to my self-esteem was still something I was working on, been a part of workplace harassment investigation, and had fallen in love with a man who I trusted more than anyone else to take care of my feeble heart, but who'd broken it instead.

However unintentionally, Logan hadn't thought about my feelings and in his quest to do "damage control" as he called it, ended up damaging *us* instead. I had never asked to be his first priority--only his sweet little girl deserved that role--but that didn't mean I would stand for being his last.

After chewing on my fingernail, to Mom's chagrin, I finally respond to my dad, coming to terms with my decision as I speak the words. "I have, and I'd like to propose an amendment to you."

38

LOGAN

*Y*es, but also because I'm evaluating a job offer from my dad.

What the fuck? Evaluating a job offer from her dad? In San Francisco? My mind whirls with a million different thoughts as I re-read her message. She's in San Francisco and because of the fucking mess I've made of us, not only did she not tell me she was flying there, but she doesn't believe in us enough to want to stay in Austin.

Getting up abruptly from the conference table where both Wayland and my publicist sit working out the terms of some of my upcoming promotions, I put my phone in my pocket and run toward the door. A mixture of panic and anguish rush through me as I think about getting to her before she can make any rash decisions.

Moving is one thing--I'll follow her to the moon if she decides that's where she wants to live--but moving because she's trying to get away from me, because she's decided to "start over" again . . .? Fuck no, I won't accept it.

Wayland brows furrow questioningly. "Where are you going?"

"It's Anisa." I don't have time to explain, nor do I care to. "Just text me with the updates and send me the documents to sign digitally. I have to go."

I'm almost out the door when I glance over at both of their perplexed faces. I address my best friend and manager. "Can you get my plane ready? I need to fly to San Francisco."

ABOUT TWO HOURS LATER, I'm getting off on a private tarmac near the Oakland airport when I get a text message from Wayland confirming Anisa's parents' address. He contacted her dad and gave him a heads up of my arrival. Sometimes I wonder how I would even survive in this industry without having someone like him by my side.

Pulling up to Anisa's house in the SUV that awaited my arrival at the airport, I take a deep breath before setting my gaze on the home that took her away from Austin. It's a grand two-story set behind large redwood trees, giving it a picturesque appeal. The long path to the front door gives me a chance to collect my thoughts, and I pray her dad hasn't leaked the news of me coming today.

Ringing the doorbell, I wait for an answer. Strangely enough, even though the house is completely different from the house Anisa lived when we were kids in Austin, I get a strong feeling of nostalgia. Like I'm here to ask her parents if she can come out to play. My throat thickens at the memories of those easy days where all we worried about was eating our ice cream fast enough in the sun so it didn't melt. How did I complicate it all? How did I lose her trust?

The heavy double doors open and someone who looks very much like what I remember of Anisa's mom smiles back at me as if she already knew I'd be behind the door. "Logan! How my eyes have been waiting to see you! You are truly very handsome."

She pulls me into a warm hug, pushing up on her toes to hold me around my back. I lean into her, both surprised and grateful for her affectionate greeting. "It's so good to see you, Mrs. Singh. You haven't aged a day."

She leans back and squints at me, teasingly. "You're still the charmer you always were, Logan Miller, but I'll accept the compliment." She turns, sliding her hand through my elbow. "Now, come. I have chai and Indian fritters waiting for you."

I walk side-by-side with her but my eyes roam my surroundings, trying to find my girl. "Is Anisa here?"

"She's taking a shower but should be down soon." She side-eyes me as if reading my thoughts. "She has no idea you were coming. Wayland told us to keep things quiet."

Relieved, I walk to the kitchen when Anisa's dad comes out of a room through the hallway. "Logan!" he greets me warmly, walking toward me with his hand outstretched. "What a great surprise."

I shake his hand and he waves me over to the kitchen table, where Anisa's mom pours out a few cups of chai and places plates out for the fritters. She proceeds to ask me several questions about my mom and Lainey, telling me she's heard how wonderfully I'm raising her as the three of us snack.

"I would absolutely love to meet her one--" She's interrupted abruptly when Anisa, wearing joggers, which hug her hips and ass, and a cropped tank top, showing the most delicious sliver of her caramel skin, comes into the kitchen. *Goddamn, the girl could turn a monk into a sinner.*

Her eyes irradiate with confusion. "Logan? What are you doing here?"

I get up from my spot at the table when I hear Anisa's dad clear his throat behind me. "Renu, why don't we give them some privacy?" he says to his wife before giving Anisa a meaningful look that I can't decipher.

Once her parents are out of the kitchen, Anisa turns back toward me, her gaze questioning. She's about to speak when I cut in, "Please, baby. If you want to take a job in fucking Antarctica, say the word and I'll be there. Lainey, me, my mom--we're all there. But, Anisa . . .." I eliminate the distance between us, placing her head between my palms. My throat closes up and my voice cracks. I've been fucking holding it all in for so long, I'm bursting at the seams. "Please don't run away from me. I can't fucking live without you. Not another decade, not even another minute."

"Logan." Her breath fans my face as her eyes close, a tear escaping through the corner of one.

"You're tattooed on my skin, *Batgirl*. Carved into my damn heart and imprinted on my soul." A sob rises out of her, and I lean in to kiss her warm, plush lips. "Open your eyes, baby. See me standing here, right in front of you, telling you that *you* control my fate. *You* decide how or where we go, but get one thing into that stubborn head of yours," I say when she opens her eyes. "I go where you go. I am where you are. You feel me, *Batgirl*?"

Her hands grab fistfuls of my shirt and she sniffles. "I didn't take the job, Logan. I couldn't."

"What?" My face must convey my disbelief.

"I thought about it, but there was no other future for me besides the one with you. And uprooting you would be one thing, but uprooting Lainey or your mom . . .?" She shakes her head. "I couldn't do that."

I search her eyes as relief soars through me for the first time in what feels like ages. "But you said your dad had a role for you."

She smiles, swiping her hand over her cheek. "We came to terms on a temporary consultation position with his internal design team. I could do it from Austin and still keep my job at *Escapade*. In any case, my dad will always have a role for me. But the only one I want is the role of your girl-friend." Her vulnerability takes over her expression. "Is that still open?"

I crush my lips to hers, pushing my tongue into her mouth, tasting what seems to be her soul and giving her my answer to her question. My lips work against hers as her hands find my hair and she arches her hips into mine, moaning. We kiss, breathlessly, breathing for one another, as our hands spell out our love on our skin. She tastes like spring but feels like summer, heating me up from the inside. Wrapping my hand around her hair, I bend her back, cementing my body to hers as I taste her deeper.

We're both panting, lust climbing between us to almost hazardous levels, when I pull away, realizing we're still in her parents' house. "Jesus, baby. I want you so fucking bad. Like, right the fuck now."

Her hand slides underneath my shirt, over my abs, scratching, feeling, wanting. "Take me home, Lo."

Sweeter words have never been said.

39

ANISA

*T*hey say true love is hard to find. But I found it in blue, gray-rimmed eyes that stay on me long after I've left the room. I found it in a smile that forms even when I've said nothing funny. I've found it in strong arms that have broken my falls before I've even slipped.

They say if you find true love, you should hold on to it. But how do you hold on to something that's woven into the fabric of your soul? How do you hold on to something you've never been without, like oxygen?

And as I climb onto his lap in the private room inside of his jet, thirty-five thousand feet in the air, lining him up between my wet folds, I look into the eyes of the man I love, seeing myself reflected within them. He's like an avalanche, sweeping away everything else that existed before him. And while the avalanche is made up of weightless little snowflakes, the sheer amount of them--the sheer amount of *him*--has the power to leave me breathless. I'll never be found again, I never want to be.

His hands slide up my bare back, gently, reverently, as I lift, giving him permission to fill me. He complies, finding my mouth with his and pushing into me, seating me on him. We moan as his body melds with mine, like a sword back in its sheath, wrapped perfectly inside of me as if he was hand-made and heaven-sent just for me. His mouth finds my nipple and I bow against him, aching with the need to release, riding him like I need to win the Kentucky Derby. "Logan," I whisper into the dim room, my knees grinding into the soft mattress below him.

"Stay with me, Anisa," he commands after nipping and sucking one peak and moving to the next. The low octave of his voice sends a torrid spark pelting through me, making me even wetter than I am, and I clamp down tighter. Watching me while giving my body the attention it begs for, his hands tighten around my waist. "Not until I say so."

My voice comes out almost like a whine. "Logan, I can't."

"You will." He pounds into me from below and I follow his movements, one for one. A trickle of sweat rolls down between my breasts as my fingers clasp his shoulders. "Say it."

He wants to hear it again, he can't get enough. Pulling his lips into my mouth, I lap his tongue with mine, pouring every emotion into our kiss. "I love you, Logan Miller."

He pushes into my body again and again, and I desperately try to control the sensation building to dangerous levels. "Again."

"I love you. Only and always you."

His hands move to my ass and he uses them to guide my body into a rhythmic circular rotation above him. I moan so loud it might as well be considered a scream. "Please, Logan."

Drumming into me harder, his breathing increases with each movement. His hand slides down my stomach and his thumb finds my heavy parcel of nerves, rolling it underneath his touch. My jaw shuts tight as the electricity shoots through me at his growl. "Now!"

I wail as my release hits me, and I feel like my body catapults into some other dimension, barely registering any other sensation besides the one burning through me. The hammering below gets faster as Logan drains me to the last drop before a rumble works up through his chest. He growls into my neck before biting down on me gently, and I feel the flood of his release deep inside me.

I CALL my parents as soon as I land in Austin to let them know I got back safely and promise to visit soon. They were a little confused about my sudden change in plans to go back home with Logan, but not enough to stop me. I got the feeling they heard part of our conversation in the kitchen--hopefully not the part with both Logan and me panting like we were having heat stroke--and knew we needed to be alone.

"What would you say about picking Lynx up from your place and coming to spend the next few days with me at mine?" Logan asks as we get into the awaiting SUV on the tarmac. He immediately grabs my hand as if even the five seconds of not touching me is too much. "You already have the days off from work."

I look at him surprised. "Don't you have to leave in a couple of days to go back on tour?"

Logan shakes his head. "Over the past couple of weeks, one of the other things I was doing was renegotiating my contract for my tours. I've decided to tour less and lean into writing and producing music. It's what I love most about my job anyway--when I'm creating. And, it'll let me be with you and Lainey more."

I smile at my multi-talented man who still shies in the face of compliments before remembering something. "Won't Lainey and your mom wonder why we're staying with you?"

He winces a little, and I wonder if he's reconsidering the idea of me coming to spend time at his house. "I shouldn't take all the credit for the song I wrote for you. Lainey and my mom helped me with it as well."

I search his face. "Really?"

"They know how crazy I am about you. Mom says she's always known, and Lainey is thrilled about us. Now, her main concern is making sure I don't screw anything more up."

"It's a valid concern." I giggle when he feigns a look of hurt and tickles me.

"So, yes? You'll come spend the next few days with me?"

Finding the tattoo of the bat in the middle of his forearm, I press my thumb on it, soaking in the feel of him being mine. Looking back at his patiently waiting gaze, I answer, "Yes," because there is no other answer.

He grins, reaching to kiss me. "What about extending your stay and moving in with me?"

I lean back, looking at him but the smile never slips my face. "You just shortened my trip with my parents. You want to talk to my dad about living with his daughter in sin?"

His hands pull me back to him so that our lips touch. "That can be easily fixed. We don't have to live in sin."

~

TWO DAYS LATER, I watch from a chair on the porch as Lainey walks next to Lynx in Logan's enormous backyard. She's been so gentle with him, understanding that he's not a spritely young puppy with endless energy. It hasn't stopped her from asking to take him everywhere though, including on the boat with us when we went fishing at the lake behind Logan's house. She'd pouted when we told her it wouldn't be safe to take him on it but when I reached down to tuck her hair behind her ear, she wrapped her little arms around me and said, "Can you and Lynx stay at our house forever?"

I hadn't answered her then, but there was nothing I wanted more. Maybe Mom and Dad would be more amenable to the idea if Lainey asked them. There's very little that anyone can refuse the little girl.

Her and my grape jelly sandwiches lay on a plate next to glasses of lemonade while I breathe in the late evening Austin breeze, praying to the weather gods to make it cooler soon. Logan shuffles out onto the porch, beautiful bare feet under his standard low-hanging jeans, holding a beer in hand. I've spent the past two nights with him, been near him almost at all times, but the surprise of him, the sheer beauty of him, still hasn't worn off. I get the feeling it never will.

"Would you want any more children?" I ask him as he comes to sit next to me, his hand finding mine before pulling my knuckles to his lips.

"Yes," he answers without hesitation. "With you, yes."

I smile, envisioning dark-haired, olive-skinned little babies, perhaps with Logan and Lainey's blue eyes. "How many more?"

"How many do you want?"

I shrug, thinking about my sister and our bond. She's been my rock--and sometimes even my hard place--my confidant, my protector all my life. And even when she went through her own crisis recently, she managed it with poise, holding her head high. She's the epitome and perfect example of a good sister, and I want that love for Lainey. "It doesn't matter as long as I give Lainey a little sister."

Logan tugs on my hand and I come sit on his lap. His warm palm slides into my shirt, resting on my belly and his eyes shine with his emotions. "How about we have as many as you want, as long as I get to have one that I can turn into a DC fan?"

Poking him with my index finger, I scoff, "No deal! This will be a strictly Marvel loving household."

His mouth finds my ear, licking my earlobe. "Fine. But we're getting started soon."

EPILOGUE 1

LOGAN - ONE YEAR LATER

"Three-Time Grammy Winner, Logan Miller Gets Hitched!"

In what wedding guests call the most exquisite wedding of the year, Logan Miller and childhood friend and girlfriend of one year, Anisa Singh, tied the knot this September in the Maldives. From private jets to transport their guests, to all-expense paid private villas, to the bride and groom dressed to the nines in Indian garb created exclusively by Stella McCartney, Logan spared no expense for his beautiful bride. The two chose the location based on Anisa's love for adventure and were spotted parasailing prior to the wedding off the coast of one of the islands.

The friends-to-lovers duo made their relationship public over a year ago and have been living together in Logan's sprawling estate in Austin. Friends close to the newlyweds say the two are also looking to purchase property in San Francisco to be closer to Anisa's family.

With everything else moving in the right direction for these two, we're curious . . .. Will they be announcing big baby news soon?

*P*utting my phone back on the nightstand after reading the article that my publicist sent this morning, I turn to see my two girls snoring peacefully next to me. Lainey had a nightmare last night and before I knew it, Anisa had wrapped my daughter around herself like a koala and brought her into our bed, soothing her back to sleep.

It's been two weeks since we got back from our honeymoon, and Lainey has been glued to Anisa like white on rice--and Anisa hasn't minded one bit. Surprisingly, Mandy and Anisa have gotten along well. Yesterday, Anisa even asked Mandy to come over for dinner so we could all "eat as a family" along with my mom.

All I can say is that I must have done some heavy charity work in my last life to have gotten so lucky in this one because there is no other explanation for the beauties sleeping next to me. The ones that 'give meaning to this whole thing,' as my dad used to say. I understand what he meant so much more now that I have it. It was a little hilly--with a side of windy and stormy--getting here, but I thank my stars for guiding me to this destination.

Anisa shuffles, pressing her face against the pillow before opening her eyes. I reach my arm over my daughter to touch Anisa's face and her dimple makes an appearance. "Good morning, husband."

"Good morning, *Batwife*," I whisper back.

She makes a face. "Nope, that's never going to be a thing."

I laugh softly. "Maybe you'll get used to it after a while."

"That's a negative." She giggles, turning her face into my palm to kiss it before looking back at me shyly. "I . . . I have to tell you something."

"Oh?" I drink her in with my eyes.

"Remember how I got off the pill a few weeks ago?"

I sit up automatically, as if controlled by some external remote. "Yeah."

Her lips tip up on one side and she takes a breath. "I took a pregnancy test last night. We're having a baby, Lo."

"Wha--" I barely even take a breath before Lainey shoots up.

"We're having a baby? Daddy!" She looks at me, any sign of sleep completely shed. "We're having a baby!" She wraps her arms around Anisa's neck and bounces in place before turning to me and giving me a hug. "I'm going to be a big sister!"

The smile that stretches across my lips has got to be the biggest one I've ever had. My heart smiles right along. Looking at Anisa over Lainey's shoulder, I say, "I told you I was like Superman, *Batgirl*! My men don't mess around."

Anisa rolls her eyes--thankfully, Lainey doesn't understand what we're talking about and scoots out of our bed to run to the guest house, likely to give Grams the big news.

I pull Anisa closer to me, lying side-by-side facing her. Placing my hand over the warm skin of her belly, I peruse her flawless face. "I love you, baby. Only and always you."

EPILOGUE 2

ANISA - TEN MONTHS LATER

*T*he house has been bustling until today. From enormous and extravagant baby gifts from Logan's friends, to my parents staying with us for a couple of weeks, to Nelly and Sydney's visit, I feel like I'm the clerk at a busy motel, checking people in and out of rooms.

It's all been well-meaning with everyone wanting to see the babies, but I'm glad that only my sister remains. Logan is in his home recording studio and my mother-in-law has taken Lainey out to see Aunt Beth while I'm finally enjoying my first bath in what seems like ages, thanks to Jeena being on baby-duty. My breasts are already filling up though, so I know I don't have a lot of time before I start leaking, but I breathe in the lavender scent in the air, letting it relax my shoulders.

Alaina--named in combination with Lainey and my name--and Lyric, her big brother, were born a few weeks early, but you wouldn't know it by the way they eat. The nurses said they were the biggest twins they'd ever delivered. I'd known it though, based on how I felt like I carried around a hot air balloon in my belly for the last three months of my pregnancy.

My eyelids are getting heavier when I hear the familiar footsteps of the man I'd recognize with my eyes closed. Since the moment I texted him that I'd be taking a bath, I know he's been nervous, thinking I'd fall asleep and drown in the tub. I swear, he's the biggest scaredy cat with the heart, soul, and growl of a lion. "I knew you wouldn't let me bathe in peace." I smile at him.

His heated gaze lingers on my engorged breasts. "I'm happy to let you bathe if you don't mind me sitting here watching you, like the creeper that I am."

I giggle. "Are you done working for the day?"

"I can be if you have something else in mind." He winks before leaning beside me in the tub. Rolling up his sleeves, he puts his hand inside the water, finding my folds.

I moan, closing my eyes. God, I want him. I'm just about to speak the words out loud when I hear the familiar cry of my little boy right outside the bathroom door. Logan gets up, drying his hand with a towel, opening the door a sliver to see who's at the door with Lyric.

"I'm sorry." I hear the wince in my sister's voice. "The doorbell rang and it woke this little guy up. I think he's hungry."

"I'm coming out," I say to her from behind Logan as he reaches out to hold our baby boy. "Let me get my robe on."

He places a soft kiss on Lyric's temple before looking at Jeena. "Who's at the door?"

She frowns almost comically. "Somebody named Wayland who says he just flew in from San Francisco. I tried to shoo him away, showing him the no-solicitation sign outside, but he claims he's here to meet the babies. Plus, he brought a healthy supply of *Fruit Loops* boxes for me that should last the next few days. He wouldn't hand them over until I let him in, though. So, I'm sorry. I've failed you."

I laugh. These two have got to have the strangest relationship--or lack thereof--I've ever seen. Even at our wedding, as the best man and maid of honor, they were threatening to light a fire with the sparks flying between them. Neither is willing to admit it though, but somehow, I think Wayland isn't the one holding them back. "When are you going to give up the charade and admit that you have a thing for the hottie downstairs?"

Jeena looks at me like I've grown an extra set of breasts--which I probably have based on how heavy they are at this point. "When goats and elephants procreate to have viable golephant babies."

Logan shakes his head, as he often does with my sister, handing Lyric to me before giving me a kiss and leaving the room. I love how close Logan and Jeena have become over the past couple of years, but even he can't get her to tell us what her beef is with Wayland.

Jeena leaves the room shortly after, giving both Lyric and me a kiss on our foreheads while I sit down on the rocker in the corner. Poppy, our eleven-year-old Maine Coon mix, meows at the door before finding her spot on my bed. I still miss Lynx, who died in his sleep a few months ago, but I'm so happy to have had the cherished time with him.

Giving my little boy my breast, I relish in the way he gratefully accepts it, his brittle little nails pressing into my skin as his soft blue eyes scan my neck. I rock him gently, softly humming the newest song by my husband. I can't believe we made all this happen, how far we've come, but I wouldn't change this remixed life for the world.

The End

ALSO BY SWATI M.H.

ABOUT THE AUTHOR

Swati M.H. prefers to call herself a storyteller rather than an author. She lives in the Bay Area with her incredibly patient husband, two beautiful daughters, and her pitbull named Sadie Sapphire. Her days start with caffeine and sometimes end with a glass (or three) of wine.

Swati's goal as a storyteller is to distract her readers from their daily grind with stories about everyday couples finding and fighting for incredible love with the help of a little luck.

Swati loves staying in touch with her readers. Find her at www.swatimh.com or through Facebook and Instagram.

ACKNOWLEDGMENTS

Inspiration can strike at any time and that is exactly what happened to me at the cusp of writing My Perfect Remix. I'd hosted a small birthday get-together for my middle-school aged daughter in our back yard with a few of her school friends. When I watched their dynamic, heard about their childhood crushes, and noticed the interaction between the boys and girls, I knew I had a story to write. One of friend-ships and attachments. One where I imagined it blooming into something more over time. Thus, came the inspiration for Logan and Anisa.

So, while my girls are forbidden from reading my books, I want to thank them for showing me the vision of being young once again and remembering what it was like to want to grow up and seek independence. Selfishly, I never want them to be so independent that they won't need their mom. :)

I'd also like to thank the man who champions all my crazy whims and shows me every day what it means to have a happily ever after—my husband. None of this would have been possible without him, not one book and certainly not three.

I've met so many amazing people in the book world and some of them have become friends that I can't go without talking to daily like Melissa Schmidt and Amy Crull who are also my alpha-readers. Thank you, ladies, for encouraging me, poking holes in the various drafts, and just being awesome.

Thank you also to Anita Arora, Mehvash Doerr, and Sandhya Dubey for being there to listen to and support me as not only my early readers but also three of my wonderful friends. Love you ladies so much!

A huge thank you to my beta readers, Marla Knob, Rachel Childers, and Anita Medeiros. Your comments strengthened both this manuscript and me as an author. Some of your comments made me giggle and squeal, so thank you for that too. Your vote of confidence means the world to me.

I'm lucky to have found an editor who truly knows my style and helps improve it. I don't envy the number of grammar mistakes she's found but I wouldn't have it any other way. Thank you Silvia Curry.

A big thanks to my PA, Stephanie Rash, and entire team of bloggers and bookstagrammers who have helped me along the way. I truly appreciate all you do for me.

And more than anyone else, THANK YOU my wonderful readers. I truly hope I did right by you and you had fun reading Logan and Anisa's story. I am so proud of their love and their fight to being together and I hope you loved them as much as I do.

Printed in Great Britain
by Amazon

23900219R00195